THE ALMOST-APOCALYPSE OF APPLE VALLEY

COPYRIGHT

DEDICATION

For those who helped form my childhood years.

ACKNOWLEDGEMENTS

This book would not exist without the support of so many people. A big "thank you" to my first readers: Marie Bailey, Berthold Gambrel, Taryn Hough, Stacylynn Margason, and Mark Paxson. This book required some major clean-up and they all pitched in more than I could ask for.

And, finally, I couldn't have written this without my wife's support as I nodded off at 8:00 pm on most nights, just so I could wake up at 4:00 am and write before my day job (#disciplineequalsfreedom).

THE BEGINNING OF THE END

Saturday, June 10, 1989 - 9:00 AM

It was a beautiful day for Owen "Rocket Man" Thom to break the all-time record.

The four kids were all on their BMX bikes, leaning over their handlebars beneath a crystal-blue sky while they loitered just in front of the electrical substation west of Lion's Park.

From the distant park, an occasional cheer from soccer-parents in lawn chairs and the referee's shrill whistle carried through the light breeze, but mainly, a low buzz hung in the air where towering steel relays, transformers, and conductors communicated with each other over thick black wires and cables.

The chain link-fenced station was poorly hidden behind a row of oak trees at the south-east foot of Bass Hill, Apple Valley's central hill where the since-passed town founder had built his house. It was rarely used and had been for decades, reigning poorly over a cobwebbed, western-style inn below where old Hollywood used to come and play cowboy in the 1950s and 60s.

The landscape was perfect for amateur weekend BMX riding. What wasn't dirt was brown and gray granite rock. There were boulders the size of tiny houses and smaller specimens that could be chucked at both friend and foe.

Owen and his friends especially liked it here because of the tiny dirt trails that crisscrossed up and down little dips, even going around a dried-up percolation pond. There were plenty of natural jumps that allowed a kid to get at least six feet of pure air (no lie), assuming the rider picked up enough downhill momentum zooming down the road to the hill-top water tanks.

As for landing?

That was easy.

Landing on both wheels and staying that way?

Not so easy.

But if anyone could do it with the semblance of ease, it was Rocket Man.

Owen's friends called him that because he'd been the 'max air' record holder since they'd first started riding here. Not that anyone took out their tape measure and penciled in official records. It was just obvious from the fact that he was the only kid in the group for whom the others would completely stop their own riding shenanigans to watch him fly like a bird over the tabletop they'd built months ago with shovels and sweat.

Owen's Redline 700SL was a brilliant chrome. He swapped out the standard black seat and handlebar grips for ones that were aqua-blue in order to match, as closely as possible, the Mongoose bike ridden by Cru Jones, his favorite BMX racer from the movie *Rad* (who cared if he was fictional).

It wasn't just his bike that stood out—it was his riding gear too. His helmet had been painted red to match Cru's with a big blue "RM" he'd spent nights and weekends carefully sketching in on each side. It's sharp-angled chin bar and dark visor made him feel almost like, if not exactly like, a post-apocalyptic road warrior sucked right out of Mad Max and dropped off in a similar bleak landscape.

When Owen took hold of the rubber handlebar grips and flexed his white-gloved hands, he became one with the bike.

His visor was flipped up right now and the kids were shooting the crap when Jake Crawford decided to be the first to dissent on their current topic of conversation.

"It's all fake anyway," he said.

They'd been taking a momentary breather, allowing their collective sweat to dry, as the discussion centered on the finer points of WrestleMania V and how Steph Morris felt that Zeus and Macho Man Randy Savage had been robbed of the title by the underhanded tactics of Hulk Hogan.

Of course, Jake would be the first to ignore the whole spirit of the conversation and throw in something irrelevant. He enjoyed stirring the pot like that.

"Fake?" Steph asked. Her voice was slightly muffled by her own neon green chin-barred helmet. Only a single green eye was visible since the other was hidden behind a curtain of pink-dyed bangs that reached her cheekbone. "When we get back to your house, let me hit you over the head with a folding chair then."

Ryan Toscano snickered.

Jake rolled his eyes. "You have to know how to do it right. I'm not going to let some amateur try, and girl or not, I'd squash you if you did."

Jake could probably squash all three of them at the same time if he wanted. He was the tallest of them all by at least six inches. Blond with blue eyes, a buzz cut, a pale face full of freckles, and enough leftover baby fat morphing into muscle to squash a whole army of kids into submission, Jake wasn't one to mess around with.

"So you're admitting it takes skill?" Steph asked.

"I'm saying it's still fake."

"Shut up and ride already," Ryan chimed in. "Or I'll hit both of you with chairs."

Ryan may not have been as big as Jake—in fact, he was even smaller than Steph—but he fought dirty. He was also pretty smart, running neck-and-neck with Owen on the mental skills, though neither one liked to talk about that.

His skin was perpetually covered in dirt or at least it seemed that way. His parents and three younger sisters looked like they'd never had the privilege of living underneath a roof. That whole clan reminded Owen of those desert Bedouins he had seen in a National Geographic video Mrs. Kirkwood put on for the class while she was grading papers.

And with that long nose and buck teeth of his, Ryan probably had some genuine rats in his family tree.

Owen looked back toward the substation. An old man with bushy sideburns and a red trucker cap sat inside his blue Dodge pick-up truck just outside of the fence. His window was rolled down and his elbow hung out the side. He seemed thoroughly engaged in his spread-out newspaper while Owen and his friends jabbered on.

"I'm ready, so I'll go," Owen said, flipping the visor back down over his face. "The rest of you can watch and drool."

He ignored the round of *pffts* and *whatevers*, knowing The Crew was actually excited to watch him. He stood on his pedals, briefly spinning his handlebars a full 360 degrees—one of his easier, but more impressive-looking tricks. He rode up the incline to the substation and wound up close to the truck. The man with the paper seemed not to notice his presence, despite the whooshing of Owen's wheels spitting up bits of gravel. An open, steaming army-green canteen sat perilously on the dashboard alongside half of a white-bread sandwich wrapped in plastic.

The man flipped the page of his paper, shook it straight, and briefly met Owen's eyes. His sun-reddened face was hard. Stoic. So much so that it unnerved Owen enough to make him look away. Even though Owen wore a visor, it felt like the man zeroed in on his pupils and was going to dive right in.

Owen and his friends typically had the run of this place on Saturday mornings, and they were all a little annoyed that this guy had come along and tainted the atmosphere.

Now it was edging up past annoying into something else.

He decided to put it behind him and looked out past the tabletop which was about fifty yards down the trail.

From this vantage point, he could see where the old Apple Valley Airport used to be. Now, it was nothing but broken up pieces of asphalt and old junk people tossed out of their cars. An abandoned pink doll factory still stood in the middle of the desert shrubs as well, just a little ways behind Church of the Valley, the Gold Strike Lanes bowling alley, and the post office.

A lot of kids made fun of this town and complained about how there was nothing to do. But Owen loved the freedom and fresh air. Most of the kids didn't have a clue just how lucky they were.

He glanced back at his friends waiting impatiently by the jump. A momentary fear, a stupid one at that, ran through him. He imagined he'd look like an idiot in front of Steph if he didn't break his record today.

Just behind him was a blacktop road that ran further up Bass Hill to a pair of water tanks. If he *really* wanted to impress her, he could have climbed that road and come back down at the jump with maximum speed.

But he wasn't suicidal.

And he wasn't exactly sure why he wanted to impress her so much in the first place.

Just as he was about to pump down on the pedals, a loud crack emitted from the power substation.

The snap was whip-like. Sharp enough to almost send Owen tumbling over his handlebars from the decibel level, but he managed to shoot his feet out to the sides and keep himself upright. The bike buzzed and vibrated beneath him like it was charged with a hidden energy.

He wanted to let go of the handlebars, but instead, his grip tightened. A keen fear slithered up his body. His breath cut itself short as the feeling traversed his rib cage and shot upward toward his brain.

And then it extinguished itself.

Owen swore he heard something akin to a sighing of relief. Like someone dying of thirst had just taken a gulping drink of water, quenching their agony.

He looked at the man in the truck who seemed not to have noticed anything at all. His weathered fingers were still holding the paper in front of his face.

Then Owen flipped up his visor and turned back toward the substation. The glare of the sun stung a little. What he was looking for, he wasn't sure. There was no sign of fire. No smoke. No cables dancing around the ground like snakes, spitting sparks of electric venom.

"Hurry up, you puss!" Steph yelled from below, sounding as if she was talking through a mile-long tunnel. "The rest of us want to go."

No guts, no glory.

Owen turned back to the intended target. He jammed the visor shut, pushed down on the pedals and listened to the wind whistle through the gaps in his helmet as he barreled down the dirt track.

Through the whole fifty yards, he couldn't help but feel that something was still wrong. Placing it was another matter.

The Almost-Apocalypse of Apple Valley

It wasn't until he reached the lip of the tabletop and felt himself floating through the air that he *knew* something was wrong. He looked to the right at his friends who were a captive audience. Jake, Ryan, and Steph were all leaning over their handlebars, all with mouths opened wide enough to shove an entire hoagie into each one.

Something definitely felt off.

Owen looked down and wished he hadn't.

His hands were still connected to the grips of his handlebars, but the handlebars themselves were no longer connected to the front forks.

They had just separated like a pair of loose Lego pieces that had lost their grippiness.

Time slowed as the declining side of the tabletop greeted him ever closer each agonizing second.

This wasn't going to end well.

His nards were already being sucked back up into his guts, anticipating the impact of either landing directly on the neck of the seat or right on top of the frame.

Odd questions piled up in his mind: Would his parents take his bike and give it away for the church rummage sale? Would his friends ever let him live this down?

Could a boy ever become a man without nards?

He let go of the floating handlebars and prepared for landing.

The next thing he felt was the soles of his British Knights high-tops disembarking from the pedals and connecting with the dirt. His knees buckled and without anything to hold onto, there was a messy sort of stutter-stop before he tumbled head-over-rear over the front wheel, the world rumbling lowly outside of his helmet, rolling several times before coming to a stop.

At least he hoped he stopped.

His vision was still spinning.

It was painful to breathe. Oxygen seemed to have a hard time getting through his mouth and into his lungs. The air had been punched out of him by the frame where the handlebars had connected to the forks.

He gasped, trying to talk.

Pain shot through his chest and stomach, and he tasted a gritty mix of blood and dirt on his tongue.

Instinctively, he reached down and cupped his crotch. Through his jeans and thick gloves, he couldn't feel much, but he hoped for the best.

Someone groaned in the distance.

Only it wasn't as distant as he assumed.

It was him.

"Holy crapola!" someone yelled.

And Owen knew *that* wasn't him.

That was a Jake saying.

And then there was that funny feeling again.

He flipped his pounding head to the side and looked up the hill at the substation. Though he was further away then he'd been at the top of the run, the tips of the cable-bearing steel towers seemed more menacing. As if there were tiny wizards living at the tops of each, controlling and doling out electricity like it was their special element of magic.

Over the bass-heavy pulse of blood pumping through his ears, Owen thought he heard rapid, heavy footsteps coming his way.

His vision was still shaky, but he noticed the driver's side door of the Dodge pickup was now propped open. Leaning against its edge was the old man who had been reading the paper. He was tall and thick—through a plaid red and black button-up shirt, his shoulders seemed ready to burst through the seams and the top of the door barely met the middle of his crossed arms.

As far away as he was, Owen thought he could see the man frowning.

Then Owen's eyelids shut out the world and told him to

go to sleep.

Sunday, June 11, 1989 - 1:00 PM

Ryan and Jake were warmongers.

The two of them crouched behind a large creosote bush
in the dirt and weed-filled lot next to Ryan's tiny two-bedroom,
vanilla-stucco house. Barely shielded from the oppressive sun,
the two boys grinned like banshees as they switched between
picking up golden ants on twigs and delivering them into enemy territory.

Ryan's gray, short-haired mutt of a cat, Fluffy, stuck its
tail in the air and decided to head back to the house since she
was no longer the center of attention.

Within spitting distance from the iconic Bell Mountain,
Ryan's parents and three sisters lived in the north-western
Apple Valley outskirts where their nearest neighbor was half a
mile away. They had a well which seemed to need redrilling every few years and a septic tank which Ryan had the displeasure
of seeing, and smelling, overflow more than once. As for the
new cable television showing up? Even if they could afford it,
the company didn't have the wires run this far out. Ryan would
have to be happy with whatever fuzzy signal the spangly an-

tenna perched on the roof could pick up, which wasn't much beyond the local TV station airing A-Team reruns and local news. His dad had pointed out one of the news anchors as a regular customer of the liquor store where he worked nights.

So, while other kids might have been able to sit inside an air-conditioned room and watch hours of cartoons and play video games, Ryan could only amuse himself with nature's gifts in the wide-open desert lots beside his house, as he was doing so with Jake this afternoon.

The little yellow guys marched up, down, and around the stick in Ryan's hand, causing him to constantly shift ends in order to avoid the things crawling up onto his fingers and digging in for a snack.

"These guys look so much cooler than the red ones," Jake said. "And they're stronger."

"Says who?"

"My dad told me."

Ryan's lips twisted like the tied end of a balloon. "How does he know?"

Jake huffed, insulted as always when being challenged. "He just knows stuff. More than your old man, anyway."

Ryan hated bringing his family into things when it came to his friends. His family wasn't exactly living on easy street and his parents weren't exactly models of worldly success.

His dad slept most of the day between night shifts and his mom worked every day but Thursday and Friday as a cashier at the local Sprouse-Reitz, a five-and-dime store in the old Apple Valley downtown.

Still, Ryan knew that his parents loved him and his sisters as much as a couple of perpetually tired parents could. At least he felt they did. Every Friday, he and the girls consistently came home to a cardboard tray of Little Caesar's pepperoni pizza sitting on the tiny, chipped dinner table and proceeded to tear apart its paper wrapping like coyotes set loose on a warren of jackrabbits.

He'd find his parents sitting on the couch in the evenings, smiling, smoking funny-smelling cigarettes and giving the kids bear hugs in turn.

Yeah, they were a loving family.

Yet, whenever he was forced to compare his family with everyone else's, except for Jake's, Ryan felt shame on top of shame.

But out here, beneath the same sun that lit upon the face of every Apple Valley citizen, rich or poor, he felt a sense of equality.

Jake released a boisterous laugh, seeming to forget the

whole tiff he'd inadvertently tried to start.

"Look at that guy," he said, pointing a fat finger at one of the latest yellow transplants wrestling with a pair of red ants. "I told you they're tougher. It's taking two of them to take him on."

The ants' limbs were flicking and sticking to each other in random, staccato bursts. Their bodies occasionally tumbled one over the other in the dirt—the red ones would get one over on the yellow one and then the yellow one would push a red one off triumphantly, getting back into the fight.

"It doesn't mean he's tougher," Ryan said. "It just means the red ones are more prepared. They're smart enough to send more people. They run things like gangs."

"*Pfft.*" Jake lifted his head and spit a fat loogie on the ground next to the anthill, pinning a yellow one beneath the slimy force field. "What do you know about gangs?"

"I've seen Colors," Ryan protested.

The gang-ridden streets of Los Angeles were as far from quiet little Apple Valley as Pluto was from Earth, but maybe that's why their dynamic fascinated Ryan so much.

It was different.

It felt dangerous.

Occasionally, his dad would give him and his sisters

money to rent VHS videotapes down at Prime Time Video. When his sisters weren't spending the weekly movie budget on cheesy horror movies, Ryan was renting Colors over and over again. He must have watched the film over twenty times now. He could spit out the Ice-T theme song lyrics at the drop of a dime. One day, he even took a red bandanna from the toolbox in his dad's garage, wrapped it around his head, and strutted around the house with a gangster lean, acting like he was a Blood.

That was one of the rare times his dad lost his smile and swatted Ryan's rear end until it was swollen like a baboon's, telling him he'd better not see him doing "some shithead thing" like that again, or he'd wind up with more than a sore butt.

Still, his parents didn't stop him from watching a movie that was wildly inappropriate for a kid his age. Come to think of it, they didn't seem to care much at all what the kids picked up for their viewing pleasure, so long as they were occupied while Mom and Dad thrashed around the bedroom behind a locked door, doing whatever cleaning stuff in there that they said they had to do.

They were cool like that.

"I've seen Colors too," Jake said, straightening up and preening like a peacock. And that's all he could say. Ryan knew

Jake wasn't going to challenge him on his knowledge, because Ryan was sharp when it came to what he did know. It's why he was in GATE.

Jake stood on his feet and wiped his dirty palms against his pant legs.

"I'm bored," he said. He looked around at the endless surrounding desert. A pair of oversized crows cawed from their perch on the wooden telephone pole that connected the only piece of civilization to the Toscano household. "I think I'm gonna go home."

Jake had ridden his bike here like he did most of the time. He lived about five miles away.

"Maybe I'll stop at Steph's on the way."

Ryan's ears perked up. Steph wasn't exactly "on the way." In fact, she lived in the complete opposite direction of Jake. Ryan had tried to call her earlier to see if she wanted to come and screw around with the ants or maybe watch a video. He actually called her before calling Jake, but no one had picked up the phone.

Ryan wasn't going to tell Jake he was actually the backup choice.

Steph was a lot of fun, but if Ryan was going to be honest with himself, she wasn't only fun in the way that Jake and

Owen were fun. He couldn't explain it well, even to himself, but whenever she was around, he felt like his feet were suspended by a bunch of helium-filled balloons. He'd get this nervous twitch in his stomach. Not the kind that made him nauseous and on the verge of throwing up, but it was more of a building excitement—like approaching the apex of a roller coaster (Ryan could only guess. He'd never *been* on an actual roller coaster).

She was one of the few people to get his random pop-culture jokes. Or at least she pretended that she did, which was good enough for Ryan.

Of course, he'd never tell her any of this. He didn't even like to *think* it. But think it he did.

"What for?" he asked Jake, just in time to see him wheeling his bike back from the house.

Jake, climbing onto the seat, took hold of the handles and shrugged his shoulders. "She mentioned something about a get-well package for Owen."

That helium-like feeling deflated a little and the nervous twitch seemed to magically convert itself into a rotating nausea.

"Oh," was all Ryan could say.

Why was he feeling something acidic creep up in the back of his throat about that fact? They *were* friends, after all. They were all friends. And Owen had hurt himself pretty good yesterday. A little something from his fellow cronies to cheer him up would be a nice gesture.

But why had Steph asked Jake and not him? Ryan had comics and other stuff Owen could enjoy while he was laid up. Not that he needed any of it. Owen was probably playing Nintendo or something, anyway.

Then Ryan also wondered why he hadn't even thought of doing something similar for Owen in the first place.

He assumed he'd see him in school eventually. Or even at his birthday party next weekend.

Maybe Steph was the true friend.

Ryan felt a twinge of embarrassment.

"See you at school tomorrow," Jake said, pedaling off into the distance before Ryan's thoughts were fully formed.

Ryan stared down at the anthill in front of his feet. The yellow ant they had mercilessly dropped off into a strange new world was now torn in half. The red ants streamed around the corpse as if it didn't matter anymore—it was just another piece of the landscape now.

A potential warning.

An overwhelming sense of sadness struck Ryan. He hated what the red ants did to the yellow ant. And he hated more that it had been his fault for delivering him unto his enemies.

He quickly stomped out the feeling by taking the tip of his scuffed Keds tennis shoe and violently grinding it into the mound, causing it to collapse into itself, wiping it from existence.

He smiled now and it felt good.

Time.

Time's a deceptive, pernicious thing. You either have too much and you're bored to death or you don't have enough and you're pulling your hair out with worry. You never have just the right amount of time you need.

Steph was dealing with the latter as Mrs. Kirkwood came around and started collecting the Scantron tests for Monday morning's reading comprehension test.

It was based on an essay about the Civil War.

For once, Steph had really, truly thought she was ready — two number two pencils, sharpened and at the ready; extra erasers (they were all shaped like sweetly scented watermelon slices); and a plastic baggie full of shelled sunflower seeds that she kept within arm's reach, just in case her incessant hunger kicked in.

And then the timer started and she froze.

She had studied the chapters she was supposed to. Memorized the set of Civil War dates she was supposed to.

She did all the things she was supposed to.

And still she froze for a whole five minutes, with a mind that seemed not empty, but overflowing with darkness like a deep pit from which not even the slightest ray of dust-filled light could penetrate. Names and facts—Robert E. Lee, Appomattox, Antietam—tried to surface, but were sucked down below, never to be seen again.

For that whole five minutes, she drew random circles on the piece of scratch paper the students were allowed, thinking about Saturday's events. She knew that what happened to Owen was only an excuse, though it weighed on her more heavily than another thought might.

The fact was Steph hated tests. It's not that she wasn't smart—at least she *thought* she had brains. She could keep up with Owen and Ryan on just about anything they talked about, but when it came to remembering dull facts, diagramming sentences, or working out long division that she just knew she'd never use in real life, she always had trouble.

She wouldn't otherwise care except that trouble led to parent-teacher meetings and threats of being held back another year if she didn't bring her grades up.

Her mom would have these little pow-wows with Mrs. Kirkwood and spill her guts about how she was a struggling, single mom and doing everything she could do for her daughter and, oh my God, how she was at her wit's end and that it would just be so much harder if Steph got held back.

It was obvious Mrs. Kirkwood didn't want to hear her sob story. *Steph* didn't want to hear her sob story.

She just wished they would both leave her alone so that she could get through school and get on with living her own life as she saw fit.

But being held back another year would obliterate those plans. The rest of the gang would be in junior high school, and she'd be stuck with a bunch of babies in the sixth grade.

As Mrs. Kirkwood came around to Steph's desk, she halted and placed a long, skinny finger on Steph's Scantron. Steph was only briefly distracted by her teacher's bland taste in press-on fingernail colors—flesh-colored. Not that Steph would have any sort of long fingernails. They would only get in the way with her playing with the boys. But she occasionally paint-ed hers in neon green or pink—sometimes both.

"Are you feeling okay, Stephanie?"

There was no hiding it: only two-thirds of the little an-swer bubbles had been filled in.

Steph got a whiff of her teacher's rosewater perfume as she swept her eyes up toward Mrs. Kirkwood's face.

Mrs. Kirkwood was wearing a magenta skirt that flowed

out just past her knees. Her collared shirt was silky and pearl-colored, buttoned all the way to the top, almost to the point of strangling her neck.

Her brown eyes were calm, sympathetic, and her brunette bowl-cut hair was like every other teacher's at Mojave Mesa Elementary School—except for Ms. Berk's curly raven-esque hair whose frosted tips settled right on top of her ridiculously big boobs.

"I just...just ran out of time," Steph said.

Mrs. Kirkwood peered up at the round clock hung over the chalkboard. "You had thirty minutes and the test only had fifteen questions." She narrowed her eyes at Steph again, this time with a little less sympathy. "That's two minutes per question."

Steph wanted to repeat a line which she'd heard one of her mom's boyfriends say—*No shit, Sherlock.*

But that would have been a very, very bad idea.

Instead, she turned her head away and looked past the annoying Loretta Mishki at the empty seat in the same row as hers, two columns over.

She wanted to visit Owen after school, but her mother had grounded her for the whole week because she came home later than she said she would on Saturday. Steph tried to explain that Owen had hurt himself and could use his friends' company. Her mom said something along the lines of how Steph shouldn't have been playing there with those boys in the first place and that because her tomboy daughter hadn't come home on time, she had been forced to cancel her attendance at a Tupperware party she'd been planning for a month.

"I know you're worried about Owen," Mrs. Kirkwood said. "But his parents tell me that he's recuperating just fine. He should be back in school next week."

Steph couldn't say a word, only nod her head slowly in response, thinking of Owen again at the mention of his name.

A crack snapped across her mind like sharp thunder. She swore she heard a similar sound at the track on Saturday when Owen was preparing his descent toward the jump. It seemed to emanate from his direction, up by the stranger in the blue truck. It was the weirdest thing, and she couldn't shake it from her mind as she recalled how it felt like her nerves were on fire, momentarily pulsating through her entire being, only to dissipate when Owen's handlebars disconnected in mid-air.

When he came tumbling down, finally rolling to a rest, he curled up into the fetal position with his hands tucked between his legs.

Apparently, he'd crushed his boys.

Steph couldn't imagine what it felt like to have icky nards that hung between your legs, but boys always talked about how much it hurt to have them hit or kicked. And Owen landed square on top of his. That alone would have made Steph double over in pain, nards or not.

But that wasn't his biggest problem. Owen hit the ground unexpectedly hard. Steph's stomach felt like it was hanging in her throat when Owen briefly fell asleep. She wasn't a doctor, but she didn't have to be to know that wasn't good.

Thankfully, he woke up after Jake slapped him repeatedly in the face, but he was still groggy.

None of them even noticed that his helmet had a long crack running all the way down the left side, top to bottom between his hand-painted initials, revealing some kind of Styrofoam inside; not until they'd managed to get him home by having him hang on to Jake's back while Jake pedaled.

Mrs. Kirkwood tapped that press-on nail on the desk a couple of times, starting to pull Steph back to the here and now. "Tell you what. I'll be in an hour early Wednesday preparing some mimeographs for the week's lessons. If you're here, I'll give you the chance to retake it, but the most you'll get is a B. Fair?"

Steph's eyes were still zoomed in on the empty plastic

chair.

"Stephanie?"

"Hmm?" She returned her focus to the freckles and wrinkly knuckles on Mrs. Kirkwood's finger. "Oh. Yes, please. Thank you."

Mrs. Kirkwood smiled with closed lips, looking like she'd just performed the world's greatest act of extreme benevolence, and grabbed the Scantron from Stephanie's desk.

Steph's vision focused just past Mrs. Kirkwood and caught Jake and Ryan grunting lightly as they threw tiny punches at each other while barely staying seated in their desks near the front. Putting them right next to each other wasn't one of the teacher's smartest decisions.

"Knock it off," Mrs. Kirkwood said, raising her voice as she picked up another student's test, "or I'm sending you both to Principal Strick's office."

The faux fisticuffs came to a halt. Ryan turned around and smiled, making eye contact with Mrs. Kirkwood.

"Sorry," he said.

Jake didn't say anything. He only picked up his pencil and started drawing on his scratchpad again.

Mrs. Kirkwood continued making the Scantron rounds.

Ryan looked back toward Steph and made fun of their

teacher, stretching his mouth with exaggerated scolding movements. He stuck out his tongue, tipping his head from side to side while he rolled his eyes, trying to make Steph laugh.

Steph cracked a brief grin, but it was mechanical.

She wasn't sure if she would be there Wednesday morning. If the only option was to try to cram all night only to fail again, what would be the point?

But maybe she could ask Ryan or Owen to help her study. She'd risk the wrath of her mom, but if she explained that it would help her pass the quiz and keep up her grades, it might be enough.

Ryan was the obvious choice since he was still here and fully functional, but she really wanted to check in on Owen and studying would be the perfect excuse. Tomorrow night was the only option since she'd have to get the idea past her mom tonight.

She grabbed a handful of sunflower seeds from her bag, tipped her head back, and savored their saltiness as they hit her tongue.

Owen would probably have asked for some.

Owen wasn't supposed to be on the computer.

He wasn't even supposed to be out of bed except to take a leak and grab a drink of water, but he'd pored cover-to-cover over three issues of MAD Magazine and two copies of Weekly World News. Spy vs. Spy always elicited a chuckle, no matter how many re-reads, but Bat Boy was getting ridiculous. Spotted hovering around the moon, holding hands with Peter Pan this time?

Come on.

But it was nice of Jake to slide the material through the window yesterday while his parents were watching the evening news in the family room. Jake mentioned it was Steph's idea, apparently not caring that the only role he played was transporting the contraband material.

Owen sort of wished Steph had come herself, but Jake said she was actually grounded because of Saturday's incident. That didn't seem fair. She didn't do anything wrong.

Jake left as quickly as he'd arrived, spending only enough time to make a joke about Owen's "cracked *huevos*" and how, when Owen died, he wanted his collection of Transformer toys because he was going to set them all up in the middle of the desert and blow them up with an M-80 firecracker, pretending that they'd walked into a trap set by Megatron and Cobra Commander (Jake relished the idea of a crossover).

Other than reading, there was nothing to do in bed except stare at shifting patterns in the white popcorn ceiling and baby-poop-yellow walls that Owen couldn't stand. His parents never asked him what color he wanted (purple). His mom just thought yellow would be cute and his dad did what he always did—*mmmhmmed* and painted it yellow.

If it weren't for the large *Rad* movie poster of Cru Jones hanging over his computer and the random assortment of Garbage Pail Kid stickers (Mom was constantly threatening to scrape those "disgusting things" off), his room would have been uninhabitable in Owen's mind.

He'd spent the rest of the previous Saturday and most of Sunday just lying there while his body gorged on drowsiness-inducing pills like a giant, fleshy leech, recuperating from Saturday morning's sudden crash landing.

He swore the pills gave him weird visions if he stared at something too long.

Case in point: the poster contained a blown-up image of

his idol soaring through the sky. Puffy white clouds surrounded Cru's outline, expanding and contracting like a giant, fuzzy halo while a blurry crowd of people cheered and swayed in the stands behind him.

Owen's back was still extremely sore, despite the medication (his bespectacled, ginger-bearded physician, Dr. Behrn, said he was lucky to walk away with only a bit tongue and a bruised tailbone, but he also gave Owen kudos for wearing a helmet).

Which reminded him.

His helmet.

His poor, poor helmet.

It sat now on the nightstand beside his bed, damaged goods that it was.

Sure, he could fill the crack with something, but his parents already said there was no way he was going to be riding for a while, like, maybe not until he was eighteen, let alone wear that helmet again when he did.

They would have thrown it away if he hadn't begged them to let him keep it in his room as a decoration.

It wasn't just his baby.

It was a symbol of Rocket Man and all that he was.

Owen still couldn't fully comprehend how it all happened. He always made sure every nut and bolt were tightened before taking his bike out. His dad taught him that maintenance was paramount—you couldn't just hope things were right. You did your best to *make sure* they were right.

Even now, he heard the buzzing of the substation gear. Felt the crackling electricity surge through his skin as if he'd become a conduit for another target.

The thoughts consumed his mind since Saturday.

That grinding, torturous memory is what pulled him out of bed while his parents were at work. He was going to go insane if he spent a single minute more lying down, feeling like he was falling into some great abyss.

The modem buzzed and squealed and hummed as it negotiated communications with the modem on the other end of the phone line.

He was logged in to The Desert Oasis BBS, a computer bulletin board system that was owned and operated by the coolest adult Owen had ever known—a man named John Pope.

Owen had never met John. Not in person, anyway. Didn't know how old he was. Didn't know what he looked like. He'd never even talked to him on the phone. His only means of contact was through the BBS.

Yet Owen liked John because John didn't talk down to him like he was a kid. John had been impressed with Owen's technological prowess from the moment he thoroughly answered a troubleshooting question John had posted on the BBS's message board.

John was what you called the Sysop, short for systems operator, of The Desert Oasis. He had three phone lines that came into his house, all connected to the computer so that people could dial in at any time of day or night without worrying about a busy signal.

Unless it was a Friday night. Those nights, you tended to wait in line as people got off work and wound down with some casual gaming and socializing.

As soon as Owen signed on, he checked his private messages. There weren't any. That wasn't unexpected—most of the discussion took place on the message forums.

He was about to log off when his monitor cleared and a blocky, blinking cursor presented itself at the top of the screen.

The Sysop had engaged a private chat.

SYSOP: HEY AMIGO. SHOULDN'T YOU BE IN SCHOOL? <G>

The <G> was the universal tag for "grin."

Owen smiled in spite of the lingering pain and typed back:

OWEN: NAH, THEY KICKED ME OUT. <G>

SYSOP: SOMEHOW I DON'T BELIEVE YOU, BUT I WOULDN'T BE SURPRISED IF YOU *DID* GET SHIPPED OFF TO A GIFTED SCHOOL. LIKE THE X-MEN.

Owen doubted there was such a thing, but he did know about GATE: Gifted and Talented Education. Ryan was bussed off to that class once a week, but Owen was never chosen for that.

It wouldn't have been his thing, anyway. They seemed to be big on all the things he wasn't interested in—art, history, and science.

Now if they'd had computers, Owen probably could have shown them a thing or two. His idea of learning was sitting down with the latest issue of *COMPUTE!* magazine and typing in the BASIC code printed in the back, trying to reverse engineer how it all worked.

OWEN: HAD A LITTLE ACCIDENT WITH MY BIKE. NOW I'M HOME FOR THE REST OF THE WEEK. DOCTOR'S ORDERS, OF COURSE.

In a classic overabundance of caution when it came to her son, Owen's mom had already decided he wouldn't be back in class until next Monday. His friends could bring his homework, of course. She even almost canceled his upcoming birthday party, but Owen pleaded enough to convince her otherwise.

The Almost-Apocalypse of Apple Valley

To be honest, as much as he enjoyed the extra computer time, he missed hanging out with his friends.

SYSOP: I'M SORRY TO HEAR THAT. YOU'RE OK?

OWEN: YEAH, GOOD TO GO. JUST HAVE TO TAKE SOME STUPID PILLS.

There was a long pause and Owen wondered if the modem had disconnected.

SYSOP: WELL, I'M GLAD YOU'RE ONLINE, BECAUSE I NEED A FAVOR.

Owen loved doing favors for John. It made him feel special, because it meant John trusted him to do something extraordinary.

OWEN: LAY IT ON ME.

SYSOP: I'M GOING TO SEND YOU A COPY OF A MESSAGE I RECEIVED OVER FIDONET.

OWEN: OK

SYSOP: IT'S ENCRYPTED WITH SOMETHING THAT I'M NOT FAMILIAR WITH. WAS HOPING YOU COULD HELP ME FIGURE IT OUT.

A giant grin grew on Owen's face. Finally, some real excitement.

OWEN: SURE. NO PROB. I GOT NOTHING BETTER TO DO.

SYSOP: ALREADY IN YOUR INBOX, AMIGO. THANK YOU! I'LL BE SIGNING OFF FOR THE REST OF THE DAY, BUT LET ME KNOW BY WEDNESDAY NIGHT IF YOU'RE ABLE TO FIGURE IT OUT. YOU CRACK IT, I OWE YOU A BACON-EGG SANDWICH FROM LOTTABURGER. <G>

OWEN: YUM! YOU GOT IT.

The screen cleared and the main menu started printing across the monitor again.

Owen hit the [R]ead Email hotkey and was presented with the message that John sent over.

The subject didn't make any sense: *Assembly Instructions.*

He hit the ENTER key and was presented a random, contiguous pattern of numbers, letters, and special characters that splashed across the screen. It filled all 80 lines of the terminal and went on for another 100 or so lines before coming to an end.

Owen raised his eyebrows. Instantly, he felt intimidated.

"How the heck am I supposed to figure this out?" he asked his reflection in the computer monitor.

He sort of hoped it would answer back like a genie in a bottle, but no luck.

He reached for the red, blue, and gray Optimus Prime Transformer that sat next to the screen and fumbled with the arms and legs. His favorite childhood toy helped him think, sometimes.

Owen knew a little about cryptography, but not much. It was lightly touched on in some *COMPUTE!* issues. There were even some text files that lived on various BBSes which dove into it a bit. Those were half technobabble, half diatribes written by guys with monikers like *Phr34kM4v3n* and *dELETEtHEnSA*.

For some reason, Owen assumed they were guys. Now that he thought about it, they could have been girls for all he knew.

He really wanted someone to talk to about this.

His thoughts wandered to Steph. He missed her the most out of all his friends. Probably because she didn't give him as much of a hard time that Jake and Ryan did for his computer nerdiness. She'd let him blabber on about the differences between extended RAM and expanded RAM and pretend to be interested. Sometimes, he wondered if she actually was. Maybe she only did it, because she was grateful that a bunch of boys let her hang out with them without hassling her.

Either way, she was always good at that stuff. He noticed that even when she was dealing with Jake and Ryan.

He ventured back to the email. He'd gotten pretty good at figuring out simple ciphers, even came up with his own that he called OwenCrypt that he tried to teach The Crew. They stopped using it after a week because it was, in Jake's words, "a dweeby waste of time."

Whatever. Owen didn't care enough to convince them they were missing out on cool stuff.

As that thought passed through his mind, he heard a sputtering car engine approach followed by tires rolling up the gravel driveway just outside of his bedroom window. He jumped up to take a peek and screamed, realizing too late how much of his back still felt like a raging fire.

He grimaced, holding in the pain, and pressed down a single row of vinyl window blinds, so he could perform recon on whoever it was. His mom and dad were still supposed to be at work, even though his mom said she'd be home an hour or so earlier to make sure Owen had taken his medicine.

It felt like an eternity for Owen's brain to register what had just shown up outside his window. He wondered if he wasn't experiencing an increase in the hallucinatory effects of the painkillers, because what he saw was too incredible to be accepted at face value.

The Oscar Mayer Wienermobile had just pulled up to Owen Thom's house.

Despite looking a little more faded than photographs he'd seen let on, it was unmistakable. Its yellow bun-shaped frame held the orangey, flesh-colored wiener in place on top, curling up at the back like a dog's tail. The windows wrapped around the front half were pitch black, making it impossible to see who was inside, but it reminded Owen of the way an airplane or helicopter cockpit was shaped.

The whole vehicle danced and fluctuated like he was seeing it through extreme heat.

He should have been excited to see it so close and in person. What kid hadn't dreamed of seeing a huge hot dog on wheels?

But now, for some reason, bile rose in the back of his throat. There was more unexplainable fear than fascination.

It sat there for an untold amount of time. Long enough for the tiny clouds of driveway dust it had kicked up to settle beneath the rubber tires.

Owen was less aware of the pain in his back now. In fact, he was unaware of it all. His brain went into survival-mode: Was the front door locked? If not, could Owen hobble there in time to make sure? Was there anything in the house he could use as a weapon?

His dad kept some handguns in the safe, but Owen didn't know the combination. He knew there was a pair of .22 rifles on the top shelf of the closet too, but he'd never thought of using them for anything other than shooting bottles in the middle of the desert. Could he actually use one in a situation that demanded it?

He released the blinds and clapped his hands to his face.

"Come on, get it together," he whispered. Why was he having such panicked feelings about this?

Sunlight peeked through the tiny slits in the blinds. Slowly, he reached forth and parted them once again.

The Wienermobile was still there. The engine was still running.

And an electric buzz began to build, vibrating outside of and searching his body once again as it had at the track near the substation.

The blinds snapped into place as Owen gripped his chest and fell back onto the bed, staring up at that popcorn ceiling once more.

"What—" he tried to ask, but his breath was short and quick, making it nearly impossible to catch air, let alone talk.

His head spun.

He felt like he was going to pass out or throw up.

Maybe both.

He heard about people who'd suffocated on their own puke. He didn't want that to be him, so he rolled himself over onto his side.

And then the Wienermobile's engine roared through the single-pane glass windows like it had glasspacks. Suddenly, the buzzing disappeared from Owen's body.

Almost if someone had flipped a switch.

Owen pushed himself up from the bed, feeling a renewed sense of strength. A strength that made him feel like he'd popped ten cans of spinach, a la Popeye. Stronger than he'd felt in days.

Heck, he was willing to say that he'd never felt this strong in his entire life.

He flew back to the window, propped open the blinds once more, just in time to see the rear tip of the Wienermobile pulling out onto his home street.

Within seconds, it was gone.

But the odd feeling of strength remained.

Owen looked down at his fists, flexing them open and shut, feeling like he could punch a hole through the wall if he wanted.

He even thought about testing it out, but a different feeling, one of fear, the voice of his dad encouraging a need to be practical, told him he ought to make sure the place was locked up tight.

He walked around the whole house and confirmed that all doors and windows were secured. By the time he got back to his bedroom, he felt like he'd run a marathon.

His computer beckoned him once again, the screen still filled with lines of gibberish that needed decoding.

But Owen felt exhausted now. The earlier restlessness, the sudden bout of adrenaline, all gone. Now, he wanted nothing more than to take a nap in his bed. To fall into a pleasant dream from which he could slowly wake.

He saved the email, turned off the computer, and slid back underneath the covers.

The computer ticked and creaked as the cooling components contracted. His ears were perked for a long time, listening for the sound of the rumbling engine and swishing gravel. His eyes focused once again on the cloud dilating behind Cru Jones. He pictured the Wienermobile approaching the dirt jump behind Cru. He saw it all happening: Cru hanging in the air, unaware of the shadowy vehicle launching behind him, towering above him like an omnipresent god.

Owen wanted to yell out to Cru. Wanted to warn him that he was about to be crushed from the monster above. But Owen couldn't find his voice. He could barely move his lips.

Before he knew it, he was fast asleep, dreaming about

something he would only sort of remember.

Monday, June 12, 1989 - 8:00 PM

Jake was in his dad's bathroom which smelled faintly of recently-sprayed Lysol. He tried to ignore the water hissing from within the toilet tank as it had been doing so for the past week. He leaned over the chipped white tile counter, holding his father's gleaming straight razor with a steady hand, keeping its cutting edge close to his face yet far enough away to avoid a repeat of the bloody mess that happened last time he'd fooled around with it.

The peach fuzz on his upper lip had shown up on the morning of March 27th. The date was marked with a big red check mark on Jake's mental calendar.

Today, on the evening of June 12th, posing and primping right before his shower, he found a real, genuine, legitimate hair protruding from the tip of his chin like a yellow needle. He didn't know how long it had been there and was a little perturbed to think that he'd missed its birth.

But the fact is that it was there.

It was real.

Yeah, it was solitary. For now. Jake was confident it

would have *compadres* soon. He was zooming into manhood.

He waved the razor back and forth slowly, centimeters from his flesh, pretending to be like his old man before work.

Jake didn't plan on shaving off his newfound claim to manhood. No sir. He just wanted to pretend. To get to know what it would feel like when he eventually had to shave every day like his dad.

On the next cycle of lifting the razor up to his right cheekbone, the bathroom door flew open, slapping against the cheap chrome towel rack. The door and rack each rang and vibrated disharmoniously for a good three seconds.

The razor tumbled from Jake's hand and bounced off the bathroom sink, hitting the brown linoleum floor with a clank.

A solitary "Shit," escaped from Jake's lips.

His dad stood in the threshold with the hallway behind him. He was a tall man, his to-the-flesh shaved head nearly hitting the top of the door frame. He was wearing his usual post-work uniform—a yellowed cotton wifebeater that exposed the smattering of random faded-turquoise tattoos that populated his chubby arms, along with a pair of seersucker boxer shorts of which the waistband was slightly overlapped by a hairy belly built on Budweiser and Fritos.

"So you like wasting my aftershave?" he said. The bathroom lights seemed to shine more harshly in the reflection of his blue eyes.

Jake looked at the plastic bottle of crystal-clear blue Aqua Velva resting on the white-tile counter just to the left of the sink. The lid was off to the side, laying upside-down.

"I haven't used any. I swear."

Jake reached down to grab the razor which lay on the tile floor. Inches before his fingers connected, he felt his father's grip pulling him upright by the back of his t-shirt. A tearing sound ripped across the tiny bathroom.

"Hey!"

Jake pulled the collar to the side and examined the rip that had started at the neck and reached down halfway to his right shoulder. The shirt was one of his favorites—pure black with a Ghostbuster's logo on the front. The one with the white ghost imprisoned behind the red "not allowed" symbol.

"But you were going to, right," his dad said more than asked.

"I was just—"

An open palm flew into Jake's face before he realized what was happening. His hand reached up too late to guard against the impact, relegated to rubbing out the resulting sting instead.

"What? You were just what?"

Jake propped open his mouth, ready to spew a bucket full of meaningless words, but muscle memory kicked in as he tasted blood pooling at the corner of his lips. He'd been through this too many times before to not learn something. No matter what he might say, it would sound like an excuse to his dad.

"Yes, sir. I was going to use your aftershave."

He let a moment's silence hang in the air before his dad said, "Get out."

Jake bent over, reaching down for the razor again.

He felt the collar of his shirt pull up into his throat once again, stinging his sensitive skin.

The tear on his t-shirt expanded down the shoulder toward the sleeve.

"Now," his dad finished.

Though he stood in place for another moment longer than he felt comfortable doing, Jake knew better than to take things any further with his dad.

He wasn't looking to commit suicide by Old Man.

In moments like these, Jake quickly dreamed of what he could do to his dad. He dreamt of picking up the razor and slicing up his wifebeater while he was still wearing it. If the old man got some cuts and scratches along the way, well, that would just be a darn shame.

The mental images of red liquid being soaked up by the old man's frayed wifebeater almost brought a smile to Jake's face, but he quickly reined it in. It wasn't worth another prickling slap.

Or something worse.

Heat rose into his cheeks. His head suddenly felt light. He realized he was holding his breath, so he took a deep whiff of air through his nose, taking harsh notice of the astringent Lysol again, and pushed past his dad into the hallway, walking straight into his adjacent bedroom.

He slammed the white paint-peeling door, seeming to rattle every hung frame in the house. Hopefully one of his dad's tin NASCAR souvenir fell off and dented itself on the ground.

"You better stop acting like a stupid little shit," the old man yelled through the door, "or I'm selling all of your crap and sending you to your mom's for good."

Promises, promises.

By the time his dad reached the end of his sentence, Jake was already splayed belly-down across his bed, his face buried deep into his pillow. He pulled the sides up against his ears to bury any further admonishments.

His dad's threats were as common as the empty Budweiser cans spread haphazardly all over the backyard porch. If only Jake could gather the threats up and sell them for change as his old man forced him to do with the cans.

Through the gaps in his bedroom window sill, the dry desert wind picked up outside. The off-white G.I. Joe-logoed curtains he'd bought himself flipped upward.

Odd music floated in on the back of the breeze. Sometimes the neighbor to the left blasted Creedence Clearwater Revival into the late hours of the night, but this was something else. Something different. This sounded like chimes and melodic tings—what one might expect to hear from an ice cream truck.

There *was* an ice cream truck that roamed the neighborhood on Saturdays and Sundays, but it rarely came by on weekdays, and never at night. At least not advertising its services.

Intrigued, Jake pushed himself up from the bed and pulled a flap of curtain away from the window.

It wasn't quite dark outside, but dusk had arrived. His bedroom faced north-west where the edge of the orange sun was still dipping down slightly behind the outline of Bell Mountain, sending its remaining rays into the cloud-filled sky.

As beautiful as the sunset may have been, Jake wasn't one to appreciate them. Besides, it wasn't the most interesting thing he saw right now.

The most interesting thing he saw sat on the dirt shoulder in front of his house.

"Holy crapola," he whispered into the glass.

It was the Oscar Mayer Wienermobile.

He couldn't see its pilot behind the tinted windows, but he pictured a guy wearing a tan-collared shirt tucked into army-green pants. He had strong, brown eyebrows and close-cut blond hair, much like Jake's. Matching yellow whiskers jabbed out like sharp sticks from his solid jaw. One hand rested on the shifter knob and the other was perched comfortably at eleven o'clock on the steering wheel.

Come to think of it, the guy reminded Jake of Duke from G.I. Joe. A non-cartoony version, of course, but it was him.

In his mind, Jake saw Duke grinning widely.

Jake wished, if only momentarily, that the man could be his father. The thought brought Jake a sudden sense of shame.

Yo Jake! Want to go for a ride? I'll even let you drive. You can get away from that big turd swilling Bud in the living room.

The idea of getting away from the old man was a tempting one. He could slide open the window and step right outside into the night air. Jake looked around the room, wondering if he'd need to pack anything. Nothing other people would consider practical, like clothes or food. He was wondering if he could pack all of his M-80s plus a brick of black cats.

If anyone would appreciate the firepower, it would be Duke.

His hand came up to his cheek, and he looked back toward the window. Visions of Duke sitting inside returned to him. As he stared into the Wienermobile's dark windows, it was like a light came on inside—or more like the dark film parted like smoke, revealing the man himself sitting inside, looking over at Jake.

The image of his idol appeared half real, half not. Like one of those new hologram pictures that changed depending on the angle at which you looked at them.

But even across the twenty yards between his window and the vehicle, Jake could see Duke clearly—so clearly that he noticed a translucent liquid, it seemed like sweat, weaving a ring around the edge of the soldier's hairline. Waxy drops streamed down his face as though he'd stepped into a sudden thundershower or out of a sauna.

Something was happening to Duke. Almost like he was melting.

Jake thought, What's wrong with you?

The words seemed to project themselves beyond his own mind.

The Almost-Apocalypse of Apple Valley

Yo Jake, nothing. Nothing at all. Come on, let's go. Let's blow this joint.

The words were his old man's. A favorite phrase that snapped him back to his bedroom, simultaneously shrouding the image of Duke again.

He let the curtains fall, but it failed to obscure the image of the melting hero in his head.

Jake almost yelled for his dad, but stopped short. What would be the point? A scenario ran through his mind where Jake's dad would slap him over and over again, telling him that he didn't care if the goddamn Pope was outside—if Jake didn't stop bothering him with stupid shit, he would take Jake's bike and toys to the town dump and personally watch them get crushed.

It was a familiar threat and one that his father seemed to be getting closer to fulfilling each time.

Still, an uncomfortable, nervous feeling rose within Jake's belly, and he thought he should at least mention it to his father.

As the thought arrived, the tinkling music cut out like it was something tangible chopped off with a gleaming, sharp cleaver.

A sharp pain shot into Jake's chest as if he'd been stabbed with a switchblade. Within milliseconds of the sensation, maybe even simultaneously, he heard the Wienermobile lurching forth onto the empty blacktop street. Its back tires spun in the loose dirt for a moment before gaining traction.

Jake grabbed his chest, falling back to the floor in front of his bed. He grimaced and groaned quietly, trying not to piss off his dad, realizing too late that the pain was already gone. It had disappeared as quickly as it arrived.

Now, an odd feeling swept in and took the pain's place. He couldn't put a finger on what exactly the feeling was—an emptiness that was not quite empty. One filled with leaking residue, just like he'd seen dripping from the pilot's face. The closest thing he could compare it to was how he felt when a lizard he'd caught and kept caged in his room had run away two years ago.

Something almost like a betrayal.

Did he lose his only opportunity to get out of here and make something of his life?

Jake didn't know which was worse—whatever this nameless thing was or the physical pain.

He stood up and placed a weak hand on the bed, gathering his bearings. His ears felt clogged up with water. The left one was ringing a little.

Again, he thought about telling his dad, but quickly

decided against it. Instead, he silently took off his clothes, showered, and went straight to bed without brushing his teeth.

Throughout the night he slipped into strange, terrifying dreams—dreams where he was chased by tiny dolls with scratched faces, their dusty dresses fluttering in the wind as their aged joints screamed with each movement. And worst of all, they were all missing some vital part like an eye or a leg.

The nightmares constantly stopped and started throughout the long night, interrupted by low thunder in the distance and even pattering rain slapping the dirt just outside Jake's window. Morning seemed to take forever to come and when it did, all Jake knew was that he did not want to leave the house.

But he would anyway.

Facing whatever it was out there that frightened him was surely better than what he'd face at home if he told his old man he wanted to stay home sick.

Steph didn't know where the whole idea of butterflies in the stomach came from, but it made a lot of sense. Only, what didn't make sense is why she felt them now. It would have been easy to blame it on the test tomorrow, but it felt deeper than that. She just couldn't put her finger on it.

While Jake was playing quarterback in a pick-up recess game of football, she and Ryan laid back and watched with their elbows resting on the cement curb of the sandbox adjacent to the field.

She was only half paying attention.

Behind them, the sound of squealing kids melded with the sound of squealing metal, composing a sort of schoolyard symphony as the chained swings flew back and forth in consistent arcs.

Three boys kicked violently at each other while dangling from their fingers to their outstretched shoulders on green-painted jungle gym bars. The girls typically were hanging upside-down on the pull-up bars, tucking their legs back until their heels hit their hamstrings, swinging back and forth with their hair hanging down like curtains while they chanted some playground rhyme.

Steph picked at the damp grass with her fingertips. The morning was cool and the sky was slightly overcast. The spots that were normally ankle-snapping divots on the makeshift football field were a new kind of hazard today—swamps of thick, brown mud due to last night's random rainstorm.

Now every single kid made a special effort to drive whichever poor soul carried the football straight into them.

Steph flicked her head, sweeping her bangs away from her field of vision.

"Ten bucks says Jake's the first to get a mud bath," Ryan said.

"You don't have ten bucks," Steph said. "Otherwise, I'd run in and push him myself."

"True," Ryan said. "I still think he'll be the first. He'd probably like it."

"Probably," Steph agreed.

She glanced at Ryan, who was grinning ear to ear, but quickly stopped like he'd been caught doing something wrong and smiled with sealed lips instead.

Steph knew Ryan was self-conscious about his two front teeth. Jake, and sometimes Owen, gave him a hard time about them, though never in a really mean way. Still, she could tell it bothered Ryan. Steph thought they made him look kind of adorable. No way she would ever say that to him, of course.

Especially lately, given how he'd been acting kind of weird around her. She didn't want to encourage him to be even weirder.

She thought about mentioning the quiz to Ryan, but thought better of it. Last night, her mom had reluctantly given her permission to visit Owen to help her study, so long as she called his parents, and they were okay with it.

Apparently, his mom thought he was well enough and that it might actually be good for him to spend an hour, but only an hour, with one of his friends.

And now she beamed a little inside, because after school today, she would hop on her bike and ride to Owen's. She knew he would help her pass, sure, but she was more excited just to hang out with him a little more.

Ryan sneezed, pulling her attention back to him, reminding her to change the subject.

"Are you going to Owen's birthday party Saturday?" she asked.

"Yeah," Ryan said. "Wherever there's cake, I'm there. Plus, he said there was going to be a *piñata*. And a magician."

It would be a welcome set of events.

One reason was because Steph knew that if she *didn't* get out of the sixth grade, it might be the last party she'd ever attend.

The other reason was that Steph much preferred the boys' birthday parties to the ones her mom threw for her. She'd tell her mom what she'd want and her mom would dutifully ignore her anyway. That usually meant there would be lace and pink and stupid Barbie themes involved.

And who could forget all the stupid, annoying girls in her class that she couldn't stand to be around? The ones who only came to her birthday parties because their parents made them?

The ones like Loretta Mishki?

Steph's eyes zoomed in on the gaggle of girls seated on silver metallic picnic benches placed beneath a steel canopy hovering just outside a pair of portable classrooms.

Loretta, perched on top of the table to ensure her place at the center of attention, wore an acid-washed jean jacket with the sleeves rolled up past her wrists, along with a pair of bright pink shorts that showed off her perfectly tanned legs. Her delicate hands rested on her knees, putting her fake fingernails on display—they were even longer than Mrs. Kirkwood's, though they were painted magenta instead of flesh-colored. Otherwise, they wouldn't match Loretta's eye-shadow. Then there was her dirty-blond hair—wavy and held in extreme place by what had to have been gallons of Aqua Net hairspray.

A hurricane could have blown through and everything but Loretta's hair would have been swept out of existence.

She was surrounded on the bench below by her cackling band of three witches who tried their best to look just like her. Giggling Tina Schaffer, Stacy Thomas, who always sounded like she had a sore throat, and the not-so-gentle giant Kim Goldnik sat beneath her like an eager audience, or more like worshipers before their idol, listening to the morning's sermon pouring out from behind Loretta's pearl-white teeth.

Steph referred to their almost-cult as the Aqua Bitches.

Wherever Loretta went, the Bitches followed.

Steph hated all of those girls an unreasonable amount. There was enough to hate about them *without* being unreason- able, but she took that hate to a level which even she couldn't explain. It wasn't like she wanted to be a part of their stupid, dumb club, even if they had asked her to (it would *never* hap- pen). But just their whole exclusive, cliquish vibe sent her mind reeling with images of violence which even made Steph feel queasy occasionally.

At least she admitted it.

And, of course, the Bitches would always come to Steph's birthday parties, but only because Loretta was there, and she was only there because Steph's mom insisted on inviting her.

"Well, maybe if you tried a little harder to be friends with them and stopped hanging out with those boys, you'd have an easier time of things," her mom would say. "You could learn a few things from Loretta, you know."

Stupid Loretta Mishki, held up by Steph's mom as the paragon of girlhood.

Stupid Loretta Mishki, who probably would have curled up and died without her adoring audience.

Stupid Loretta Mishki, who wore a jacket and shorts at the same time, because yeah, that made total sense.

The Bitches gleefully came to Steph's birthday parties only to talk trash.

So, yeah, she was really looking forward to Owen's party, because she knew they wouldn't be there. It would be an actual party where she could have actual fun.

"I bought him a switchblade," Ryan said.

"Huh?" Steph said, halfway conscious of her waking thoughts.

"I said that I bought him a switchblade. Owen. For his

birthday."

There was a dry booger hanging from Ryan's nose, flapping side to side every time he exhaled. She decided not to mention it.

"You bought him a knife?" she asked, her eyes wide open. "Are you crazy?"

"Not a real one," Ryan said, rolling his eyes. "One of those combs that pops out."

"Oh," she replied, relaxing again. "Cool."

As much as Owen would probably like that, she had something else in mind for him. Something she couldn't afford completely on her own, but that she could at least help put a few dollars toward.

A brand-new helmet.

She didn't know if Owen would accept the money for it, given how partial he was to the current one, but she'd seen the damage—it was beyond repair.

Now that she learned that Ryan had already spent money on a gift, she'd propose he return it for a refund and help support the new Rocket Man Helmet Fund instead.

"I was thinking, What about—"

"Get him!"

Steph's question was interrupted by the shout which

seemed to come from nowhere. An onslaught of clumsy foot-falls and grunts rose in volume as a group of bodies beelined toward her and Ryan.

The two of them lifted their heads just in time to see kids chasing after Jake who had the football tucked inside his breadbasket like something precious.

Steph and Ryan scrambled to their feet. They had been sitting just out of bounds, but with the group of boys continuing on their chaotic trajectory toward the pair, it was obvious that momentum had no respect for rules.

Jake was running full bore, clearly trying to make a go for the end zone that was the school blacktop. All ten kids who made up the other team were on his tail. They closed in on him like a pack of wolves.

His face was drawn up tight and his shoulders bounced from side to side in sync with his pumping legs. There was something else in his face though—like he wasn't just trying to score a touchdown. Like he wasn't just running from the kids on the other team.

Steph thought he looked like he was running from the Devil himself.

His head occasionally twisted back to keep track of the predators on his tail. She saw a grimace form, pulling his eyebrows down and in across his forehead like he was furiously concentrating, only that wasn't quite it. The fact that Steph couldn't put into words what she was seeing left her frustrated.

As the mass of tiny humans careened down the sidelines, closer and closer, Steph stepped over the cement lip and back into the sandbox, feeling rough, loose particles invade her Vans slip-ons. She yanked on Ryan's arm, pulling the hypnotized boy back to safety alongside her.

It was unnecessary though. Jake course-corrected and quickly swung back toward the middle of the field. Knowing him, he probably thought he was being clever. And maybe if he were a different player, it would have been clever. The problem with Jake was that even though he was big, he was slow.

Sure enough, one of the faster kids, little Adam Nielsen, got a grip on the back of Jake's shirt, pulling its front tight against his round belly. It slowed him down even more. Other hands followed Adam's until Jake was rendered nearly invisible by a multi-colored blanket of flesh, hair, grass-stained jeans, and Rude Dog t-shirts.

The pile of little football star wannabes was pressuring him, pulling him down with all of its collective might.

An unnerving scream rose from Jake's throat, almost a cry.

It turned into a scene that reminded Steph of a drawing she'd seen in the book about Gulliver, the giant being tied down by all of those little people.

And then it happened mostly as expected.

Jake, in his infinite unwisdom, had headed straight towards the closest mud pit.

A massive cheer went up as Jake went down.

"Get off me!" she heard. "Get off me!"

It couldn't have been timed better: the end-of-recess bell went off just as his chest plopped down right into the puddle, sending a splash of brown sludge onto anyone within a radius of five feet.

One by one, the kids scrambled away, laughing, flinging the freshly stirred-up mud at each other.

The predators scattered with their fresh coat of brown body paint, laughing at both Jake and themselves. But when Jake's body surfaced, he wasn't laughing or smiling at all. Instead, there was another expression on his dripping face—one of surprise. Steph might even say fear. Like someone had unexpectedly dumped a bucket of cold water on his head which he immediately took to be acid.

Steph looked at Ryan who was grinning again, but this time not seeming to care if she saw his two front teeth protruding into the air.

"I really wish you would have taken that bet," he said.

The Bitches laid in wait.

Steph wasn't an idiot, but the tiny minds of four particular girls seemed to think so.

Though those four pitiful excuses for human beings often hung around together, it was never near the bike racks, and it was never at 3:00 p.m. when the school was for all practical purposes, a graveyard. Nearly every kid had been picked up by their parents or were halfway through their bus route.

The only bike left in the rack was Steph's.

In other words, they had no reason whatsoever to hang around that particular spot if it wasn't to "run into" Steph.

Paused behind the southeast corner of the cafeteria building with her green and black Teenage Mutant Ninja Turtles backpack slung over her left shoulder, she wasn't necessarily hiding, but certainly hesitating.

The Bitches stood face to face with each other, gabbing about God knows what. Loretta was leaning into her groupies, arms crossed, wearing her signature jean jacket and excessive ruby red lipstick. Steph was surprised Loretta managed to talk at all, in between blowing giant pink bubble-gum bubbles that expanded beyond rational possibilities, popping, and then being chewed back into optimal blowing condition once again.

Steph would have paid twenty bucks just to have the opportunity to jab her finger in the bubble so that the gum spread all over Loretta's face, messing up her ridiculous make-up or even getting tangled in her hair.

Fat chance she'd get away with it though. The Aqua Bitches may, by all appearances, seem like prisses, but Steph had seen them throw down before—especially Big Kim Goldnik, the tall one who could launch a softball like a rocket and whose long pony tail poked at her lower back as she walked, just above her butt. She seemed like an honorary Bitch, only because she was desperate enough to fit in with the cool crowd and Loretta needed the additional muscle.

Steph turned back a little and leaned against the brown stucco. The rough texture poked the back of her head.

She couldn't wait here forever. Her mom would give her crap for being late. She'd ask Steph if she was spending too much time hanging around those boys again. Not that she'd outright ban Steph from doing so, but the attempt to shame her daughter would be in full force.

After taking a deep breath, Steph pushed herself off the

wall, straightened her back, squared her shoulders, and walked toward the girls like she owned the place. She was the Terminator (if only they had made a movie where the bad ass robot was a girl).

Once Steph was halfway to the bike rack, Loretta stopped talking. Head Bitch lifted her chin to an angle of forty-five degrees while her eyes remained focused on Steph. Simultaneously, her elbows came into contact with the ribs of Tina and Stacy. Kim had her back to Steph and was the last to catch on, laughing like a dumb donkey as if their conversation was still continuing. Stacy harshly shushed her.

A shot of fear hit Steph's stomach. Skipping past them suddenly became an enticing possibility. She could walk home—maybe be thirty minutes late—and just pick up her bike tomorrow.

But there were still three days left in the school week. Who's to say they wouldn't be waiting for her tomorrow as well? Or the next day? And who's to say they would let her off the hook if she walked? Even with the backpack, she could outrun three of the girls, but Kim would probably catch her and sit on her back, rubbing Steph's face into the dirt, while the other girls caught up.

If that happened, Steph could fight back. She'd fight

dirty. She had absolutely no qualms with that.

But she didn't want to fight. That was a last resort. She decided to take a different tack. She would just ignore them. Pretend they weren't there. Pretend they weren't real, but merely figments of her imagination.

Avoiding eye contact, she was ten feet from her bike. A cloying mix of cheap drugstore perfumes wafted through the air, punching Steph in the nose.

The girls said nothing as Steph reached her bike and started flipping through the dials of the chain lock. The combo was three digits and Steph knew them by heart. Still, she was so self-conscious now, she had trouble remembering what the correct answer was.

Her hearing felt so sensitive, picking up every minute sound around her: a murder of crows flying overhead; the low rumble of a car engine entering the faculty parking lot just behind the school cafeteria; she even thought she heard the judging eyes of the three girls swiveling back and forth in their sockets between Steph and each other.

The first digit was a three.

What was the second?

It was a warm day and the sun seemed even more merciless now than it had in the past two weeks. A bead of sweat found its way from the tip of Steph's hairline to her eyebrow. It fell onto the cement below, leaving a tiny puddle of evidence. The sweat glands on her palms were starting their business now too.

I know this number, Steph thought. I know this damn, stupid number.

"Hey," Loretta said.

Steph heard her. Tried her best to ignore her. To focus on the second number, but it wasn't coming.

"Hey," Loretta repeated.

Six?

No. No, that wasn't it. Her thumb flicked the little white dial continuously, cycling zero through nine on the black digits.

"Hey, Boy George, she's talking to you," Stacy said in her squawking, parrot-like voice.

Steph stopped for a moment. The Ninja Turtles weighed heavily on her back. Heavier than they'd ever weighed while she struggled to remember three stupid little numbers. It was hopeless. She couldn't concentrate. Not until she got rid of the Bitches.

"What?" she asked, looking back at them. She noticed a glint of white plastic sticking out of Loretta's left jean jacket pocket. The top was square and cracked open slightly, like a lid.

Were those cigarettes?

"I saw you sitting with your new boyfriend on the playground earlier," Loretta said, chewing rapidly like a cow with a wad of cud who'd ingested six gallons of Jolt Cola that day.

There was a dramatic pause while she blew a bubble that almost stretched across the whole of her face. More than ever, Steph felt the urge to pop the damn thing, hoping it would collapse across Loretta's nose and mouth, suffocating her.

"Does your other boyfriend know about him?"

"Huh?" Steph replied.

"The nerdy one. Oliver? Austin?" Loretta shrugged with exaggeration and looked at the Bitches like anyone outside of her little world had hardly been worthy of her attention.

Steph glared directly into Loretta's eyes. For the briefest second, her stomach dropped, and she stumbled backward slightly as a tiny red glow pulsated around Loretta's pupils and quickly disappeared.

"Owen," Steph replied, rankled that Loretta didn't even know his name. "And he's not my boyfriend. And neither is Ryan. I don't have a boyfriend."

Loretta grinned, showing off her perfect smile as if she'd stepped out of an Aqua Fresh commercial.

"Sure. Whatever." She chuckled slightly. The Bitches copied her. "Your boyfriend. The first boyfriend. He's a little dweeb, though I guess he's kinda cute."

"Eww," Stacy and Tina said harmoniously.

Loretta laughed again. Something ugly between a grunt and a giggle.

For some reason that had not yet manifested itself to Steph, the fact that Loretta thought Owen was "kinda cute" pissed her off beyond rational thought. Maybe it was because Loretta had gone through six "boyfriends" before the whole school year had even come to a close. She cycled through them like she did her wardrobe. Steph wondered if Loretta maybe even thought of them that way. She'd seen the way she treated them—adoringly for a small slice of time, holding their hands during walks at recess, letting them buy her chips or soda from the vending machines next to the water fountains.

But then, inevitably, she would get bored. Loretta never seemed to actually break up with any of them. The unlucky guy would just find himself with extra quarters in his pocket and no hand to hold the next day because it would be occupied by someone else's.

Owen would be too smart to even think of doing that.

Right?

Again, she tried to ignore the cawing of the crows, the

idling engine, the shifting eyes.

Steph put her focus back on the lock. She realized that her thumb had subconsciously landed on the number one.

That was it.

Cool.

One number left. Just one stinking number left, and she could ride away from these stupid girls and their stupid lives.

"Do you think I should ask Oliver out?" Loretta asked. She looked around at the Bitches. "I think I'm going to ask him out."

The tiny puddles of sweat on the cement were piling up now, forming an obscure pattern of connect-the-dots. Steph's cheeks felt flush with hot anger. She wanted to tell Loretta and her Bitches to stay the hell away from Owen and any other of Steph's friends.

Not that she cared who Owen held hands with. At least she didn't think she did. He could hold hands with any girl he wanted to, right? Just so long as it wasn't Loretta or one of the Bitches. My God, how that would absolutely destroy Steph, as much as she didn't want to admit it.

The third number clicked into place and the lock snapped free. It felt like opening a can of soda. All the pressure of Steph's inner tension was released. She fumbled with the plastic-covered chain, coiling it up and stuffing it into her backpack.

"You do what you want," Steph said. "He'd never go out with you anyway."

Steph hoped she sounded confident. But now she wondered if Owen had ever mentioned Loretta? Or any of the Aqua Bitches for that matter?

Steph searched her mind's tenuous alleyways and byways, digging for a past moment, a fragment, where that may have happened. She didn't think so, but the idea that Owen might actually have feelings for one of them struck her as a fearsome possibility. They were the popular girls, after all. Wouldn't it be weird if he *didn't* have a crush on one of them?

During the moments of searching thought, a pair of hands, hands that weren't Steph's, placed themselves on the handlebars of her bike.

They were chubby hands. Fat and ugly hands.

Kim Goldnik hands.

Steph raised her face to meet Kim's chin and never felt so small in her life.

Loretta and her two other stool pigeons walked up and stood beside Kim.

"I don't like you," Loretta said.

"The feeling's mutual," Steph replied.

"The feeling's mutual," Tina and Stacy mocked.

"You're annoying. You're stupid. You're poor. But worst of all, you're ugly..."

Loretta rattled off a laundry list of things about Steph that may have affected her at any other time, maybe even to the point of tears, but right now, the only tears that were springing forth were generated by the notion that Owen may have thought about holding hands with Loretta Mishki once or twice.

"Look, the baby's going to cry," Kim said, her voice sounded deeper and more domineering than normal. The words were charged with electricity that Steph almost felt running through her entire body.

The cawing of the crows gathering near the school's green dumpsters intensified. Whoever had pulled into the parking lot seemed to be revving their engine for no good reason.

Steph stood there like a dumb ox, unable to move. With one hand on the seat and the other in the middle of the handlebars, she felt like her options were nonexistent. Kim wouldn't let her move the bike. She felt the force of the big girl's hands holding fast.

"Cry, baby, cry," Tina teased.

"What do you want?" Steph finally asked, her voice cracking. "Please, just leave me alone."

Loretta didn't give Steph the relief of a fast answer. Instead, she seemed to take pleasure in the streaming tears of her compliant victim.

"I want you to do exactly what you're doing. I want you to cry. I want you to know that you're a worthless, dumb girl and that I could take your boyfriend—assuming I even want to."

There was nothing Steph could say. The energy was still surging in her, but it felt like half-juice. That if she were to wind up and sock Kim somewhere in the face with all of her might, it would peter out halfway, only giving Kim a love tap.

Yeah, that would only piss her off.

Loretta elbowed Kim in the arm. "Let's go," she said. "She's got enough to cry about for now."

From behind the safety of her bangs, Steph risked a quick glance into Kim's and then Loretta's eyes. They glowed a red fire, reflecting the heat of the afternoon sun. They latched onto Steph for an uncomfortable amount of time.

Finally, Kim pushed the bike backward into Steph. The back of the seat jammed into Steph's hip, making painful contact with the bone.

Steph winced. Something felt odd about the bike, but she was too distracted to try to figure out exactly what it was.

The Bitches started to drift away.

Their backs were to Steph now as they headed toward the staff parking lot. The four of them, if anyone else were to see them, maybe walking in the Victor Valley Mall or just down the street, would probably think they were innocent, everyday adolescent girls enjoying their time together.

Prior to today, Steph had only maintained a healthy level of dislike for them.

For some reason beyond Steph's comprehension, they now had taken things to a new level. These weren't just 'girls being girls' anymore. These girls were demons. These girls were pure spirits of evil that happened to live in the bodies of children.

She let the bike lean against her body so that she could crumple her fists and squeeze them together. Thoughts of what she could have done to Kim passed through her brain. She was feeling that electric charge now and was certain it wouldn't give out. Certain that it would provide enough juice to pass through Kim's layers of flesh, bone, and muscle, all the way out of the back of her head.

Steph blinked. Such a vision disturbed even her. She wanted to hurt them, hurt them all, but not anything like that. She wanted to make them pay, but not literally kill them.

Right?

Before turning the corner of the cafeteria, Loretta paused and turned. Almost with a psychic intuition, her friends turned in sync.

"Oh," Loretta said. "Say hi to your mom for me."

The Bitches cackled and then continued on their way.

Steph exhaled deeply and slowly, like air from a balloon whose neck was being slightly pinched. This newly formed nausea would go away. She would get on the bike, feel the wind in her face, and ride to Owen's. The studying would take her mind off what just happened. Seeing him would turn things around.

But in the back of her brain, just like the cawing of the desert crows and the revving of the engine, images of Owen and Loretta holding hands during recess nagged at her.

Steph put her hands back on the handlebars and began to pull it out from the rack.

It felt like she was pulling dead weight.

She glanced down and saw what had felt so funny earlier. She exhaled again, this time with greater force.

Both tires were flat.

SYSOP: ANY LUCK?

The gray block-cursor blinked ominously. It was a foreboding symbol.

Owen had logged into The Desert Oasis to play a quick round of Trade Wars, a BBS strategy game where multiple players took turns trying to conquer the galaxy, struggling to dominate over each other while engaged in interstellar commerce.

He'd been trying to distract himself and was successful: for a brief moment in time, he honestly forgot about the encrypted message.

Normally something like that would weigh on his mind until he figured it out, but Owen's thoughts were pulled toward other events more than normal.

The cursor continued flashing in and out of existence, awaiting a response. Owen could have logged out. Could have claimed his computer spontaneously rebooted or the modem malfunctioned.

But he knew that John was expecting an answer. To not reply would be to take John's friendship for granted. It seemed

John trusted Owen to do something extraordinary and a large part of Owen didn't want to let down the coolest adult in existence.

OWEN: NOTHING YET. STILL DECIPHERING.

It was the truth, though not the whole truth. Owen had spent some time on it in the morning, but his head was still occupied with other things.

First, the Wienermobile loomed largely in his thoughts. Why had it come to his house? Was it a simple mistake? Maybe it was supposed to go to some local event and the driver got lost, so he pulled into the driveway to look at a Thomas Guide or something.

Of course. Why not? That made complete, rational sense.

But even as he recalled the prior day's events, the feelings and images that had coursed through his body at the very same time the car showed up still reverberated within.

But that was just the meds, right?

Those thoughts had occupied his brain for most of the day, but they were later impeded upon by the second mental albatross: Steph stopping by to study.

Or, more accurately, *not* stopping by to study.

Based on her quick phone call the previous night, Owen expected Steph to show up soon after school let out. He made sure to shower twice. He couldn't explain why he did that. She'd never complained about the way he smelled before.

Yet, in the end, it didn't matter.

She never showed up.

He felt slightly worried at first and thought about calling her at home, but he really didn't want to talk to her mom. Ms. Morris always gave Owen the cold shoulder, and inevitably, Steph was always busy if she didn't pick up.

What if she decided to go somewhere else? He didn't want to get her in trouble. He decided to leave it be. Maybe try tomorrow to find out what happened.

Owen focused on the screen again, realizing John had already typed out a response.

SYSOP: NO WORRIES, AMIGO. TAKE YOUR TIME. HOW'S YOUR BACK FEELING? PLEASE DON'T TELL ME YOU'VE BEEN OUT RIDING YOUR BIKE ANYWAY.

Owen's fingers were poised over the keys. He debated whether he wanted to tell John about the crazy visions the medication was giving him, but he doubted John cared. He would probably just make a joke about it or worse—really have thought Owen was off his rocker and decide to cut ties.

He glanced at the ruined helmet sitting on his bedside stand. The crack between the *RM* seemed to have expanded over the past two days. More of the helmet's foam stuffing seeped out, exposed like a lower layer of sediment.

The pain in Owen's tailbone still radiated—especially when he'd been sitting for a long time or whenever he sat down on the hard toilet seat to go number two. But it was transient. Standing and pedaling might actually feel good. Even just to ride around the driveway out front and launch from the tiny lip between the cement driveway and street would be liberating.

OWEN: SOMEBODY'S GOT TO GO OUT AND SAVE THE WORLD. WHY NOT ROCKET MAN?

John replied right away.

SYSOP: WHY NOT, INDEED. WELL, I NEED TO HIT THE SACK. EARLY MORNING MEETINGS. I HAD THE BBS SEND AN ALERT OVER MY SPEAKERS WHEN YOU SIGNED ON. JUST IN CASE YOU FIGURED THINGS OUT.

Owen's heart sank into his stomach. Even though John had said "NO WORRIES," Owen couldn't help but feel he'd let his only adult friend down. He'd certainly let himself down. The knowledge and skills he had separated him from the average kid, even the average adult, and John was one of the few people to recognize it.

OWEN: LET ME GIVE IT ANOTHER SHOT. I'M NOT TIRED AND I'VE GOT NOTHING BETTER TO DO TONIGHT.

SYSOP: SOUNDS LIKE THE OWEN I KNOW. <G> I'D BE A BAD ADULT IF I SAID "YES, PLEASE GO AHEAD." SO I'LL JUST SAY DO WHAT YOU WOULD NORMALLY DO. AND IF YOU *DO* HAPPEN TO STAY UP, AND *DO* HAPPEN TO FIND AN ANSWER, SHOOT IT OVER TO ME IN A PRIVATE MESSAGE. <G>

OWEN: <G>

The chat screen refreshed itself and Owen was presented the main menu.

He hesitated there for at least a minute, mindlessly bouncing the selection cursor around the options before deciding to take his turn in Trade Wars.

After using up all his turns selling fuel ore and taking out a couple of planets, he was tempted to log off. The meds did make him tired, practically lethargic, but it wasn't enough to keep his brain from chastising him for slacking. He knew that he wouldn't be able to sleep anyway.

Angrily, he jammed his fingers on the keyboard until the encrypted message was in front of him. It sat there, and he thought long and hard about it.

Assembly Instructions

How would he even be able to begin deciphering this? He'd analyzed the pattern. It wasn't a simple substitution cipher. If it was, John wouldn't have bothered to send it over.

Maybe the key was in the title. The contents had to do with some sort of assembly code—an arcane programming language that was specific to computer processors.

He saved the data to a local file, disconnected from The Desert Oasis, and proceeded to review a text file which he downloaded from another BBS the day before (Owen had to make a long-distance modem call that he knew his parents would ream him about in a month, but it was the only BBS he knew about with the most extensive collection of text files). It was titled *The Crypto Keeper's Cookbook*, a play on another favorite text file of Owen's, *The Jolly Roger's Cookbook*, which was itself a derivative of *The Anarchist's Cookbook*.

All the information contained in these files felt like forbidden knowledge. What kid wouldn't be drawn to such things?

With *The Crypto Keeper's Cookbook* displayed on his screen, Owen scrolled through the various cipher methods listed, looking for something that might be a close match.

He had to take things methodically. Often, it was simpler to eliminate what the encoding language wasn't than to identify what it was.

Any of the letter-only ciphers like Amsco and Beaufort

were eliminated immediately.

Number-only systems such as Pollux didn't make sense either.

Now something like Gromark, with its combination of characters was a possibility, but the message didn't add up to anything when Owen ran through that.

At some point, Owen typed in *time* at the DOS prompt.

3:30 a.m.

And he'd barely gotten anywhere.

The answer wasn't even on the tip of his tongue. It wasn't anywhere *near* his tongue.

Every time he believed he was close to something, he came up empty. He may as well have spent the evening downloading some illegally shared "warez" game to play.

The full weight of exhaustion hit him as his head hinged back, revealing the popcorn ceiling. His back screamed out again now that it realized just how long it had been shoved into that chair.

Sorry, John, you're going to have to give me more time or figure this one out without me.

Owen jabbed his index finger at the power button and turned off his computer.

Simultaneously, a loud crack outside of his window sent

him reeling backward in his chair, nearly tipping the whole thing over. He stretched forward as quickly as he could and grabbed the edge of his desk, straining his back in the process, but maintaining his balance.

Goosebumps marched up his arms and across his neck.

The cracking sound was all too reminiscent of the one he'd heard at the dirt track. His body had a visceral reaction as it recalled the odd sensation from Saturday.

What's the deal with that?

Still feeling somewhat shaky, he reached down and grabbed his lower back, attempting to massage out the pain he'd induced.

Light flashed across his window, briefly lighting up the entire bedroom through the thin facade of his puke-yellow fabric curtains. His eyes were drawn to the shadows they drew across the back wall.

A slow, rolling thunder, like a pot of water coming to a boil, penetrated the assumed safety of the house. Owen suddenly felt vulnerable.

Two more successive flashes outlined his helmet. It stood out in relief against the textured bedroom wall. The crack running up and down the helmet was also illuminated each time, seeming larger than life. In Owen's vision, it was growing as he watched—growing from a tiny crack to a threatening chasm, and he was afraid that if he took a wrong step, he'd fall in and keep on falling for eternity.

A second loud snap of electricity whipped and shook the window.

It was the final straw for Owen.

Like a frightened puppy, he shoved his chair into his desk, scrambled back into his bed and cowered beneath the sheets. He started to recite the Lord's Prayer. It didn't hold any special meaning for him, but he'd heard it recited enough in church that it seemed appropriate and came to mind without effort.

"Our Father who art in Heaven—"

CRACK

Even through his thick Transformer-themed comforter, he could see the light illuminating his room as if it were the middle of the day.

"Hallowed be they name. Thy kingdom—"

BOOM

A thunderous fist punched the exterior of the house.

"Thy kingdom come, Thy will be done, on Earth—"

A rapid succession of snaps and house-shaking thunder made it feel like the whole world was on bum wheels—the kind you find on most grocery store shopping carts. He could have sworn the bed was spinning, circling down the chasm that had expanded from his helmet.

It was enough to shut Owen up.

He needed to get his bearings, to listen, to hear what was happening in the dark beyond the cramped mirage of safety that was his blankets.

After what must have been at least a full minute, the violent noises had not returned. Instead, it was replaced by a droning background noise which built to a steady volume. Through the comforter and sheets, drumming and clicking sounds could be heard from just outside.

Owen slowly withdrew from the temporary shell of his making. Muffled sounds soon became clear.

Raindrops.

Friggin' raindrops.

Of course.

A sense of shame ran through his body—what, was he four years old again? Why was he acting like a little baby afraid of some inclement weather?

He glanced at his helmet where the *RM* seemed to be glowing like a light bulb which still retained some latent electrical charge.

He laughed to himself.

At himself.

Rocket Man.

Rocket Man wasn't someone who cowered in bed, scared of loud noises in the sky.

Rocket Man wasn't someone who felt helpless in the face of a problem like John's email.

And then there was the final truth which shook him the most—maybe Owen wasn't Rocket Man after all.

Wednesday, June 14, 1989 - Some time in the AM

In between pops of thunder, the pitter-patter of rain

hitting the dirt outside of his window, and even at one point,

the growling of some animal like a revving car engine, Owen

Thom's dreams stopped their rapid cycle and found their focus.

He stood beside Steph on the precipice of a giant cliff.

Behind them were Jake and Ryan. When he turned around, he

couldn't *see* them. He only felt their presence and heard them

talking to each other in low tones. He knew that they were

there, but they were sort of background pieces. He didn't know

what they were discussing.

Below, the entire town of Apple Valley was spread out—

a tapestry of tarred roof-tops on brown dirt lots, surrounded

by clumps of weeds and asphalt streets, some which curved

and connected to the main thoroughfares like Highway 18 or

Navajo Road. Owen wasn't able to judge the exact distance, but

if he had to compare it to something, it was like they were in

an airplane, looking out the window about at a level where the

clouds might be. He wouldn't have been surprised to hear a pi-

lot's voice come over a fuzzy intercom—"We're at our cruising altitude of 26,000 feet..."

But something about the town made it seem closer in some respects.

All Owen knew was that his hometown looked like one of those miniature models like in the introduction to Mr. Rogers.

Despite the seemingly high elevation, Owen was sweating from the heat.

"We should throw rocks at it," he heard Jake say clearly for the first time.

Ryan laughed and enthusiastically agreed.

"Don't," Steph said. "You'll hurt someone."

"No, we won't," Jake said. "No one will even know it's us."

"Come on, Owen," Ryan said. "Let's do it. I even found you a good rock."

Owen looked at Steph who was staring back at him. There were tears in her eyes. Pleading tears that she quickly wiped away.

Owen rarely turned away from a good rock-throwing. It's just something boys loved to do. It was hardwired into their system, probably since the caveman days. If there was a rock that fit in your hand, it had to be thrown.

Still, Owen didn't like the look in Steph's eyes. "Guys, I

don't think we should."

A clack pulled his attention down to his British Knights. A perfectly-sized gray stone, smooth like it had been washed over the centuries by the running waters of the neighboring Mojave River, bounced and rolled next to his right foot.

"Come on," Jake said.

"Yeah, Rocket Man," Ryan added. "Don't be a puss."

Owen looked over at Steph, still teary-eyed, shaking her head.

But still, something compelled Owen to reach down.

He was being pulled in two different directions, and he truly believed that if he didn't make a decision, his head would detach from his neck and roll off the cliff.

The pull was too great. What did Steph know about throwing rocks? He swiped the stone from the ground and stood at attention, feeling the polish with his thumb, testing the weight in his palm.

It felt good.

It felt so right.

Steph was full-on sobbing at this point, her hands furiously wiping away the snot and tears now. There was the occasional "please" and "please don't" escaping her lips in a low whisper. Owen tried to ignore her. Her pain and fear were contagious, like he was present at an extremely sad funeral. He fought back the urge to turn on his own waterworks. He didn't want to hurt her.

Jake said, "Let's go, Rocket Man."

"Ignore her," Ryan said.

Owen's resolve was weakening. His grip was beginning to loosen around the rock until he felt another hand on his shoulder.

It was hot, almost searing, and Owen ripped himself from its grip. He flung himself around to see it was Ryan, but yet, it wasn't.

The person had Ryan's frame, but there was something wrong with his face. It was a lot like the adult movie channels on the local cable system where the screen showed nothing but a jagged, scrambled image that occasionally manifested itself into something more coherent and exciting.

Steph was suddenly quiet now. Her complexion was ruddy underneath the eyes. The tears had stopped, like she'd exhausted herself.

There was no longer any debate or time for hemming and hawing. Owen felt that he was at the moment of decision now.

"She doesn't really care about you," Ryan said. "She doesn't want you to have fun."

The Almost-Apocalypse of Apple Valley

Owen peered down at the tiny town below and watched the microscopic cars circle around the streets, ferrying passengers to and fro.

And before he knew it, his left arm was stretched behind his head in a wind-up pitch, his front leg lifted high for leverage, and he was fully engaged.

Steph let out a little yelp as the rock left Owen's palm. Instead of zooming out of focus to match the miniature Apple Valley below, the stone did the opposite.

It grew like a balloon.

And it kept growing.

It expanded and swelled until it became a crater-less meteorite the size of Apple Valley's central hill where the race track existed—the very landmark it seemed to be aiming for, though Owen hadn't consciously tossed it there.

Or had he?

In his head, he heard the rising crescendo of a thousand panicked screams. They didn't sound like they were coming from below, but he knew they were. And he knew the source: they were the children playing soccer, the parents cheering from the sidelines, the mailmen delivering magazines, the dog catchers, the hairstylists, the burger flippers, the mechanics— the citizens of Apple Valley. Normal people who thought they controlled their own lives and realized in a painful instant that that wasn't the case.

Then came impact.

The monstrous stone slammed into the hill. A rumble reverberated from the giant hole, spreading all the way to the cliff on which they stood. Soon, it was followed by a slow-motion rise of dust, forming a cloud of grime and debris which stretched all the way up to their perilous perch.

Owen began to cough uncontrollably as the material entered his nostrils and mouth, tunneling into his lungs.

Then Steph started in as well.

Then Jake and Ryan.

Together, the four friends collapsed to the ground. Owen wanted to hug them all, seeking mutual comfort, but he looked down at his body and realized something horrible had happened—his head had been removed from his neck after all. His lifeless body lay a few feet away.

Owen Thom screamed himself awake, just in time to see his mom and dad flinging open the door.

"What's wrong?" his mother asked, rushing over to the bed to hold him tightly.

Owen said nothing, only whimpered with his hands gripping his head, ensuring it stayed in place, listening intently to the occasional shock of thunder outside his window.

He caught a glimpse of his broken helmet still retaining a slight glow.

"We're *definitely* keeping him home for the rest of the week, Hal."

Owen snapped out of his trance, looking up to his mom's eyes locked on Owen's dad. "Mom, what about my party?"

"We'll see," she said, rubbing his back. "You need to focus on getting better."

"Oh, we're having the party," his dad said. "I've already paid for everything."

Then and there, Owen decided that he would stay in bed, stay off the computer, and do everything his parents said.

Wednesday, June 14, 1989 - 10:00 AM

It had exhausted itself and its Attendant, but It was satiated. They both slept in their own way and the dreams were good. This place would work out fine. Just fine.

There had been concerns at first. There were always concerns, mostly from the Attendant, but that was the Attendant's job. If the Attendant wasn't concerned, that put everything at risk.

And there's always *some* risk. Truly great rewards never come without great risks.

But the rewards here were beyond anything It had ever experienced. The children here were so full of power. So full of Capability.

While the kids played and lived in ignorance, the Attendant and It would work.

Yes, this tiny desert town would work out fine.

Just fine.

Saturday, June 17, 1989 - 11:00 AM

The smell of grilling burgers and hot dogs drifted through the open kitchen window and into the dining room, but it wasn't enough to pull Owen's attention away from the cake sitting on top of the table.

The centerpiece was almost radiant in appearance, but not so radiant that Owen wouldn't be happy to stab it with a fork and spill its chocolate guts.

Even a week full of ice cream—whenever he was hurt or sick, Owen milked his mom's sympathy for all it was worth—couldn't keep him from drooling over his favorite combination:

Devil's Food with chocolate frosting.

A pair of number-shaped white wax candles with red outlining proclaimed to the world that he was turning twelve—*had* turned twelve as of midnight.

The only problem was that the design on top made him feel like he'd turned half that. It was supposed to be a reasonable imitation of Rocket Man on a bike wearing his RM helmet, flying off a jump—a symbol of his derring-do and launch into manhood.

But his parents had changed it at the last minute, deflating any notions that they were going to actually let him grow up.

Apparently, they thought replacing Rocket Man with a generic picture of a cartoony rocket ship blasting off toward a cratered-moon might discourage him from continuing down the path of BMX racing and pursue what? Astronomy?

That fact would have made Owen sad if he wasn't so dedicated to getting back into riding shape. In essence, he didn't really care what they thought.

Rocket Man wasn't going to give up easily.

Surrounding the cake was an orderly demonstration of colorful paper plates, cups, napkins, and party hats. Everything was yellow with the matching pattern of drifting rainbow confetti, even the plastic tablecloth.

In the normally spacious living room next door, a crowd of thirteen kids and a few grown-ups gathered. *Eye of the Tiger* pumped through Owen's mother's silver boombox while Jake and Ryan took turns rapping each other with their knuckles on bravely presented forearms—a game they liked to call Monkey Bites. Steph sat on the ground nearby and shook her head in disgust.

Not that she adequately hid the slight smile formed on

her lips.

Sometimes, Owen thought he totally understood her. She was mostly one of them, but it was times like these that he was reminded that in the end, she was still a girl. And to The Crew's growing occasional disillusionment, she seemed to be aware of that fact more and more every day.

That was okay, though. Owen didn't mind as much as Ryan and Jake seemed to.

He was just so happy to see his friends here, all gathered for a birthday celebration that he'd narrowly missed. His parents had come to a compromise of keeping him home from school the rest of the week, but allowing the party to move forward as scheduled.

Now that The Crew was back together again, it just felt right. They were all so much more than the sum of their parts.

Owen admired the rest of the scene. The other kids hanging out were really just background.

Adam Nielsen, Thomas LeGrande, and William Jackson, to name a few, had all been invited, but both they and Owen knew the routine—each of them provides some cheap present found last-minute at Sprouse Reitz or Thrifty and Owen provides the food and entertainment. That was it. That was the contract. Come Monday morning, they'd resume their roles as mere classmates.

It was the same sort of school birthday party relationship Owen imagined happening every Saturday across the country.

Eye of the Tiger ended, and his mom's custom mix-tape started playing Kenny Loggins' *Danger Zone* just in time for Ryan to nurse his left forearm like a newborn, admitting defeat in Monkey Bites. He and Jake headed toward the punch bowl sitting beside the cake. They were breathing heavily as they passed Owen. Despite the air conditioner pumping cold air through the entire house, sweat caked their hair like they'd just finished running a marathon.

Owen walked over to Steph and slowly took a seat on the floor beside her.

He was practically feeling normal now. Last night, he'd finished his final pain pill, thankful to have his head in the game again, so to speak.

Knowing that, he tried to be cautious with his movements. He didn't want to pull a muscle or reinjure something that might short-circuit his chances of riding sooner rather than later. He had big plans to get back on the bike on Monday and test things out. Big plans.

"I'm glad you could come," he said, smiling.

"Me too," Steph replied, grinning back. She snapped her

head, flicking her bangs from her eyes. For Owen, it was a familiar, comforting movement that he'd missed the past week. "Are you coming back to school on Monday?"

"Yeah," Owen said, rolling his eyes, feigning disgust at the notion. He didn't want to fully admit that he looked forward to getting back into routine. "I guess it'll be better than being stuck in bed all day."

"Yeah," Steph said, rocking her head back and forth in sync to the music. "True."

The song filled long, awkward gaps in conversation.

Why were those gaps there? They only seemed to be a recent phenomenon. Owen couldn't put a finger on it, but the previous week, before the accident, everything between him and Steph seemed to be...different. Maybe that was even the case with Jake and Ryan. At least a little. But nothing to the level of awkwardness that he felt toward the only girl in the group—a fact of biology that seemed more obvious now than it ever had.

Steph broke the painful silence. "Hey, you know Loretta?"

"Mishki?"

"Yeah, kind of. Why?"

Steph was slow in her reply. "I dunno. I can't stand her. She's just, like, totally annoying, right?"

There was a look in Steph's eyes that reminded Owen of a dog begging for a bite of food to be handed down from the dinner table. It honestly made him uncomfortable, so he decided to change subjects as smoothly as he could.

"She's all right. Hey, guess what? John sent me a crazy email."

There was no reply and Owen was worried she was going to keep pushing things in a weird direction.

"That's cool," Steph said.

Owen wasn't entirely certain which statement of his that response was intended for. He decided to assume the last.

"It was coded. Something he wanted my help with."

Suddenly, he was gripped with a terror that told him he'd made a big mistake. His lips tightened as if that made a difference in what was already done. John trusted Owen to look at the message, but how would he feel if Owen told someone else about it? John hadn't specifically said he *couldn't* tell anyone else, but...

The idea gave Owen pause.

"Oh? Did you crack it yet?"

Well, it was too late now. Owen directed his eyes at his feet and pulled off loose pieces of carpet fuzz that accumulated on his shoelaces. "No. I was thinking I should show it to Ryan."

Sure, dig the hole even deeper.

"Yeah, why not?" Steph asked.

Owen shrugged, knowing he wouldn't do anything of the sort. He had to stop it now. Stop it at this conversation with Steph.

"I'm sure I'll figure it out now that I'm feeling better. The meds the doctor gave me made me kind of tired and my brain didn't seem to be working right."

"Did it ever?"

"Ha. Ha." Owen laughed sarcastically, his smile coming back.

"Did you get high?" Steph asked.

"What?"

"From your meds? Did they make you high? My cousin had a problem with something like that. Had to go to some rehab place."

Owen thought about the question in relation to the anti-drug *D.A.R.E.* program that occasionally came into his classroom. Crack cocaine and acid made you high and ruined your life. But medicine prescribed by a doctor? Owen guessed some effects were like the *D.A.R.E* officer had described — the hallucinations; the swings in body temperature; the unexplainable fear that just gathered within his gut like a tornado.

But he'd also been told that taking drugs, even once, made you want to take more. Personally, he couldn't stop taking the pills soon enough. They made him feel miserable. Out of control. He didn't like being out of control.

Even when he was flying through the air at the mercies of gravity, he still felt a sense of control over many things—how the bike was angled for landing; how tight or loose his muscles were for impact; how he would react and steer once he hit the dirt on the other side.

He thought back to the past Monday. A mix of fear and anticipation of relief bubbled up in the back of his throat. He decided that any relief would have to come from talking to someone about what he'd seen. Why not Steph?

"Maybe," Owen said. "I mean, I saw the Oscar Mayer Wienermobile."

Steph raised her eyebrows.

"But that may have been real," he added quickly.

"What?" she asked with a sort of laugh. "No way."

"Way."

"Where?"

"Here. Outside of my house. In the driveway."

"What was it doing?"

"I don't know. Just sitting there." He didn't want to

mention the sensations that had hit him soon after he'd seen it. Just thinking of the paralyzing pain in his chest quickened his breath. "It took off before I could figure it out," he said finally. "Maybe it got lost."

"Wow," Steph said. "I would have run out of the house and hopped inside."

Owen shivered at the thought. Whoever was inside, lost or not, he was pretty certain that he didn't want to go anywhere with them.

"Hopped inside what?" Jake asked, returning to the group, still breathing heavily. He pulled the waxy paper cup of punch away from his mouth, revealing a red stain surrounding his lips like he'd been loose with a tube of lipstick.

"Nothing," Owen said before Steph could tell them. He didn't want Jake or Ryan to know. Why? Owen wasn't certain, but it felt like something special between him and Steph. Their own little secret.

But that was only a part of it—he was afraid that Jake and Ryan would sense the fear that it triggered and harass him about it. He was supposed to be Rocket Man, despite what the cake showed. He wasn't supposed to be afraid of anything.

Danger Zone stopped.

"Don't you have any rap music?" Ryan asked after chugging down his cup of punch. "I should have brought some of my tapes."

"You know my mom doesn't let me buy any of that stuff."

"Not even like Run D.M.C or The Fat Boys?"

Owen shrugged. He liked rap, but not to the extent that Ryan did. That boy was obsessed.

"Next time, I'll bring my non-parental advisory mixtape," Ryan finished. "It's got those guys, EPMD, Boogie Down Productions, Spoonie Gee, Salt-N-Pepa—"

"Hey! Tetherball!" Jake said.

Everyone turned their attention to the pair of sliding glass doors connecting the dining room to the backyard. Through them, they saw Adam Nielsen and some other kid unwinding the rope from the tall metal pole which stood in the back yard.

It was a custom Tetherball setup that Owen's dad had built, held in place by a cement-filled tire.

"I'm going," Jake said, already halfway to the doors, eyeing Adam like the kid owed him money. "You guys can come if you want. Doesn't matter to me."

Just then, the doorbell rang. Owen's dad clapped his hands together loudly and proclaimed, "Oh, I think that's the entertainment."

Saturday, June 17, 1989 - 12:00 PM

Owen had never heard of a female magician, let alone seen one.

Wasn't that a witch?

But this woman didn't look like a witch—neither her clothing nor her face indicated such.

She didn't have the long, crooked nose, the requisite moles parked randomly along her face, nor the sharp, black pointy hat. When she smiled, her teeth were actually white and straight like pillars of perfectly carved ivory.

Her outfit was that of a standard magician: the black top hat with the crimson banding just above the brim, the black coat, the red cummerbund, and all the way down to the black slacks and polished black shoes.

Then, of course, there was the cape which was a blood-red velvet on the inside and pitch-black on the outside.

No, she didn't look like a witch. Owen may have even ventured to say she was kind of pretty, at least for someone probably around his mom's age.

And, to be honest, the outfit was pretty rad.

Of course, Steph thought a female magician was the coolest thing in the world.

"Why shouldn't there be girl magicians?" she asked, leaning into Owen as they sat on the fuzzy, brown living room carpet. The bay window had its curtains pulled to the side and the noontime sunlight pressed itself into the house. "Guys can't learn any special tricks that a woman can't learn too."

Owen had no answer. It's not like he could prove it one way or another when it came to magic.

He'd seen what Steph could do with her bike, and he'd honestly never thought she *couldn't* do anything that boys normally did. Then again, Owen didn't think of her fully as a girl. She wasn't like the ones who gathered in corners of the playground or classroom, hands cupped from mouth to ear, whispering uninteresting gossip to each other.

Still, a female magician just seemed so...unusual.

Owen, Steph, Jake, Ryan, and the other kids that Owen's mom made him invite were gathered in the living room now. The chocolate-colored love seats and coffee table had been pushed to the edges so that a wide-open space could be made for the children to sit down.

The Crew was seated in the front row.

Owen's dad had found the magician, maybe in the Yellow Pages. The entertainer would perform her tricks in front of a rapt audience before the little tyrants were released for cake and presents, followed by Owen's favorite part—the bashing of the *piñata*.

As Owen sat, watching the magician place a tape in his mom's boombox, Owen felt that familiar unsettled feeling in his stomach that he thought had gone away. He blamed it on the meds probably upsetting his insides. Maybe this was still a lingering side effect.

He jumped slightly when he heard the loud click followed by blaring trumpets and strings.

"Welcome to the greatest show on Earth!" the magician yelled over the soundtrack.

Her tiny elfin-like hands were on her hips as she looked down at the mostly eager kids.

Steph elbowed him in the ribs and tossed him a look like he was an alien. "Dude, are you okay?"

"Huh?"

Owen took a moment to assess himself and realized he was shaking like a leaf in the heavy High Desert winds.

He closed his eyes and took a deep breath, quickly trying to come up with an excuse.

"You look like you're going to ralph," Steph said.

"Pfft," Owen said. *"You* look like you're going to ralph," he replied, feeling like the world's most spectacular idiot afterward. It wasn't his best comeback, but he hadn't had the mental wherewithal or time to think of something clever.

Steph rolled her eyes in response.

"I'm just a little cold," he said. And he was, despite the four adults fanning themselves in the corners of the warm room at the same time. Despite the fact that Owen's dad refused to turn on the air conditioner before two p.m.—his way of avoiding the electric company's "highway robbery."

"Oohhh-kaayyy," Steph said.

It was early summer in the Mojave Desert. Unless one stuffed one's self inside a freezer, there was no such thing as being cold.

Owen tried to throw her off with a smile, but he knew he failed. He looked to his left at his other friends.

Ryan was distracted by picking at the dirt beneath his fingernails, but Jake appeared to be all ears, listening intently to the Mysterious Mariska. Owen had never seen him pay this close of attention to anything in his life.

The orchestral music subsided into a low, repetitive drone of strings and the magician's voice seemed to match as it took on a soothing, almost hypnotic quality.

"I'm the Mysterious Mariska."

She scanned the audience. The grin on her face stretched six miles wide. "Who here believes in magic?" she asked.

A couple of hands shot up immediately. Kids that Owen knew, but didn't necessarily call friends.

"That's it?" the Mysterious Mariska asked, her voice cracking. Her brow furrowed in serious disappointment. "How can you children, so young, so open, not believe in magic? All of you should believe." She flashed the youthful crowd an admonishing look, part joking, part sinister, and Owen noticed for the first time, just how thick her black eyebrows were—like someone had taken a couple swipes with a Marks-A-Lot.

"Well, I suppose it's okay," she said, smiling again, reaching behind her back. "I'll make believers out of you all before all is said and done."

With a quickness that defied modern physics, she pulled out a handful of rainbow-colored confetti and sprinkled it over the front row of kids. The tiny, glittery pieces floated down as if a rainbow exploded.

A few of the kids laughed and reached for the pieces like they were flakes of gold. Owen might have done the same if his back was completely better, but he still had a little pain whenever he overreached.

For the next ten minutes or so, the Mysterious Mariska ran through the household variety of magic tricks—pulling different colored cloths out of a magic wand, bending a spoon with her mind, and making a coin disappear and reappear in one of the kid's pockets.

And then she walked over and stopped the music playing from her portable boombox.

Besides the flapping makeshift fans of the adults, the room was filled with an eager silence. Owen had a feeling everyone was looking forward to this part wrapping up, so they could get some refreshments.

Owen wanted to think about cake and candy and the pile of colorfully-wrapped presents sitting on the table beneath the living room window.

"I was told that it was someone's very special day today," the Mysterious Mariska proclaimed to the kids, her face zooming around the audience.

Her eyes zeroed in on Owen, and he immediately felt like he had been zapped with a spark of electricity that formed a bridge of current between them.

Owen wanted to look away, but with the current now flowing, it felt much like a Band-Aid—tearing it off would be painful. Maybe worse than leaving it where it was.

"In fact, I was told that it's *your* special day today, Owen Thom. Is that right?"

Owen couldn't speak. There was a lump caught in his throat. All he could do was nod.

"Please, come up for my most special trick of the day," she said. The corner of her lips turned up, and then she mercifully broke the current between them, smiling at the rest of the kids and parents.

Owen's legs weren't working. None of his body seemed to be working. Gravity accelerated, pressing down on his limbs and torso to ensure that he wasn't going anywhere.

"Owen, get up there," he heard his mom say, covering her mouth with some embarrassment.

Then he felt the electrical current reestablish. The Mysterious Mariska's eyes seemed to glow like brake lights in the night. Owen's limbs began to untangle themselves, unfolding against the gravity which had held them in place.

"Get up there, dweeb," Ryan said.

"I'll go!" Adam Nielsen called out, but everyone seemed to ignore him.

"This is the most special trick for the most special boy of the day," the Mysterious Mariska replied. "Owen Thom. Please, come up."

And with that command, Owen felt himself rising. He was standing now, unfeeling except for the buzzing hum of energy coursing through his veins like his entire body had fallen asleep.

Owen stood in front of the other kids, in front of the adults, and what felt like in front of the entire town of Apple Valley.

He could smell the magician now, and she smelled of meat. Sweet meat, not unlike the occasional steaks his dad would grill on warm summer evenings. Owen stood up to just below her chest. She leaned forward and her face was inches from his own now.

Her lips were moving, half-silently, but the words she was saying were unintelligible. Then she stopped and smiled, presenting Owen those white teeth with streaks of magenta lipstick now smeared across in parts. A new dose of fear shot through him, but it felt completely pointless. He still had no control of his body.

"So, birthday boy, what is it you're wishing for the most today?"

Her breath was just as sweet smelling as the rest of her, but there was a hint of musty staleness emanating from the back her throat.

The Almost-Apocalypse of Apple Valley

Deep down inside, Owen knew what he wanted. He'd known what he wanted for a week now, and yet, the thoughts no longer seemed able to make themselves present within his mind. It was like being asked to answer questions about a story he'd been asked to read for school. He knew the answers were there, floating somewhere within the confines of his consciousness, but they were lost among the stream.

The buzz between Owen and the Mysterious Mariska now felt uncomfortably strong. His teeth chattered.

"Seems like the cat has your tongue," the magician said, turning to the audience and grinning. "What do you think, kids? Does the cat have Owen's tongue?"

Owen's head turned on its own accord. The faces of the kids seemed to match the feelings within Owen—blank, obedient, without color. Their heads nodded in synchronicity, even The Crew's, snapping up and down like they were being controlled by invisible puppet strings.

The Mysterious Mariska straightened up, reached behind her back with both hands, and brought them around again. They were no longer empty.

In her palms was a calico-colored kitten that couldn't have weighed over a pound or two. Its sonorous purrs lined up perfectly with the humming of the electrical current still flowing.

But Owen's eyes locked on to one specific thing. Hang-ing out of the cat's furry lips, beneath its moist pink nose, was something fleshy and long, streaked with a deep crimson red.

Owen started to open his own mouth, and simultane-ously, so did the cat. Expecting a meow, Owen was instead con-fronted with a roar that echoed infinitely across the living room, piercing his ears.

He closed his eyes and wanted to scream, just as he had wanted to in his dream, but as he did so, a throbbing pain pulsed within his mouth. The cat's roar overwhelmed any at-tempt Owen made at vocalization. Owen's hands shot up to his ears to mute the sound, but it was of no use—the roar poured through the microscopic cracks in his fingers and continued on its merry way straight into the center of his brain.

Tinny wetness pooled around the corners of Owen's lips. He went to lick it up, but nothing happened.

There was nothing to lick it up with.

Panic danced around in his mind. He shoved his hands into his mouth, feeling for the tongue that had been there since he'd been born. But his fingers felt only the warmth of his teeth, gums, and a mix of saliva and blood that he couldn't taste.

"Yes, kids," the Mysterious Mariska said, stroking the kitten's furry spine and cooing at it slightly, "indeed it does appear that the naughty cat has Owen's tongue."

And then the kids broke out into uproarious, echoing laughter. Even the adults chimed in. Owen's dad grabbed his paunch as if it might pop off the rest of his body and roll away if he laughed any harder. His mom's hands were clamped to her face, doing a poor job of hiding the tear-inducing giggles that were written across her forehead and crinkled eyebrows.

Between the current, the deafening roar, the laughter, the missing, yet expected, taste of blood, Owen's senses were over-whelmed. He felt himself collapsing now, unable to fight off gravity any longer, but something kept him suspended.

It was the Mysterious Mariska's eyes. They held Owen in a death-grip, a painful suspension that denied him any sense of relief.

"What do you say, Owen? Would you like your tongue back?"

The laughter continued.

Owen couldn't answer. He grew more desperate by the second, furiously wiping away the flavorless blood streaming down his chin until his wrists and the back of his hands looked like they'd been dipped in red paint.

"I'll give it back to you on one condition, birthday boy."

Anything, Owen thought. He'd do anything.

"Stay out of trouble and mind your own business. Do you understand, young man? Do you and your friends a favor. Don't mess with magic. It's bad for you."

Mess with magic? Owen struggled to comprehend what that meant.

"Take your vitamins. Stay in school. And most importantly, stay away from the track."

Stay away from the track.

The words echoed in his mind, and he wanted to argue back. Violently. Staying away from the track would be like taking away a piece of Owen's body—not a useless part like a pinky toe or an ear lobe, but his heart and soul.

Despite the damage he'd done to himself a week prior, the track was the place where life itself seemed to flow into Rocket Man every Saturday. A sacred locus of rejuvenation which repaired the damage that the other six days of everyday life inflicted.

But he found himself nodding and nodding, making his vertigo even worse.

"I promise!" he shouted, generating a sharp pain in himself that radiated from his chest and shot through every single nerve ending.

His hands shot up to his mouth and grabbed his tongue at the realization that it had returned. He looked at the magician and saw that her hands were empty. In fact, they were no longer in front of him, but still behind her back.

"Well, I'm glad you're so enthusiastic," the Mysterious Mariska said, smiling a befuddled smile down at him, and then projecting it back out at the audience.

Things had changed in an instant. The laughter among his friends and adults was still there, but the tone was lighter. The sinister feeling was gone, even the one he had sensed from the magician standing before him.

He met her eyes once again and there was an airy sense of familiarity instead of the oppression he'd felt earlier. A warm feeling like that of a doting aunt.

"But you didn't answer the question," the Mysterious Mariska said. "What is it you're wishing for the most today?"

Owen was too entranced by the fact that he'd had his tongue again, that the entire atmosphere had changed in an instant, that he didn't realize he was supposed to answer the question.

So Ryan answered for him, shouting out, "A Barbie doll!"

The other kids laughed even harder now. Owen looked down at Steph, who was also trying to stifle her own giggles with her tiny hands held fast to her lips, but she stopped instantly when she saw the pain that Owen was transmitting through his eyes.

"Well," the Mysterious Mariska said, "the magical creatures from the other side told me otherwise. They told me that twelve-year-old Owen Thom would like a brand-new Transformer."

Mariska brought her hands back around again in front of Owen. He closed his eyes and felt around the back of his teeth with the tongue that was still attached.

Bravely, he opened his eyes again.

There was a present there, a rectangular box with a string of yellow ribbon tied around red Transformer wrapping paper—Optimus Prime had his strong, blue metal hands wrapped around the steel shoulders of Megatron as they wrestled for control of the future.

But Owen didn't want to take the present. He didn't want to touch anything that had been in the Mysterious Mariska's hands, no matter how non-threatening she appeared at the moment.

Though the laughter had subsided to the point of chuckles, Owen's face burned with embarrassment. It wasn't just the laughs. It was what he had promised the magician. Maybe no one here knew what he'd promised, maybe it had all been in his head, but *he* knew, and that fact hurt him more than he could say.

He saw a gap to the kitchen and instinct took over.

He ran around the crowd of children, through the kitchen and down the hallway, all the way to the other side of the house and into his bedroom where he slammed the door, twisted the knob lock, and took refuge.

The pain in his lower back was beginning to throb again, but he sat down at his desk, turned on his computer, and tried to forget everything that happened as the PC went through its boot-up sequence.

Owen shut out the world.

But then a pair of crows cawed pushing themselves in from the distance just outside of his window. A great shadow passed over the cracks in his window blinds, casting a menacing darkness, extinguishing the little of noonday light that flowed into his bedroom.

The caws diminished but the shade remained.

Something glinted in his eyes from outside.

There was a knock on Owen's door, followed by the familiar voice of his mother, but it sounded hundreds of miles away. It was background. It was all background but the flash.

Owen gripped the armrests and pushed himself up from the chair. His arms shook, trying to hold the weight.

"Leave me alone!" he heard a faint echo of his voice saying.

Finally, he was on his feet, leaning over the hot CRT computer monitor, feeling the heat rise into his chin where it penetrated his flesh like a smoldering fire.

With his thumb and index finger, he spread open a pair of window blinds at eye level.

He froze in time.

There it was, sitting in the driveway. Sitting in the exact same spot.

The Oscar Mayer Wienermobile.

In his mind's eye, he could penetrate the blackness of the windows. He could see what was inside—could see its long, smoke-like, black-as-night body slithering and zooming around the yellow and red fabric seats, leaving a trail an inch thick until the entire cabin was coated with a film of sticky grease.

It had no eyes per se, but Owen knew it saw everything. It never stopped moving. Never stopped gyrating. Never ceased its energetic output.

It seemed almost anxious, yet giddy at the same time.

And then it stopped.

Owen heard the far-off, futile twisting of his bedroom doorknob followed by more knocks and shouts.

But even more, he felt that the creature had found what it was looking for.

Had found *Owen*.

It looked at him in a way that Owen couldn't explain, but shook him to his very core.

It was calling out to Owen. Challenging him.

It hated him and Owen hated it.

And then something broke the hypnotic current between them. The squealing of the house's front door jarred them both from the tenuous, unseemly conversation they had established.

A pair of voices and shuffling footsteps followed. The dim shadow suddenly lifted from the sky, releasing the noon-day sun once again. It blinded Owen to the point that he jumped back and released his grip on the blinds so that he could put his hands over his eyes.

The commotion at his bedroom door had stopped, but Owen continued to hear the conversation outside.

His stomach stirred. Simultaneously, he wanted to look and not look. The indecision tore at every inch of his insides before he decided he couldn't take the tension anymore.

He leaned forward and parted the blinds once more,

conjuring up a cartoony Sunday School image of Moses parting the Red Sea.

His father and the Mysterious Mariska stood just in front of the Wienermobile. She gripped her black leather case with one hand while the other was extended, receiving a folded wad of green cash from Owen's dad.

She accepted it with that toothy, snow-white smile. Her face shined brightly, practically glowing. The winds kicked up in a sudden gust, sending a flurry of Apple Valley dust between her and Owen's dad. Owen noticed the clouds had formed in the sky once more.

She quickly stashed the cash in her pants pocket and held on tight to the top of her black hat. Her cape took on a life of its own.

Owen thought he saw the outline of things—of crea-tures—form beneath the cape itself as it flapped in the wind.

He saw sharp double horns and pointed ears.

Bulging eyeballs and twisted, split tongues.

Edged, jagged fangs and thick, iron piercings.

Then his mind shot back to the inside of the Wienermo-bile. To the thing he had detected inside.

Mariska reached to open the passenger-side door. A pulse of fear bolted from Owen's chest to the rest of his body.

The Almost-Apocalypse of Apple Valley

He had to run out there. Had to warn his dad.

But like a dream from which he couldn't awaken, his movements were caught in a thick syrup of time. His brain moved a million miles per hour while his ligaments flexed and stretched a millionth of an inch per year.

Before he knew it, the car door was open.

And there was nothing inside but those empty yellow and red seats.

Mariska removed her hat, and placed it on top of her briefcase on the passenger seat.

The wind was really kicking up now. So much so that Owen couldn't hear a thing. But he realized Mariska and her father were saying their goodbyes. She walked around to the driver's side door and got inside.

The engine turned over and rumbled lowly, parts of it cutting through the wind which now seemed to be fading. The car sounded just as it had when it pulled into the driveway the prior week.

The front door squealed once again, slamming shut.

Owen's dad was back in the house now.

In this brief slice of existence, there seemed to be only Owen, Mariska, and whatever vile thing thrashed and flailed within the Wienermobile.

Owen sensed it stirring. Agitating again. Like it had been a video game that was paused, only to be resumed mid-battle.

The passenger-side window began to lower, slowly like cold syrup being poured over french toast.

First, Owen saw the hat. It was back on the Mysterious Mariska's head. Then came the eyes which were focused on Owen like she'd been watching him the whole time. Next, the nose followed up by the unnerving grin.

The window stopped. Owen swore he saw the black, smoky texture, pass in front of her face.

The goosebumps returned. Owen didn't know how long they had been engaged in the staring contest, but all he knew was that he couldn't let her win. If he did, that was the beginning of the end—only he had no idea what that meant.

Stay away from the track.

YOU stay away from the track, Owen reflected back.

The Mysterious Mariska blinked like she'd been slapped across the face. The black smoke thickened until it reached the point where the magician was nearly impossible to see.

And then the dark window shot back up, closing off the interior of the car from the outside world.

The Wienermobile's tires spun, kicking up gravel as it sped away from the house and launched back onto the blacktop streets.

Where it was going, Owen didn't know.

But despite his reticence, he intended to find out.

Saturday, June 17, 1989 - 1:00 PM

Owen and his parents sat in the quiet living room. It was empty now and rearranged. The furniture was back in its normal place. His mom and dad sat next to each other in the love seat while Owen sat cross-legged, deep in what was normally his dad's recliner.

On the white porcelain counter sat one-third of the chocolate cake, sans candles. What was left of the paper plates were stacked up next to it and a single goody bag with Owen's name on it rested alone on the counter, almost sad in its solitary repose. A small pile of unopened presents sat on the living room floor in front of the fireplace.

Owen felt a flush of embarrassment cross his entire body. The realization that on Monday, he'd be facing the kids who saw him running to his room like a little baby at his own birthday party hit him like an armada of incoming dirt clods.

And that didn't even count facing The Crew. What sort of misery would they heap on him?

From his bedroom, he'd heard all the parents' cars arrive, their doors slam shut, and then their just-as-fast departure. Only after his mom had knocked on the bedroom door one last time and confirmed everybody had left did Owen show himself.

Now the cheap, replica miniature grandfather clock sitting atop the entertainment center ticked in the background as he stared outside into the backyard. He couldn't see it from his vantage point, but heard the metal clip which held the Tetherball to its rope clinking off the pole in the breeze.

What he could see was the top half of a bicycle *piñata* carcass swaying on a piece of yellow nylon rope that hung from a porch crossbeam. It was the one bike-related birthday item his parents had bought before his accident that they hadn't been able to exchange for another dumb rocket.

Only an hour ago, it had been filled with Tootsie Rolls and Jolly Ranchers. Now, all that remained floating were the tattered blue handlebars and forks.

"Do you want to tell us what got into you?" his dad started, breaking the barrier of awkward silence.

Owen looked at him, but didn't answer right away. His dad removed his thick, heavy eyeglasses and rubbed at the reddened indents they'd left on the bridge of his nose. Then he swept a loose strand of gray hair back onto the top of his head, putting it back in its preordained spot. He returned the glasses to the designated slot on his face, making his eyes appear larger than life once again.

How could Owen even begin to tell them what he'd experienced? How would they believe a word he had to say and not dismiss it?

"You missed the *piñata*. You missed blowing out the candles. You missed the rest of the magic show," his dad said.

Mentioning the magic show brought back Owen's goosebumps. He sank back into the refuge of the recliner, wishing it would suck him all the way into oblivion until it was safe to come out again.

"I'm worried that accident did something to his brain," his mom added in, talking about him almost as if he weren't there.

She fiddled with her thin, brown watchstrap while resting her hands across her lap. Despite the bright red lipstick and a thick layer of foundation that only seemed to highlight the wrinkles spreading out from her eyes, her expression was naked and vulnerable through her lucid, chestnut-colored eyes.

"His brain's fine," his dad said, irritated. "It's his attitude that needs fixing. This whole act today seemed rather ungrateful—"

"He just had a major accident, Hal." Mama bear was coming to Owen's defense, making him feel even more embarrassed about the situation. "How do you know he's okay?"

Owen's dad exhaled loudly through his nose as he crossed his arms and leaned back into the love seat, exposing his farmer's tan. "Because the doctor—"

"I'm fine, guys," Owen interrupted. "It's just..."

"Just what?" his dad asked.

Owen's mom leaned forward with raised eyebrows.

Owen knew he had to say something. He could lie. He could say that, yes, he was definitely still not feeling well. But at the least, that would only lead to more coddling from his mom and more disgust from his dad. At the worst, she'd take him back to the doctor. He wasn't sure he could handle either situation, so he started with the car.

"Why does the magician drive a Wienermobile?"

The clock ticked a few times and the Tetherball clip clanked outside twice while he waited for a reply.

Owen's dad and mom exchanged glances and then his father looked at Owen.

"What on Earth are you talking about?"

"I told you, Hal," his mother said, placing a hand on her husband's wrist and scrunching up her face in concern. "I told you these quacks up here didn't look at everything. We need to take him to another hospital to run more tests. Maybe Loma

Linda—"

Owen's dad held up his hand.

"Answer us, Owen. What Wienermobile?"

Now Owen was at a loss for words. It wasn't even a question that Owen had expected his father to ask. He saw for himself, for goodness' sake. He was out there.

"Didn't you—when you—when you handed her the money—"

"*What. Wienermobile,*" his dad repeated, emphasizing the question posed more like an angry statement.

"I saw you outside," Owen said. "When the Mysterious Mariska left." He glanced at his mom which was a bad idea. The look on her face said that he was her poor little baby and she would never let him out of the house again. Never let him be confronted by the big, bad, dangerous world that could scramble his brain even more.

"Are you talking about her car, Owen?" his dad replied.

The emphasis on Owen's name grated on his nerves.

His dad continued, almost to himself, "Wienermobile? Is that some sort of derogatory slang term you kids are using these days? Not everyone can afford a Mercedes-Benz, kiddo."

"No!" Owen shouted, leaning forward in the chair, trying to keep his frustration from boiling over. "I'm talking about the actual, honest-to-goodness metal hot dog in a big metal bun, Wienermobile!"

Owen watched his dad's lips shiver and curl slightly. Owen knew his father wanted to laugh, but his father was probably also thinking that it would shoot gargantuan-sized holes through any credibility he had as a parent.

"Owen, she drives a tiny, old beater. A rusting Volkswagen Rabbit. It's almost as far from the Wienermobile as one can get."

"No," Owen said, shaking his head, refusing to believe that his own eyes could have been wrong. His own, newly sober eyes.

He looked up at his father, "I'm telling you the truth. Why are you lying?"

"Lying? You're accusing me of lying?" He looked at Owen's mom with incredulity. "You need to be careful, young man."

"Hal," his mother said, stopping with her single word of warning.

Owen had enough and just wanted to go back to his room, turn on his computer, and talk to John. That's what he should have done in the first place.

"Either that or you need to clean your glasses, old man!"

Owen clapped his hand to his mouth, but he knew it was too late. Where the words came from, Owen couldn't say. They just came cracking out like the electricity which had cracked at him from the substation. Like the electricity which had cracked at him in his own bedroom.

The cracking appeared to be contagious.

It scared Owen.

His father's eyes popped wide open like something out of a cartoon, made even more cartoony by the thickness of his eyeglass frames.

"Grounded. One month."

"Hal," his mother interceded once again, this time with a different emphasis—that her husband was headed in a direction which he might regret. It's amazing what a mom can say with so few words.

"No, Judy. It's final. Not up for debate. No disrespect in our house. Not to you. Not to me. Not to anyone." He waved his hands around at the leftover cake and decimated *piñata* swinging in the wind. "After all we did for you today."

"Dad, I swear—"

"I'm not done." Owen had never seen his father so angry. He thought he even saw a sort of red glow reflecting from his lenses. He raised three fingers and ticked one down.

"One, no riding your bike during that time."

"No!" Owen said. He leapt up from the chair and onto the carpet, only sort of realizing that he did so without feeling any pain in his body.

Next finger.

"Two, no computer."

"You want to stimulate your noggin"—he pointed at the dust-covered set of Encyclopedia Britannica books lined dutifully behind glass cabinets in the entertainment center—"there's your new computer."

Thoughts of John and the email came to Owen's mind.

For a whole month? How could he explain it to John? How could he get *anything* to John?

Owen balled his hands into fists at his sides. It's not that he wanted to punch anyone, especially not his father, but if he were given the opportunity to go three rounds with a *piñata* which may have resembled his dad, he'd eschew the wooden bat.

"And three..."

That last word was given such power, reinforced by his dad's still-red glare, that Owen knew he'd better be very, very careful about his response.

The last finger came down slowly.

"I'm throwing away that helmet of yours."

Now Owen wanted to cry. His whole body shook, and he only allowed a tear or two to stream down his face. His mom got up from the chair to hug him, but Owen's dad reached across her lap and held her in place.

Owen's instinct was to race to his bedroom, grab the helmet, and hold it for dear life until they pried it from his hands. But he knew it would do no good. It would just make things worse.

Still, he'd rather be grounded for a whole year than lose his helmet—it was like losing a piece of himself.

Losing his entire identity.

"It's broken and not safe. And you won't be needing a new one until you can show us that you know how to behave."

Owen tried to comfort himself. Tried to convince himself that maybe his dad was right and that he could always buy a new helmet.

But there was no convincing. He knew it wouldn't be the same.

"I'm going to get up now, and lock your helmet in my car so I can take it to the garbage dump on Monday, and then start taking apart your computer. The fact is, I don't trust you, Owen, and you really need to spend the next month figuring out how you're going to earn my trust—*our* trust—back. Because this attitude needs to go. Do you understand?"

Owen didn't answer right away. He couldn't. He was only half-listening to his dad. The realization that he wouldn't be able to ride his bike for a month at all, let alone with The Crew, started becoming real.

At least he'd see them in school and could play during recess. His parents couldn't take *that* away.

Could they?

"Do you understand?" Owen's dad repeated.

Owen's mom threw her husband's hand off her lap and stood. Owen looked at her, feeling final defeat at having mommy come to rescue her baby boy, but he'd be lying if he didn't also feel an ounce or two of gratefulness.

She approached her son and knelt down before him, gripping his shoulders gently, holding court with his face so that their noses were inches apart.

"Mom, you believe me, right?" Owen's voice cracked slightly.

Of course, she would believe him.

She *had* to believe him.

That's what moms were made for, after all.

Her sympathetic eyes searched his, looking at Owen as

if she were trying to detect something, anything, deeply wrong that only Mom could fix.

"Honey, you look sick. Pale. You look like you're not feeling well." She turned and looked back at Owen's dad. "I still say we need to take him to the hospital."

Owen's stomach sank. Even his mom, his last line of true-hearted loyalty, had lost the faith.

"He's fine," his dad said, getting up from the couch and heading into the hallway.

Owen's mom returned her attention to him. She lifted her hand and started stroking his hair.

Owen rubbed away the tears from his cheeks, following up with rubbing away the snot that gathered beneath his nostrils.

Just like a mom, she magically retrieved a tissue from her pocket and began to wipe his nose for him. Owen tilted his head back and grabbed the Kleenex for himself.

He could only put up with a certain amount of babying.

"Everything's going to be all right, honey," his mom said, continuing to stroke his head.

Owen was glad she was so sure, because right now, he didn't think anything would be all right ever again.

"It'll happen," Mariska said.

The words were slightly garbled since her fists were jammed into her cheeks, supported by her elbows on the bolted-down, square Formica breakfast table.

She sounded as wiped out as she looked, make-up half wiped off and a desperate sleep in her eyes.

The whole of her rusted, white, single-wide trailer shook slightly, creaking in the winds generated not only by the air currents outside, but from within the confines of her tiny abode.

They came from the Thing racing in chaotic patterns inside.

Here, sitting on the lone folding chair parked in front of the table, she was only Mariska.

She wasn't Mysterious among The Worm.

She wasn't even *the* Attendant.

She was just *an* Attendant.

Her tired eyes had a view of the narrow living room spread out in front of her. It was a mess. On the right, backed up against a wall of cheap wood paneling, was a set of three wire racks that served as an entertainment center. She'd picked them up from a TG&Y five-and-dime store that was going out of business. The racks held a tiny nineteen-inch Zenith TV that was connected to a refurbished silver VCR. One end of cables connected to the roof-top antenna was screwed into the back, but she hadn't had time to actually mount the antenna since arriving in Apple Valley one month ago.

Stacks of magazines—wrinkled copies of *Time*, *Fangoria*, and *Genii*—and magic how-to books remained toppled over the pair of cheap oak coffee tables bookending a faded blue fabric futon pushed up against the opposite wall. Most of her free time, time in between the birthday parties and caring for The Worm, was spent reading them beneath the porous yellow lamp light.

On the floor, there were more self-sustaining landmines. Piles of fast food wrappers and soda cans with bendy-straws still tucked inside their open tabs. Piles of notebooks with scribbles that contained information that she probably should have burned at some point in case people showed up that shouldn't and stuck their nose where they shouldn't.

But she was tired and that often won out against her paranoia. She wasn't going to do anything that wasn't on the *Need To* list.

The Almost-Apocalypse of Apple Valley

The place had been orderly once. Mariska may have even been dumb enough to straighten things out once or twice since they arrived.

But cohabitation with someone as unpredictable as The Worm made regular cleaning a fool's errand.

Her eyes lazily shifted, unable to keep pace with The Worm writhing and twisting around the inside of their shared home. It occasionally blotted out the outside world visible through cracks in the shade-drawn windows. They lived on an acre-sized dirt lot in the Marianas, a part of Apple Valley on the south-east fringes which butted up against Lucerne Valley to the east and the White Mountains to the south which served as the northern vanguard for the forest town of Big Bear.

Now that The Worm was back home, free from the confines of the cramped vehicle, it expressed a mix of giddiness and impatience.

Giddy at having more room to move around.

Impatience that everything was taking so long.

It swirled and wrapped itself around Mariska's face like a translucent scarf, pushing stringy bits of its not-quite-body into her mouth and nose.

For a brief, horrifying moment, Mariska's airways were clogged.

Hurry.

Mariska's hands shot up to her face, trying to pull The Worm away. Deep down, she knew that it was futile—The Worm wasn't something that could be physically grasped and manipulated—but it wasn't up to her. The human instinct reacted before logic could kick in.

Hurry, before I get too hungry.

The Worm pulled back and flew away, resuming its lap around the inside of the trailer.

Mariska fell forward onto the breakfast table, almost smashing her nose in before catching herself with her hands. She coughed and drooled tiny puddles all over the surface.

Apple Valley was her last chance.

Not *their* last chance.

The Worm constantly reminded her that it would find a way. It wasn't the expendable one.

Mariska had learned that too late.

But now they were here, shacked up in a small California desert town called Apple Valley whose only apples Mariska could see were on display in the grocery stores.

Still, Apple Valley was special.

Not just because the skies were clear and the cost of living was cheap—many of the residents moved up here from Los

Angeles and other places "down the hill," as the locals called it. But those qualities could be found in spots all over America.

Not true when it came to a Magic Zone like Apple Valley.

Magic Zones were rare. Ninety-nine percent of places in the entire planet, almost all two-hundred-million square miles of it, were just average. There was nothing special or unique about any of them. Nothing that could sustain something like The Worm.

In a Magic Zone, The Worm could live for centuries without needing to pack up and move on.

There were places it could survive, sure, but there weren't places it could *live*.

Places where it could *really, truly* live.

What made a place a Magic Zone?

Mariska had never been privy to that answer. The Worm had never thought to say, and she'd never thought to ask.

In all honesty, she no longer cared.

The only reason Mariska packed up her belongings, discarded her old life, and headed west from Cherry Hill, New Jersey, was because The Worm was getting hungry.

It needed to feed and Cherry Hill had long since lost its designation as a Magic Zone.

That was not good.

Because the loss of magic meant Death.

The Worm told Mariska how he had seen its Mother die. Killed, because she had grown greedy in a Magic Zone that was near depletion. So greedy that she almost took The Worm with her.

But The Worm found a way to escape Death and strike out on its own.

Mother had an Attendant who died in the chaos. One that would have been suitable for The Worm.

But The Worm was forced to find a new Attendant if it was going to carry on.

And, oh boy, did it find one.

Mariska had been seventeen, fit, and full of Capability when it discovered her. Her daytime hours were spent scooping up vanilla and mint chocolate chip ice cream in a parlor in Atlantic City to summer tourists. During those times, the sweltering summer days, The Worm felt her yearning, but it was dim.

Not so in the evenings.

When the stars sparkled from above and the moon projected its pale glow through graycast clouds, The Worm felt her the most. Those evenings she spent in the tiny bedroom of her mother's two-room shack with the door shut, enraptured in psychedelic rock music while practicing magic tricks, were evenings that promised The Worm a long and happy future.

She would make a fine Attendant. She would be able to take care of The Worm during those times it couldn't take care of itself.

Like when it needed to move to a Magic Zone.

"I need to rest," Mariska said, using the long white sleeve of her shirt to wipe away the last bits of sticky snot running from her nose. "Now we know a little more about what we're up against. Just give me a little time."

Time is not a luxury. Time is a gift.

She flinched as it quit circling the room and bounded toward her once more, halting inches from her face.

She hated when it spoke in near-riddles. There was just enough there for her to grasp the meaning, but enough vagueness to leave a fog of fear settling in her stomach.

"I know that," she said, her chin up, attempting a show of defiance. If she couldn't feel confident, at least she could act confident. The Worm seemed to respect that. Sometimes.

I'm worried.

Worried? Mariska couldn't remember The Worm ever using that term. She wasn't sure how she should feel to hear that.

Worried that I'm here and will starve. I cannot starve, Attendant. You cannot let me starve. It will be very bad for us both.

She didn't doubt that.

"I will get you what you need," she said. "But we need to be careful. I didn't like the feeling I got after the birthday party today. You heard the boy's thoughts. I don't think these kids are going to be as simple to deal with as you think."

The Worm was practically still a child itself. Mariska feared it would be its own worst enemy—*their* own worst enemy. An insatiable hunger and desire to come here might blind it to the complete dangers lurking in this Magic Zone.

And, oh, were there dangers.

Like most anything in the universe, there's a balance of good and evil—an almost-scientific law that every bit of bad always comes with a counterbalancing good.

Magic Zones were no different. If anything, the threat for the scales to quickly tip in an undesired direction were greater, because the consequences were greater. The heavier the weight, the bigger the crash, should something cause a shift.

He is nothing we cannot handle. There are ways to weaken him.

But not too much, The Worm was quick to add. *He must still be full of Capability when I feed. But he can be subdued. There is an opening. We saw into the other.*

Mariska knew exactly who The Worm was talking about.

It wasn't wrong. There always seemed to be one domino that could be pushed so the others would fall. Where there were humans, there were human emotions, and the right ones could be manipulated like light switches, casting light on the others.

It was obvious at the birthday party, but only to someone who was paying attention.

Don't disappoint me, Attendant. I'm growing hungrier by the hour.

Mariska had no choice. Not a real choice, anyway. If she didn't take care of The Worm, then what happened back in New Jersey would be a drop in the bucket. The Worm's mother had done some horrible things on her way out, but she was old and ancient.

The Worm was young, relatively speaking, and filled with Capability it had acquired over the years. Capability that could be expressed with a mere flicker of thought. If it didn't get what it wanted, what it *needed*, to continue living, it would make everyone pay.

"I have some ideas," she replied. "I'll take care of it tonight."

The Worm shivered, racing through the trailer again, shaking it with enough violence that the entire home threatened to tip onto its side. Futilely, Mariska gripped the edges of the table. More books, ceramic dishes, and hung pictures of deceased magicians crashed onto the floor, leaving a mess. A bottle of bleach she'd been using to clean spilled out onto the tiny patch of kitchen linoleum, sending heady fumes into the air.

It meant The Worm was happy.

It meant The Worm would be getting its way.

This would probably last its typical ten to fifteen seconds, but it was always violent and still managed to scare Mariska half to death.

She was certain The Worm knew that.

Ryan woke up in the middle of the night, thirstier than he'd ever been in his life.

He was pissed because he'd been having a great dream. A fantastic dream. The best dream, he was convinced, that he'd ever had in his entire life.

He had been at the beach, laying on a long blue beach towel spread across the sand, having his chest massaged by two Sports Illustrated swimsuit models posted on each side of him. Through a pair of rainbow-tinted Oakley Razorblade sunglasses he'd never be able to afford in the real world, he gawked up at them, thinking them unaware, but knowing deep down that they knew he was staring like the little horndog he was. The girls both wore the smallest bikinis he'd ever seen in his young life. He knew their faces, their bodies, but couldn't remember their names. They were coating him with thick suntan lotion—the one with the sugary coconut scent that was his favorite.

Next to Ryan was a shirtless Mr. T. laying back in a lounge chair, soaking in the summer sun with his hands behind his head. He wore only a pair of gold-frame sunglasses, red swimming trunks, and the signature, glinting gold chains of varying lengths and sizes draped over his neck and across his chest. Ryan wondered if they were hot to the touch. And then he wondered if they wouldn't eventually burn a path right through Mr. T's skin.

"This is the life, ain't it boy?" Mr. T. said in that signature gruff voice.

"Yes, sir," Ryan replied. A smile stretched across his face, threatening to split his head in two.

Just behind them were a pair of bodyguards standing tall, glancing around the beach—two also-shirtless Crips covered in tattoos. They each had a blue bandanna draped over their mouths like Old West bank robbers, sagging pants, and an AK-47 held lovingly in their arms. They were obviously charged with protecting Ryan and Mr. T.

From what, though, Ryan couldn't say.

The bikini models had just asked Ryan if he wanted to go skinny dipping. He was just about to jump up onto the sand and pull down his shorts when his vision zipped out like Fluffy scrambling for cover whenever Ryan caught him peeing next to his bed instead of using the litter box.

He was back in his room now.

Back in stupid reality.

He kicked off the sweat-soaked sheets and exhaled loudly. Loud enough to send his three little sisters stirring in the larger bed to his left.

No matter how hard he tried to fall back asleep, he couldn't. Despite his burning eyes, closing them only seemed to make falling asleep harder. His stomach was a little queasy—maybe he shouldn't have eaten that extra bowl of Mr. T cereal before bed. But maybe part of that queasiness was knowing that he'd never get to skinny dip with the swimsuit models.

Oh well.

Now he was parched and didn't have a cup of water anywhere within reach.

He pushed himself out of bed, wobbling slightly like a beached whale, and was shocked by two sensations, neither of which he was sure came first: the squishing sound as his feet hit the floor, or the cold sensation that seemed to zoom up his ankles until it hit his torso.

"What the..."

He looked down, his eyes already having adjusted to the dark, and saw what appeared to be the outline of a wet spot in the carpet.

The acrid odor of cat pee seemed to be released on impact, shooting straight up his nostrils.

"Fluffy, you stupid piece of—"

And then he was falling.

His words were cut off as if his speech had been cut cleanly by a pair of scissors.

His stomach jammed itself up against the rest of the organs in his chest until they became a compressed pile of juicy meat and muscle. Ryan felt his cheeks shooting up past his ears, his lips expanding and his teeth and gums exposed to a force that he'd never experienced in his life.

Air rushed into his eyes, forcing him to close them. He tried to reach his arms out to stop. To grab something, anything. But the force was too great, and they remained pinned to his side as if he were going down one of those giant, nearly vertical hundred-foot waterslides.

He wanted to scream, tried to scream, and maybe he did, but the rush of wind flying past his ears made it impossible to tell.

The journey downward was rapid. Neverending. Frightening beyond anything he'd ever experienced in his life.

His heart was pumping like a machine gun, one of those AK-47 automatic rifles toted by one of the Crips bodyguards, shooting a billion bullets per minute.

He wanted to curl himself up into a fetal position, but

couldn't.

He began to whimper.

So many images raced through his mind: his parents and sisters watching him like a barely engaged audience, dead still as if they were in an old photograph. The swimsuit models, pointing and snickering at him. Stupid Fluffy, running around in circles with his tail swishing, proud of the practical joke he'd pulled.

And then just as quickly as Ryan was falling, he was floating—like he'd been dropped into a pool of water, but without the splash.

The surrounding liquid was warm on his skin. It reminded him of the community center pool on an August afternoon.

He opened his eyes and wondered if he'd even done so, the world was so pitch black around him.

He stuck his limbs out from his sides, finding that the sensation of falling had left him, happy that he was able to control his body again. Resistance met his arms and legs like he was indeed swimming.

And then something odd struck him.

He was breathing. The air, or water, or whatever he was in, felt thick, sliding in and out of his respiratory system.

But he was breathing.

That seemed to calm him for some reason.

At least until he realized that he didn't know if he was upside-down, or right-side-up, or something in between. He was lost. Without bearings.

He tried to scream, but again, his voice was lost in the thickness of this world.

Be calm, boy.

A familiar, disembodied voice echoed from all around him. It was disconcerting, not having a single direction to reference.

Again, Ryan tried screaming at the top of his lungs until his breath ran out. The whimpering came again.

He'd never felt so scared of anything in his entire life, discounting the time his mom threatened to leave him at the gas station after he'd stolen a pack of gum, only to actually do it, forcing him to walk home in the dark for an hour.

She was in tears when he got home, apologizing profusely for what she called the biggest and only mistake she'd ever make with him again.

It didn't seem like that would happen here.

Be calm.

A relaxing sensation overcame his entire being. Suddenly, the blackness disappeared, like someone had flicked on a light switch.

He clamped his eyelids, shutting out the harsh white light.

A warm breeze flickered over his exposed flesh. It carried the scent of coconut tanning oil. Beneath him, Ryan felt the comforting fabric of the blue beach towel once more.

Slowly, he blinked his eyes, adjusting to the world around him.

He shuddered as multiple pairs of hands touched his chest once again, but the following feminine giggles calmed him.

The swimsuit models were back and his recovering eyes confirmed they were still wearing those tiny bikinis.

Only there was one major difference. They weren't random models anymore. They were girls he knew—Kim Goldnik, Stacy Thomas, Tina Schaffer, and the one he really couldn't believe: Loretta Mishki.

These were all the popular girls. Girls who'd never so much as acknowledged Ryan's existence, and now here they were, giving him their full attention.

He turned his head and glanced behind him. Between him and an array of palm trees, the Crips were gone, replaced by a pair of Bloods. They were just as menacing—in fact, they looked like the exact same guys—only sporting red bandannas instead of blue.

"Yo, Ryan. You need to chill."

Mr. T. was in the same spot, lying on his own towel a few feet to Ryan's left. His chains were glowing now. Glowing red-hot like they'd been sitting in a blazing fire. There was a tiny amount of smoke rising from Mr. T's chest and Ryan thought he even heard sizzling, popping sounds.

Need to chill?

It seemed like a possibility again. His heart no longer felt like it was going to extricate itself from the rest of his body like a prisoner breaking out of Alcatraz.

Seagulls called out in the distance.

Yeah, he could chill.

"You know, kid, there's something not right with your friends."

"Huh?"

"Those little punks you hang out with," Mr. T. said.

"What's wrong with my friends?"

"They're no good for you. They all think they're better than you. You're actin' like a fool, Ryan. And you know what I think about fools."

Ryan wasn't looking for pity. He felt enough of that coming from Steph's direction lately.

"Especially that kid with the helmet. What's his name? Ramen Man?"

"Rocket Man. Owen."

"Yeah, Owen. You know he thinks he's better than you, right?"

Thoughts of recent events spun through Ryan's mind. He couldn't pinpoint any exact incident where Owen had pissed him off or said something that had hurt his feelings, but there was a general emotion—something he wasn't fully ready to admit to—that rankled him inside.

Owen was smart, but Ryan always thought he was smarter. Who was in GATE, after all?

So Owen had his computer. If Ryan's parents could afford to buy him one, he'd have one too.

"And not only that, but he's movin' in on your girl," Mr. T. said.

Ryan tried to feign shock at the notion.

"What girl?" he asked.

But he knew.

He knew exactly what girl before Mr. T. sat up, pulled his sunglasses off, and leaned over with a serious look on his face. The chains seemed to weigh heavily on him, and now they were glowing even hotter than before—more icy-white and sea-blue than a glowing orange.

"You know. And you know that I know. So don't even try to front."

Ryan didn't say anything. He tried to focus back on the girls rubbing his body with more suntan lotion. Loretta raised her eyebrows seductively and continued massaging Ryan's chest.

Ryan tried to remind himself that his friends were exactly that—none of them would do anything to upset him on purpose. He felt a tiny sense of shame that he'd even remotely considered Owen something of an enemy.

"Owen wouldn't do anything like that. He doesn't even like Steph." The words rang hollow as he spoke them. "And neither do I," he added in for good measure. "Just friends."

"Whatever you say, fool. Just remember, lyin's not good for your health."

Ryan knew lying was mostly bad, to be used only during times of stranger danger, but he'd never considered it to be anything that would affect his body.

"Ryan?"

"Yeah?" He gazed at the man who watched over him every night as he slept.

"You know what you gotta do. And that's one to grow on."

Ryan watched as Mr. T's left eyeball soundlessly popped out of its socket and rolled down his arm, coming to a stop on the sand next to Ryan.

"See you soon," Mr. T. said, laughing with that gruff laugh of his. The next eye popped out with a quiet puff and rolled down beside the other like a pair of morbid dice.

Ryan's mouth felt dry again, propped open by a mix of fright and disgust.

Then he realized the hands had stopped rubbing, and he felt something wet splash onto his chest and roll down. It was another eyeball.

Followed by a second.

He looked up and saw a grinning Loretta with empty sockets hovering above him like an old crone. Her face shrunk in on itself. An implosion of flesh and bone.

And then the entire world around Ryan started disintegrating, like yellow glitter coming unglued from construction paper for a school art project, twinkling away into a great nothing.

The darkness that had surrounded him before was returning.

For lack of a better word, Mr. T. "melted" into his towel, which was itself melting into the sand, which was itself withering away into the abyss.

Ryan hopped to his feet, standing on his own towel as if it were an island of refuge. Thankfully, it maintained its shape.

He stared down at the other girls who were still lounging in the sand on each side of him. They all still smiled, but now with dark, bleeding sockets and faces falling in on themselves.

Their hands were still reaching out, palms filled with dollops of white sunscreen, until one by one, they melted into the sand as well.

Everything picked up pace.

The pair of Bloods that stood behind him didn't so much melt as collapse into grains of unreality. The palm trees, the ocean, sky—it all fell into oblivion. Erased from existence.

Everything went away until it was only Ryan, floating on his towel amidst the blackness again. His stomach knotted itself up.

And then the towel disappeared like someone had yanked it out from beneath his feet.

He was falling again.

Screaming with his eyes shut.

Then something hit him across the cheek, stinging him

into consciousness.

"Shut up!" Gabriela, his youngest sister, screamed in his face.

The falling sensation was gone.

Ryan was lying on his back.

He blinked a couple of times, adjusting his eyes to the sliver of early-morning sunlight that peeked through the thin curtains of his bedroom window.

"Yeah, we're trying to sleep!" Mary and Julie, his other sisters, the twins, yelled simultaneously.

He sat up and looked around. Gabriela was standing beside the bed. In the very same spot where he'd fallen down into the void.

"Move!" he yelled, pushing her away hard enough to make her fall back into the wall next to the bedroom door and bang the back of her head.

"Ow," she said, reaching up to rub her scalp. She sat right below the spot where Ryan had long ago pinned up a full-spread photo of Mr. T. from one of those A-Team fan magazines.

He was posed with his arms crossed, resting above the pile of gold chains. There was no smile on his face. Only pity.

But at least he had eyes.

"You a-hole!" Gabriela yelled, pushing herself up and

running out of the room. It was followed up with a distant, "I'm telling Mom and Dad!"

Mary and Julie were both quiet in their shared bed. Only the whir of the brown, spinning pedestal fan in the middle of the room penetrated the silence.

Ryan gripped the sheets, holding onto them for dear life. He was nervous, scared even, as he tentatively looked over the side of the bed.

The only thing that greeted him was the fuzzy brown carpet, dry as a bone.

Then he saw Fluffy leap out from under the bed and chase after his sister.

He looked back up at Mr. T. and thought about what he had said about his friends. That's what they were, right? His friends? They would never do or say anything to change that. To push him out.

To make Ryan the fool.

Instantly, his thoughts solidified on an image that he didn't know was real or not. In his mind, he pictured Owen and Steph sitting at one of the crowded cafeteria lunch tables. Underneath, in the shadows, their hands slowly inched toward each other until they met, their fingers interlocking like threads in a perfect pattern.

He'd never actually seen that happen.

Had he?

No. No, they were all friends. Just friends.

Until Steph was ready to accept that Ryan may be ready for something more. Then maybe *they* could be more than friends.

But Owen and Steph?

Ryan knew one thing for certain: he'd never let it get to that point.

Sunday, June 18, 1989 - 9:00 AM

Steph was outside of her apartment, straddling her bike on the cement walkway that ran between two rows of housing within the single-story complex, seconds away from the freedom of the wind in her face when her mom poked her head outside of the door.

Tucked between her mom's shoulder and ear was the cordless phone. She managed to simultaneously shake her head to whatever was being said on the other end while ensuring the phone didn't drop onto the ground.

Without a word, only wide, determined eyes, she wiggled her "come here" finger at Steph, who was still fiddling with her helmet strap.

The cool, cloud-covered morning beyond the complex beckoned Steph. She thought about ignoring her mom, taking off and pretending she didn't see a thing, but she imagined that would only lead to a worse outcome than the one she anticipated was already lined up for her.

"Mmmhmm," her mom said, closing the door behind Steph as she stepped back inside. "I see."

181

Steph pulled off her helmet, placing it on the worn carpet beside her mom's half-painted, cotton ball-stuffed toes. The living room was a mess—their two cheap love seats were packed with half-opened cardboard boxes of Avon material. On the coffee table was an army of tiny nail polish bottles, jars of night cream, and other accouterments to make women more desirable for men.

The rest of the tiny two-bedroom apartment was a labyrinth of other boxes stuffed with Tupperware and health supplements that may or may not be approved by the FDA.

"Yes, I'm very sorry to hear that."

Steph cleared a space for herself on one of the love seats and placed the soles of her feet on the edge of the coffee table.

"Unacceptable," her mom said, either to the person on the other end or to Steph, maybe both, as she came by and smacked Steph's legs away from the table.

"Thank you for letting me know, Mrs. Kirkwood."

Steph rolled her eyes and her chest sank, even though she figured out before she'd even stepped back through the door that that was who the other party was.

"We'll be having a discussion right now." Her mom looked down at her toes, wiggling them back and forth, admiring the sheen of the recently-applied polish in the apartment's subpar lighting.

Her mom hung up the phone and placed it back on the charger sitting on the kitchen counter.

"Do you *want* to be held back? Is that what you want?"

The questions came from behind Steph's head. She didn't turn around or say anything. It was pointless.

"Because that's what it seems like."

Her mom came around to the other love seat adjacent to Steph's, entering her line of sight, but remained standing in front of it.

"I thought you were going to study with that boy, Orson."

"Owen," Steph said, forced once again to correct her mom. "And I was. Only those stupid bitches—"

A stinging slap resonated across her entire face. Her ears even rang for a second.

"Language, young lady."

Her mom's slaps were rare, but common enough that they didn't faze Steph like they were probably intended to.

"Fine. Those *girls* gave me flat tires and I had to drag my bike home." She glared up at her mom. "Don't you remember?"

For one half of a split-second, there was a bit of hope in Steph's heart. Her mom was going to take her side. Her mom was going to believe her and do the right thing.

"I'm very busy, Steph. I don't have time to dwell on your schoolyard dramas. Plus, none of this stuff you go on about would even happen if you'd tried to make friends with girls in the first place."

"What?" Steph asked. She was incredulous.

Her mom continued on as if she'd never stopped. "Instead, you hang around that group of boys like you're one of them. And look where it's gotten you." She reached down and took hold of Steph's bangs. "I can't even get you to have a proper haircut."

Steph was ready. Here came the part she'd prepared for.

Her mom started with a couple of sniffles. At least two. And then she would wipe away a little wetness from the right eye.

"I just don't know what to do with you anymore." The words came out in a pained tone. Steph quietly mouthed them as her mother spoke them. "I'm at my wit's end. I'm trying to raise my daughter to be a young lady so that she'll grow up and marry a good husband who will take care of her so she doesn't have to spend every waking hour trying to scrape by."

"I don't need anyone to take care of me!" Steph said. She saw herself marrying someday, but she'd be damned if it would be anything like her mom said.

"Oh yeah? You think you can go out there"—her mom pointed at the door—"and take care of yourself?"

"If I had to. Better than you do."

Yeah, she probably shouldn't have said that.

Her mom's tears dried up like they'd been sucked up with a vacuum. An unsettling silence filled the air. Steph leaned back, waiting for another slap, but it never came.

"You're grounded."

Now that stung.

"One month. No bicycle. No TV. None of your 'boy' friends. You come home, you go straight to your room, and you study. You only come out for meals and to use the bathroom."

"Mom—"

"I let you go to your friend's birthday party, because I thought that maybe I was being too hard on you. But it's clear to me that I haven't been hard enough. If I had a good man around here..."

Steph turned her head and let her eyes drift toward her helmet on the floor, trying to ignore the ugly disposition on her mom's face.

"One more thing. After I finish my nails, I'm going to ring up Loretta's mom."

Steph whipped her head back around. Dread rose in her stomach. This was bad. This was really, really bad.

"What? Why?"

"If I'm going to turn you into a real girl, it's time you start spending time with one. I'm going to arrange a little get-together."

Now Steph wanted to turn on the waterworks. She could have taken the grounding. Though it wouldn't be the same as Saturday rides, she'd see The Crew at school. No problem there.

But this?

This was a nightmare.

Monday, June 19, 1989 - 8:00 PM

The clink of the softball being slapped with an Easton bat weaved through chain-link fences, in and out of cinder block dugouts, and over small five-row stands filled with the families of grown adults playing team sports.

Owen didn't understand why softball leagues were such a big deal for grown-ups in Apple Valley. Volunteering to play organized sports seemed foreign to him. Why would anyone put themselves through that on purpose?

Of course, he kept his thoughts to himself. The old people could do whatever they wanted, so long as Owen got to hang out with his friends outside of school.

Since his dad was on the same team as Ryan's, there wasn't much anything Owen's parents could say to keep him at home. Leaving him alone might mean he'd spend whatever time he had trying to hook his computer back up again. As much as he hated the distrust, he saw the opportunity and took it.

So here he was, hanging out with his friends at the Apple Valley Community Center, sitting in a brown plastic swing on the playground away from the spectators. Just behind them was a tall metal rocket ship that had once been painted red, white, and blue, but whose paint cracked and rusted due to time and lack of care.

It didn't matter. Kids still crawled around the thing like ants, sliding down the scalding metal slide in the heat of summer afternoons.

Jake was there too. The only one missing was Steph who was suffering her own punishment for her failed test—she told Owen that Mrs. Kirkwood called her Mom and ratted her out.

In Owen's hands was a warm Styrofoam cup with the grabbing-end of a plastic spoon sticking straight up.

He loved a good pepper belly: a stomach-warming concoction of hot chili con carne, neon yellow nacho cheese, and Fritos chips sold at the concessions stand.

"I don't want your nasty cooties," Ryan said, looking disdainfully toward the cup.

"Good," Owen said. "I didn't offer you any, anyways."

"Whatever," Ryan replied. He stuck out his tongue. Beneath the bright field lights projecting from fifty yards overhead, Owen could see Ryan's nasty tongue dyed purple by an excess of Fun Dip powder. "So, are you going to tell us what scarwey-warwey magic twick fwightened the poor wittle baby at his birthday party?"

Owen figured that Jake would be the one to hassle him about the very thing he dreaded would come up, not Ryan. Rat-face had been incessant since coming back to school that morning.

How much could Owen tell his friends? He hadn't mentioned anything at recess all week, and they hadn't brought it up.

"I...I just wasn't feeling good. I think I drank too much punch."

Owen felt like a failure, not being able to tell his friends the truth. If he couldn't trust his friends, who could he trust?

But maybe he'd start small. Baby steps for a big baby. He swore to himself that he'd mention it to Steph the next time he saw her. Her absence tonight seemed to weigh extra heavily on him.

"Nice! You went and puked the rest of the day?" Ryan snorted and looked at Jake to see if he'd have a similar reaction. Jake did, but barely. He seemed a little distant. A little on the periphery.

There were only two swings, both occupied by Jake and Owen, so Ryan was leaning against one of the metal support poles, dragging a path through the sand with the heel of his shoe.

"When are you going to be off lock-down again?" Ryan asked.

"Supposed to be until the end of the month," Owen replied, "but I'm hoping for early release on good behavior."

"Good luck with that," Jake said, finally piping in. "That wouldn't even be a possibility for me."

"Yeah, but your dad lets you get away with all sorts of stuff. You got to come here and he probably didn't even notice. I wish my parents didn't notice sometimes."

Jake seemed to tighten his grip around the chains holding up his swing. He stared at the ground like he was burning holes into it, Superman style, saying nothing in response.

Owen dipped his spoon into the pepper belly, delivering up a mouth-filling bite. "At least I'm not the only one getting screwed over," he said, halfway mumbling as he chewed. "I wish Steph could be here."

Ryan's head snapped up as if Owen had offered him a thousand dollars.

"Why?"

"Why what?"

"Why do you care about Steph? Aren't we good enough for you?" Ryan's voice was mostly joking, but Owen thought it seemed a little forced. Kind of like when someone was asking a question that they pretended not to care to know the answer about, but deep down, the answer was the most important thing in the world to them.

Owen decided he'd throw out a snarky reply. "You guys are all right. But we all know Steph's a lot cooler."

He had a feeling that if he could see Ryan's face in the light of noon, it would be beet red. He could see a bit of it now beneath the field lights, in the cool dusk, but he didn't need the full picture—there was just this vibe that Ryan constantly put out which broadcast his emotions. Owen decided he'd better try to short circuit the situation before it grew out of control.

"I didn't tell you guys, but my dad made me throw away my old helmet. Steph gave me birthday money to put toward a new one. I wanted to tell all of you my ideas for how I was going to paint it. Maybe you could help—"

"Who cares," Ryan said. "She wouldn't care."

Owen was silent for a few seconds, trying to process Ryan's reaction. So much for short-circuiting. Why was he acting so weird?

"Dude, what's your problem? I just thought—"

Ryan jerked his body away from the swing set and started walking away. "No one cares about your retarded helmet, *Rocket Man*. You should just paint a big wiener on the side. It would be more fitting."

Owen didn't say anything until Ryan was halfway back to the softball field. The word "wiener" triggered something different altogether in his mind.

Finally, he asked Jake, "What's his deal?"

Jake shrugged, still looking a little sullen like a mistreated dog.

Owen stared down at his pepper belly. It had cooled some and now the still-lingering salty, savory smell was making him a little nauseous. He wanted nothing more than to throw it away. He pushed himself off the swing, looking for one of those big, old metal oil drums that served as a trash can.

He scanned the park, and before he spotted one, he spotted something else.

The hairs on the back of his neck stood up. He felt the Styrofoam cup slip from his hands, plopping into the sand beneath his feet. The tiny impact of its contents hitting his pants leg barely registered.

Jake actually laughed, or so Owen thought, but like a far-off echo, that barely registered too.

A slow rumble hit Owen's eardrums, vibrating a familiar pattern.

An unsettling pattern.

An unforgettable pattern.

Alongside the community center playground ran the side street, Powhatan Road. And alongside that side street, sitting there on the dirt shoulder, headlights turned off but releasing a sort of ethereal glow along its entire body, was the Wienermobile.

The vehicle was only twenty yards away.

"Holy crapola," Jake whispered, or so Owen thought.

"Do you see that?" Owen asked.

From the corner of Owen's eyes, he saw his friend nodding.

"You—you too?" he asked.

They were both frozen, vision locked on the Wienermobile.

The wind kicked up suddenly, cutting through the iron bars of the rocket ship slide, whistling and humming a discordant tune. The rumbling engine was the only other sound making its way through Owen's consciousness.

"What do we do?" Jake asked. His voice was almost pleading, and his hands were clutched at his chest like he was suffering from massive heartburn.

Owen didn't have an answer, but his mind raced through potential ideas.

His first thought went to his parents. He wondered how much trouble he'd get in if he made a beeline for his mom while his dad was playing. If he tried to drag her over, tried to convince her that her son wasn't crazy, would she see?

Or would she only see a beat-up Volkswagen Rabbit?

But Jake could see it too. So Owen couldn't have been completely insane.

Or was it possible for two crazy people to see the same thing?

Owen briefly looked around for Ryan, but he was nowhere to be found. Probably back at the field already.

Would he be able to see it too?

The engine revved and it pulled Owen back to Jake's question.

"Let's go see it," Owen said.

The impulse shocked even him.

It was as if, all of a sudden, he'd been topped off like a gas tank with some sort of confidence fuel.

Jake's jaw dropped and his hands returned to the swing chains like he was going to fall off a cliff. "Are you stupid? What if it's a child molester or something. And he's got a gun? I'm not letting some a-hole get into my pants."

It sounded like Jake was trying to convince himself not to

go.

Owen didn't think it was a child molester. At least not what he thought a child molester normally was.

This was something worse.

So why did he want to confront it?

His head ached a little. It felt like something, like *someone*, was trying to pry apart the boarded-up windows of an abandoned house, only it wasn't abandoned at all—it was Owen's house and the boards were there for protection. They seemed to be holding, but Owen didn't know for how long that would be the case.

"I've seen it before," Owen said. The confession rolled out of his mouth like a tidal wave, impossible to stop. "The magician. She drove it."

Jake's hands were back at his chest. He seemed to be struggling for air—breathing hard like he'd just finished running the football from one end of the recess field to the other.

"Me too," Jake said. "I saw it too. It came to my house."

Owen and Jake's eyes unglued themselves from the car only for a moment to confirm that neither of them was lying to each other.

"The magician, you said?" Jake asked. "The one from your party?"

Owen could only nod. He wasn't a hundred percent certain he was even doing that.

The intensity of the boards being pried from his mental house cranked up. A crack sounded off in his brain—like one of the boards had come flying off the window.

And through the boards, he saw something black flash through the exposed daylight. Whatever it was, it zipped by several times, creating a strobing effect before coming to a fast stop.

Slowly, a pair of red eyes revealed themselves. They gazed into Owen's house, into Owen's mind, never blinking.

Only penetrating.

Like they were searching for something.

Owen's resolve was beginning to give.

"Maybe you're right. Maybe we should—"

The engine revved once more.

Come for a ride. Don't you want to have fun?

Owen heard the voice loud and clear. Its raspy familiarity brought back the bad memories of his birthday party to the forefront again. The embarrassment, the shame, he felt at running away started to return.

The door of the Wienermobile cracked an inch, bleeding a combination of sensory data. There was an intense rainbow of light. It reminded Owen of the three glass prisms which hung from the drop-down ceiling near the windows in Mrs. Kirkwood's class, splashing a myriad of color against the inside walls in the early morning.

"Do you hear that?" Jake asked.

"Hear what?"

"The music. The ice cream truck music."

Owen didn't hear a thing. Oddly, not even the ambient sounds of the community center at night penetrated his ears. All of his sense power seemed to be concentrated through his eyes like the sun through a magnifying glass. He saw only the churning lights of the prism.

Ride the Rainbow Trail. Hell Track is nothing in comparison. Ride the world's biggest bike jump and feel the glory, Rocket Man. Feel everything fall into place. She'll think you're the best!

An urge flowed through Owen—he deeply wished he had his bike right then. Wished he had his helmet so that he could strap it on, crack be damned, and take on the biggest, most awesome jump he ever had the pleasure to witness.

He saw everything so clearly.

"I see the jump. I see the rainbow."

"What?"

"The rainbow."

"What rainbow?"

"The rainbow! It's right there!" Owen yelled, or at least tried. His words were coming out in a flat, monotonous tone that he couldn't change.

And then he saw himself wearing his helmet. Saw the crack running down the side, but it didn't matter. He stood at the top of the Rainbow Trail, straddling the Redline's frame with his feet planted confidently on each side.

Surrounding him were not just hundreds or thousands of onlookers, but millions, all floating in the surrounding space, all filled with anticipation of what would be the greatest, most triumphant moment in the history of the human race.

One person was separate from it all, though. One person who could have replaced the millions and Owen wouldn't have batted an eyelash.

Floating to his left was Steph, her hair characteristically hanging over her right eye, gazing at Owen as if he were the greatest hero she'd ever encountered.

Rocket Man would make the jump for millions, but in his heart, he knew he was making the jump for her. The feeling felt natural, but at the same time, scary. Owen felt a lack of control that he wasn't used to.

He kind of liked it.

The Almost-Apocalypse of Apple Valley

But then the rainbow began to strobe, as if something with Predator-like invisibility crossed its path over and over again—like a pianist's hands quickly sweeping back and forth across piano keys.

Something else was happening in the background—in the world outside of the Wienermobile. Almost like something happening just outside of the known universe.

In the outer limits of his vision, Owen saw something moving toward the rear of the car.

Suddenly, the Wienermobile's door slammed shut.

Everything went away and it hurt.

"No!" Jake cried out, his voice filled with pain.

Owen felt it too. Felt the loss of the rainbow. Felt his only chance of ever getting on his bike again and the only chance to ride the most awesome jump in the world, both disappearing before him.

Sound rushed into his ears like they'd become unclogged. In the distance, rising in the air, there was a tiny clink followed by the shouts and whistles of softball fans.

The Wienermobile's engine revved.

Something else revved its engines as well.

Owen realized it was the thing that had arrived behind the Wienermobile. The thing that had floated in from another universe.

The thing that was a familiar-looking pick-up truck.

It took Owen maybe half a second to place it—it was the blue Dodge pick-up driven by the man from the morning of Owen's accident. The man who had been parked outside of the Lion's Park electrical substation. The man who'd watched Owen fly off his bike and whose intense eyes he felt even now—like they'd never stopped looking.

The silhouette outline of the man's baseball cap and round face was all that was visible now.

The truck engine revved again.

So did that of the Wienermobile.

In turn, each engine grew in its furor, building to a screaming tempo. They seemed like warriors facing off for battle, shouting in an effort to demoralize the other side. The truck's engine was a low, rumbling growl—slow, confident. The Wienermobile's was high and chaotic—like a screeching cat, its hair standing up on its back with sharp claws at the ready.

Finally, there was a loud click and the screech hit its apex. The Wienermobile's rear tires spit up dust and loose gravel as it sped away, eastbound down Powhatan toward the neighboring star-lit town of Lucerne Valley.

Two conflicting feelings slammed into Owen like a pair

of runaway semi-trucks: relief at having the tension broken up, yet an enduring sadness at losing the opportunity to ride the Rainbow Trail.

The pick-up truck's engine returned to a steady, idling rumble. It kicked up briefly. Then it rattled to a halt. Once again, the air carried only the sounds of the softball field. Even the whistling hum of the wind that had earlier passed through the rocket ship was gone.

There was a squeal as the driver-side door swung open. The man inside sat there for a moment, motionless. Owen felt a tiny fear beginning to take hold of him again. It was nothing like what had been brought on by the Wienermobile and the presence of whatever it was that drove the dang thing, but it was a very real, soul-gripping fear nonetheless.

Finally, the man stepped out and slammed the door closed. Only the top of his cap was visible above the truck cab. He started walking around the hood, turning toward the latched gate that was the only exit and entrance to the playground from outside of the park.

"We should go," Jake said. He was on his feet now, angling toward the softball fields.

Owen heard him, but showed no indication that was the case.

"Owen."

Owen, leapt off the swing, slowly. He still held on to one of the chains, swaying on his feet. It felt like the ground was moving beneath him in wave-like patterns.

"Owen."

Owen heard the call, felt the tug on his shirt sleeve, even knew it was Jake, but his friend sounded distant as Owen watched the man lift up the latch and swing the gate open.

Another rusty squeal.

So many parts of Owen's body were straining against the very idea of standing still. He was experiencing the fight-or-flight instinct that Mrs. Kirkwood talked about during science period, but heavily on the flight side of the equation.

Even though most of his anatomy was telling him to take heed and get the heck out of there, Owen liked to think himself a fighter—to think himself brave like Cru Jones taking on Hell Track.

Images of the glorious Rainbow Trail jump flashed through his mind once more.

Next thing he knew, he heard Jake's shoes tip-tapping rapidly away from the swing set.

Owen was alone.

The man approached the swing set. Details filled out

as he got closer. The sideburns were still there. The cherry-red cheeks barely hidden beneath.

"Owen Thom?" the stranger asked, maybe four feet from Owen now. Owen's head reached the man's chest. He could punch him in the belly and kick him in the nards if he had to. It wouldn't be hard. If the man tried to cover Owen's mouth to keep him from yelling, he'd chomp down on the stranger's hand until it bled.

No, Owen wouldn't go down without a fight. In fact, he was itching for a fight now. Those previous thoughts of flight disgusted him.

Adrenaline pumped through his system. The strange, familiar adrenaline he'd felt in his bedroom when he'd watched the Mysterious Mariska leave his house.

"Yeah," he replied, coming back to the present, throwing away every bit of D.A.R.E training he'd ever received by stating exactly who he was. "What do you want?"

He noticed there was no quivering in his voice. That fact made him feel even braver. He straightened up his back and puffed his chest out, letting go of the swing chain.

The man seemed briefly taken aback, but then his surprise morphed into a smile. He stuck out a hand. Its callouses and wrinkles were clearly visible beneath the park lights.

"We need to talk, *amigo*."

Tuesday, June 20, 1989 - 5:00 PM

Owen found yet another loophole in the world of being grounded—the library.

He produced a pretty genuine-looking handout from Mrs. Kirkwood that instructed her students to go to the Apple Valley Library and perform research on any topic. Each student had to deliver a four-page report on said topic at the end of the week.

First, Owen's dad insisted he just use the encyclopedias he'd so readily pointed out after the birthday party, but Owen was ten steps ahead. Like any good journalist, he had to cite multiple sources and the library was the best place for that. He even threw in something about having to make use of the Dewey Decimal system.

His dad dropped him off just outside the old, single-story stucco building on Outer Highway 18. Its windowed front blocked out the afternoon sun with yellowed curtains that had once been white. Owen noticed John's truck right away, parked on the side of the building. Thankfully, there was no Wienermobile or Volkswagen Rabbit anywhere in sight.

Setting a pick-up time of 6:30 p.m. and confirming that Owen would be fine on his own, his dad pulled out of the parking lot, a grateful smile of relief on his face at not having to stick around.

Once inside the closed confines of the building, the first thing Owen noticed was actually how well the curtains kept out the purring engines and general road noise from Highway 18.

It was deathly quiet.

He soon realized a lot of that was due to the fact that there only appeared to be two people in the whole building — himself and the librarian.

"Can I help you?" she asked.

Her silver hair was tied up in a bun, and she wore her glasses well. They were the black, narrow-framed type that made people look sort of like cats. A shimmering chain of fake pearls hung down from the temple tips resting in the nooks of her ears.

She looked like she had stepped out of a museum exhibit titled "Generic Librarian."

"I'm just looking," Owen replied after rubbernecking around the building, not seeing John anywhere.

Her eyebrows dipped below the top of her frames.

"We don't have any computer games in here."

The tone in her voice implied that kids these days didn't come to the library to "just look."

"I'm not here for that. I need to do a report. For school"

For a brief moment, Owen wondered if he hadn't made a mistake coming here. Or at least shored up his story first.

"Owen," a voice whisper-yelled from the back of the library. "Over here."

He leaned past the front of the desk and peered down a narrow alleyway surrounded by shelves filled with plastic-sleeved hardcovers. Against the rear wall, John sat in a steel folding chair behind a small card table, a large book spread open before him.

"Like I said, I'm just looking—for my uncle. He's supposed to help me. Found him! Thanks!"

Owen scrambled toward John, feeling the eyes of the librarian drilling into his back the whole time.

It was the first time Owen could remember ever stepping foot within the town's library, and to be honest, it was a sorry-looking place. It smelled slightly of mildew and dust. On his way to the rear, he navigated past hundreds of uncatalogued books sitting in portable carts and even more piles knocked over haphazardly across the floor. The carpet was coming up in spots, revealing the raw cement below.

Owen was glad he didn't actually have to produce something from this mess.

As he approached John's table, he felt some trepidation. He had a difficult time connecting the words on the computer screen with this man who looked like he'd spent more time tilling fields on his John Deere tractor than dealing with the latest technology.

"Hey," he said.

"Hey," Owen replied, taking the chair opposite. It kept some distance between them. Still, he could smell the lingering coffee on John's breath.

Owen peeked over John's book. Interpreting the upside-down words, he saw they said something about pottery.

"It's nothing," John said. He inclined his head toward the librarian. "Just something to keep the old bat off my case."

That made Owen smile. He may not have looked like John, but it sure sounded like him.

"Just you?" John asked.

Owen nodded.

"Look, I appreciate you not mentioning anything to your friends," John said. "Not just yet."

Owen nodded again.

John hadn't said much the night before other than they

needed to talk about "current events" and asked if Owen could meet him at the library the next day, just the two of them. He handed Owen the official-looking printout that he'd passed on to his parents.

Owen felt a mix of emotions when John asked him to keep this little meeting to himself. Especially since Jake seemed to be seeing the same things he was seeing. All day, Owen had wanted to talk to The Crew about what he and Jake had seen in the park.

Ryan and Steph probably wouldn't believe them, but the case was growing stronger that something strange was going on.

On top of that, Owen couldn't help but feel that things had gone awry since the accident at the bike track. It was like Owen's world had taken a turn for the worse. He wasn't sure he could put it into words, but it almost felt like The Crew was disintegrating before his very eyes. The conversations during recess were more stilted and everyone seemed to be getting into trouble for *something*.

Owen had a feeling it all tied into what John wanted to talk about, but he couldn't be sure. "My dad took away my computer," he said. "I haven't been able to work on the thing you sent me."

John waved his hand. "I understand. I've sent it to some other friends and I'm hopeful we can figure it out in time."

"In time for what?"

John paused for a moment. He took off his cap and set it on the table, revealing thinning gray hair. The bags beneath his eyes seemed to magnify. Owen realized the trucker hat made John look younger.

"You've been seeing some strange things lately, right?"

Relief flushed through Owen's body like a stream of cool water. To not have to explain what had been happening to him felt like a minor miracle.

John continued, "Things that make your blood run cold? Things that make the hair on the back of your neck stand up?"

Things that make me feel like I'm not myself, Owen wanted to add, but he only nodded.

"It's why I came to the park last night," John said. "I knew something was going wrong. There was someone else there in that car and I had to flush him away."

"Her. The Mysterious Mariska."

John chuckled, but Owen didn't think it was funny.

"Ah. Sorry. It's just that it seems ridiculously fitting. Wouldn't matter if she called herself Pretty Pretty Princess, though—she's bad stuff, Owen. But she's only a part of the problem. She's just a worker bee."

"Huh?"

John looked over Owen's shoulder briefly. Owen had a feeling he was keeping an eye on the librarian. He then leaned over the table and whispered, the smell of coffee coming through strong again. "We don't know its real name, if it even has one, but we know it by many names—The Presence. The Black Smoke. The Worm."

Those names each meant something different to Owen, and he believed they could each apply in their own way.

"Why is it here though? What does it want?" he asked.

"It wants you."

"Why?"

"Well, not you in the sense that it wants you specifically. It wants what you have. What you can do. Which I guess is as much *you* as anything. And when I say you, Owen, I don't just mean *you* you. It wouldn't mind that, but this thing is greedy. It wants what you and your friends have. What you all create. Certain kids combined with their environment generate what I'll call 'the magic of youth'. It only exists for a short period in life, but to something like The Worm, it's chocolate cake with the power to sustain it for centuries."

He wanted to go further down that train of thought,

thinking that he didn't *create* anything except headaches for his parents, but Owen realized something about what John had said earlier. "You said 'we.' Who's 'we?'"

John leaned back again, settling in his chair. "That's a longer story and one I hope we can talk about another time. Just know that I was a kid once too, believe it or not. I missed most of my childhood because of something like this thing and I wasn't the only one. Others did too. We all found each other, through vague newspaper ads and BBSes, just like I found you." He concentrated on the ceiling for a moment, then looked back at Owen again. "Think of us as guardians. Or maybe more like scouts."

Owen asked the next logical question: "So, if it's so bad, and you already know about it, why haven't you guys stopped it?"

"We wouldn't be having this conversation if we could," John replied. "We can't stop it, *amigo*. We can barely see it. But we can see enough of it to keep track of where it's headed and to warn others. What it did to us...let's just say it left a little part inside each of us that no matter how much we wish, ain't never gonna go away."

Owen frowned. He reached down and grabbed his stomach, thinking of the movie *Alien* where the little creature burst out of the guy's belly after the mom had latched onto his mouth and laid its eggs.

"Don't worry," John said. "It hasn't gotten to you yet."

The 'yet' part seemed to be the only word Owen heard. He tried desperately to keep himself together. To hold back the waterworks.

"I'm just a kid," Owen said. "I don't know how to beat the Mysterious Mariska or some worm thing."

"But you can," John said. "Well, at least we *think* you can."

"You *think* we can?" Owen fought back the feelings of despair.

A harsh "shhhh" came from the librarian's desk. Owen was already on edge and his irritation almost forced him to yell, "We're the only ones in your stupid library, lady!"

But he held back.

John sucked in a little bit of air between his lips. "Meeting you like this, telling you this stuff—it isn't easy for me, *amigo*. It might even be easier to tell a kid he has incurable cancer, because at least the ending's certain, laid out for all to see."

He leaned in toward Owen again. "But if I just let that pair come to Apple Valley and wreak havoc, I'd never let myself live it down. Besides, this feels different. This feels like it's going to be so much worse if we don't nip it in the bud."

Great, Owen thought. What makes me and The Crew so special as to warrant something 'so much worse?'

John's eyes locked onto Owen's like Maverick locking onto a Soviet bogey. For the first time, Owen realized it didn't make him feel uncomfortable. "The first thing we need to do is separate The Worm from his pet, Mariska."

"How do we do that?" Owen asked.

"There's always something that binds them together. An object. Something. If we can find that and destroy it, then The Worm is next to powerless."

Owen thought hard about what such an object could be. His mind journeyed back to the birthday party and his focus landed on a single item.

Her hat.

That had to be the connection.

"You're going to have to trust me on this one," John said. "Can you do that?"

If John Pope had asked him that question a couple of weeks ago via Sysop chat, the answer would have been un-equivocal. Owen would follow him off a cliff if the man had asked. But now Owen had not only himself to think about, but his friends as well.

They didn't seem to have a say the way Owen did. The amount of responsibility sitting on his shoulders right now weighed down on him like all the library books surrounding him combined.

"Yes," Owen said.

John picked up his hat and rubbed the bill between his fingers. "Now that you know what I know, I think it's time you get the others involved. Get them ready. It's up to you how you want to bring them into this. You know them better than I do. They're your friends. The Worm and Mariska, they're going to throw everything at you. Try to break you up in the process. Don't let it happen."

And with that, John pushed back the chair, making it scrape loudly against the floor. He flashed a smile over Owen's back toward the front of the library as he placed the cap back on his head.

"Wait," Owen said, grabbing John's wrist.

John looked down, his eyebrows raised.

"The email. What was the point of that?"

"Honestly, I don't know. It may not be anything. It may be everything. Every time the creature and its helper come to town, it's like there's always something which shows up myste-riously—something that can help get things back in balance. As scouts, we keep our eyes open for anything unusual. I suggest you start doing the same."

With that, John rubbed the top of Owen's head. "Don't worry, *amigo*. You're not in this alone. I'll be in touch, but if you need anything beforehand..." He reached into his back pocket, pulled out a creased leather wallet, and withdrew a business card.

"If you don't get me at home, my pager number is on there."

Owen said nothing as he heard the soles of John's boots click away and then the street noise tunnel through the shelves from the front door.

The book John had been reading was still sitting there, open. It would be another hour before Owen's dad would pick him up. Owen thought about grabbing a hardcover from the shelves, maybe a Stephen King or something sci-fi, but he didn't feel much like reading.

Instead, he just put his head down on his arms, closed his eyes, and thought about the conversation he'd just had.

He wanted to trust John. Wanted to believe him.

But if Owen Thom felt anything right then, it was alone.

Combined with crafting the dreams, the latest group of kids stepped all over Mariska's last nerve at her latest after-school birthday party.

It was a noisy affair at the Chuck E. Cheese in Victorville. The birthday girl, a redhead with freckles and rosacea that mapped across her face in a pattern that resembled a combo connect-the-dots/Rorschach test, pulled hard on her cape in the middle of a card trick, causing it to tear into two on the left side.

Mariska could sew it—she had the skill—but it was just one additional annoying thing that weighed on her.

That little girl had some Capability—nothing like the group from Saturday—but all kids have it. It was enough for The Worm to stretch Mariska's limits just a little more, serving as an appetizer for the upcoming main course.

She admitted feeling some pleasure at the look on the little girl's face when the animatronic Elvis-looking lion hopped off the stage and proceeded to knock off everyone's head with the butt of his red guitar, leaving a trail of rubbery pizza and corpses in the dimly-lit party room.

But now the Mysterious Mariska was wiped out, eyes closed, lying completely naked on the living room carpet after a cold shower. Her hands were folded across her chest, fingers tucked into each other in a lace-like pattern.

She was so tired.

Entertaining at parties.

Contriving the dreams.

The Worm was pushing her hard.

It was hard trying to make a living *and* be an Attendant at the same time.

Brain fog crept in, making it difficult to focus on any single thing.

She wondered if the Magic Zone could feel things like a real person, and if so, did it feel just as exhausted after The Worm did its feeding? Could the Magic Zone feel anything at all? Was it something real and living or was it just inanimate food like a piece of cheese?

She supposed even that was living. A vague recollection from some long-ago school lesson reminder her that bacteria gave certain cheeses their tangy flavor.

Mariska started to giggle.

When her own life force had essentially been sucked out of her, her thoughts often went to the silly. But that was okay.

Everything was quiet for the moment. Calm, even.

The Worm slept. It had been sleeping since Monday night in the second bedroom, wrapped up like a cat looking for the tightest possible cardboard box to squeeze into.

It would probably continue sleeping another day or two. Mariska wasn't the only one who grew tired after feeding.

Still, even though The Worm claimed to do most of the work, everything was channeled through the Attendant. Without the Attendant, the magic couldn't be pulled from the children, manifested into something edible.

Mariska always thought she wanted to perform *real* magic. Magic that was truly from another realm. Something beyond sleight-of-hand and cheap props.

But now she found herself yearning more and more for the simplicity of the everyday stuff. She didn't want to say that she was done with being an Attendant. Just the thought shook her to her very core, turning up her senses to eleven in case The Worm stirred.

What would she be without that role? Without that power?

Was it even possible to just *stop*?

The trailer shook slightly.

Mariska's hands tightened their grip on each other.

Was The Worm sensing her thoughts, even in its sleep?

No. No, it must be those High Desert winds kicking up.

Please, please, don't wake up.

The movement subsided.

Her hands took almost thirty seconds to return to their normal, tensionless state.

The Worm stirred occasionally. That's all it was. She knew that consciously, but subconsciously, a bile rose up in the back of her throat, knowing that any relief she felt was only a temporary relief. That was always the case.

Living with The Worm was a constant state of tension. It was a lot like having an alarm set for 5:00 a.m. because you had to make an important appointment and you woke up every hour or half-hour, staring at the red LCD numbers which had only moved incrementally, but nonetheless pushed you closer to the time of reckoning.

No, there was no early exit point from the path she'd chosen.

In fact, she had a new problem.

The man with the baseball hat.

He'd shown up last night at the community center when The Worm decided it wanted an evening snack. Every muscle in Mariska's body tensed at the man's arrival. The Worm was surprised too, but it quickly turned to annoyance.

It told her not to worry. The man was essentially power-less. They would have to take care of him, though. He would only interfere and make things more difficult.

Mariska had wanted to ask how and why, but she sensed that she'd be better off keeping her mouth shut.

Quickly, Mariska sat up. The curled tips of her wet hair slapped the sides of her cheeks.

A question arose through the fog: How could she use the man to her advantage? She could slip away from The Worm if she could find a way to transfer the role of the Attendant, right? Could the man be forced to take the role?

It wasn't that easy.

Nothing was ever that easy.

The Worm stirred again.

In the kitchen, the plates that hadn't shattered in the last outburst of The Worm rattled in the cabinets, ready to break free and follow their brethren into the shard-filled underworld.

Mariska had to stop thinking about this. She raised her hands to her temples and rubbed with her fingertips, as if she could massage away the thoughts—squeeze them out so that they would disappear into thin air.

She chuckled quietly.

Something like that would take Magic.

Real Magic.

Wednesday, June 21, 1989 - 5:00 PM

"Mom, please. I swear that I'll be good and I'll do better on my tests."

In the salon mirror, ugly tears streaked down Steph's cheeks and pooled onto the dark brown nylon bib. Citrus scented shampoos and chemically sharp rubbing alcohol permeated the air. The *snip-snip-snip* of scissors sprung from the stylist standing behind a stone-faced Loretta Mishki, who was seated in the barber's chair on Steph's left-hand side.

"See, doesn't she look beautiful?" Steph's mom asked, nodding toward Loretta, completely ignoring her daughter's pleas. She and Loretta's mom hovered behind the two girls like a pair of old crows, their arms crossed and grins painted on their faces that would make the Cheshire cat jealous.

"You'll look great, honey!" Loretta's mom said to Steph. Her perkiness burned holes in Steph's ears.

The woman was just as tanned as her daughter, but the constant exposure to the sun had done its damage—nearly every part of her exposed flesh was wrinkled and freckled. Yet she tried to cover that fact up as much as possible with bright pink lipstick and layers of make-up that gave her daughter a run for her money.

snip-snip-snip

"I'll be done with Loretta soon. How do you want hers?" the stylist, jerking her head toward Steph. She was loudly chewing a piece of gum, running a comb down Loretta's hair.

"As close to Loretta's as you can get," Steph's mom said.

"No," Steph said, but it only came out as a whisper.

Her eyes swung back toward Loretta. Loretta's face was still and focused on the mirror. She pretended to be oblivious to the situation, but Steph saw a crack starting to form on her lips, their corners turning slightly upward. She swore that she even saw that familiar red glow flash in her eyes. The one she'd seen at the bike racks.

"I'll do what I can," the hairstylist said, lifting her eyebrows and glancing down at Steph like she was being asked to fly a 747.

"They could practically be sisters," Loretta's mom said.

"Aww," Steph's mom replied.

Steph wanted to vomit.

Being grounded was punishment enough. And then there was this idea of a 'play date.' But this was taking things too far. This wasn't a play date—this was a play nightmare.

Her mom hadn't even told her about this part until they got to the Mall of Victor Valley. She thought they were going to meet at the food court, probably do some shopping at Wet Seal (Hot Topic or Spencer's was more Steph's speed), and then call it a night.

Steph could have handled that. Sure, she'd seethe the whole time, but it would be over and done.

But here she was now, before anything else had even taken place, sitting in a Regis hair salon while shoppers walked through the mall's Muzak-filled hallway outside, oblivious to the horror taking place inside.

A half-hour had passed, maybe more, and it was done. Steph held back the tears this time, but not for lack of trying. They just wouldn't come. She stared in the mirror at what the gum-snapping butcher had done, too devastated to cry anymore.

Now she was just numb.

Her hair wasn't a like-for-like as Loretta's—it wasn't long enough—but the look was close. It made her think of a long-haired poodle bred with a mop.

Steph just wished her hair would fall out.

"I did what I could," the stylist said.

Steph's mom stepped up behind Steph and crouched

down, examining all angles of the new hairdo like it was a piece of artwork.

"My little girl," she said.

Fifteen minutes later, they were all seated in the food court. Steph's corn dog sat in a cardboard tray, still drizzled with mustard with a single bite missing—the one she took before she realized she had no appetite.

She was seated across from Loretta while the mothers sat across from each other at the table next to them. Blurs of people walked behind Loretta, carrying plastic trays filled with plates of orange chicken and slices of pizza. Water trickled from surrounding fountains. Echoes of piano music reverberated across the court from the raised platform behind them.

The moms were laughing and talking way too loudly about the latest guy Steph's mom was seeing. They were babbling away like they were best friends—Steph's mom living vicariously through Loretta's, and vice-versa.

Steph tried to avoid making eye contact with Loretta. She decided it was the only way she was going to get through the rest of the evening without completely losing it.

"I called your boyfriend last night," Loretta said, stirring the pile of chow mein sitting on her paper plate.

Steph wasn't going to bite. Wasn't going to listen. Wasn't going to give Loretta a moment of her time if she didn't have to.

But her emotions betrayed her, and she had to say *something*.

"Sure you did," she said.

"Yeah. Owen."

She got the name right. The Bitch got the name right.

No, she was just messing with Steph. She wouldn't have called him.

"I felt bad that he'd gotten hurt," Loretta continued. "I wanted to tell him that I was glad he was feeling better."

"He's fine." It didn't matter, Steph realized after she said it. Loretta didn't *really* care about him.

"Yeah, I know."

Steph couldn't help but look up from her corn dog and into Loretta's eyes. She had to see what was there.

Big mistake.

Her eyes were definitely glowing now.

"I was thinking of asking him to go out with me," Loretta said. She stirred her noodles once again, flicking her eyes between them and Steph.

Steph pictured herself grabbing the corn dog from her tray and jamming it all the way into Loretta's ugly mouth, punching it through the back of her throat where it would fly out the other side and slap onto the food court tile.

The imagery made her shudder.

"What do you think?" Loretta asked. "Do you think he'll say 'yes?'"

"Not a chance," Steph said immediately.

Loretta was nonplussed.

"I think he'll say yes. They all do. Let's face it—between me and you, the winner's pretty obvious, no matter how much your dumb mom tries to turn you into a girl."

The cackles rising up from the moms indicated they had no clue what was happening at the table next to them.

"Stay away from him," Steph said. It wasn't what she intended to say. In fact, she had no idea from where the forceful words arose.

"Yeah, I'm definitely going to ask him out tomorrow."

Saying anything else was an exercise in futility. Steph spun her corn dog around on its stick, painting it in the yellow mustard, ignoring Loretta until the moms finally decided that it was getting late, but they absolutely, positively, had to do this again.

They hustled to the car since it started to rain. When they got inside, Steph's mom reached across and gently caressed the back of Steph's head.

"I think this is all going to work out."

"Sure, mom."

As they pulled out of the mall parking lot and on to Bear Valley Road, something caught Steph's eye.

It was momentary.

A flitting piece of time.

But it played out in her head like a movie on slow-mo.

In that brief span, through the passenger-side mirror, she could have sworn she saw the tail end of the Wienermobile drive around the corner of the Mervyn's department store, disappearing into the wet summer evening.

Wednesday, June 21, 1989 - 11:30 PM

None of them were supposed to be here, but Owen bet on the stamina of nearly-teenagers outlasting that of his forty-something parents.

It was late—probably close to midnight—but nobody had a watch or was really keeping track.

All four kids were gathered inside the two-man, nylon tent, a single flashlight tilted up to provide illumination. From the outside, it resembled a tiny green pyramid with rounded corners. The entrance flap was slightly unzipped, allowing a little bit of *Dude Looks Like a Lady* to filter out from the portable radio speakers.

Owen hoped the low-volume drone would cover any discussion, should his parents wake up.

Owen's backyard was expansive, mostly covered in a rectangular patch of verdant green grass, surrounded by a dark-red wooden fence that ran the length of the house and stretched out just enough to accommodate the lawn and an oval-shaped Doughboy pool.

They all came at Owen's behest. He hadn't given them

the details as he wasn't sure of them himself. He only knew he had to convince them that it was in their interests to go after the Mysterious Mariska.

There was only one sleeping bag and it was his. As much as he would have normally loved hanging out all night with his friends, there was too much weighing on his mind, not to mention the fact that he was still grounded.

When he told his parents that he wanted to camp out in the backyard, they were only a little bit suspicious. Either they felt bad about everything he'd been through pain-wise and wanted to give him a little leeway, or they were more trusting than he'd taken them for.

All that mattered was they gave him the go-ahead, and as a result, The Crew was together again which meant Owen could break the news and formulate a plan.

But first, Owen wanted to ask Steph about her hair.

Everyone gathered tonight wanted to ask her about her hair.

It was the elephant in the tent.

Except no one asked, because the first thing Steph had said when she'd been the last to arrive was, "Don't ask."

With all of them gathered together again, there was a certain level of empowerment fizzing in the air. Owen couldn't put his finger on it, but it was reminiscent of the vibe that ran through him whenever the Wienermobile was nearby.

Only, in a good way.

And much more powerful.

We have several dedications tonight coming out of Victorville.

Dude Looks Like a Lady ended and the DJ for 103.1 KVVQ came on. The radio station was broadcast out of Victorville and was a local favorite with the kids. Nearly every night, the DJ would come on between songs and announce the dedications.

Marcy wants to tell Albert that she loves him with all of his heart and that she's sorry about what she did to his Mustang.

Oh, Marcy, the DJ continued. *I sure hope you didn't go and do something drastic.*

The disembodied voice laughed, almost a little too long.

You should forgive her anyway, Albert. Women do crazy things when they're in love.

And with that, the DJ launched into *Love Shack.*

"Your parents sure have a funny way of grounding you," Ryan said. His back was pressed against one side of the tent with his arms wrapped around shins, pulling his knees up to his chest.

"Yeah," Jake added. "Must be nice."

Owen held a finger to his lips. "I told you, I'm still

grounded. Don't be loud and mess this up."

Steph was the quiet one tonight, which was unusual. She sat with legs crossed, her back to the tent's opening. Through the flapping opening behind her, a field of stars greeted Owen on a magical-looking night.

That also struck him as unusual, because it had seemed that the summer was going to bring rain upon them every day. Now, summer was actually behaving like summer again.

"Hey," Jake said, knocking his elbow into his backpack which was sitting in the corner of the tent next to him. "I brought some goodies. I'm thinking we ought to give Adam Nielsen a little surprise tonight."

Adam happened to live a couple of houses away. Owen knew what his friend meant by goodies. Jake had obviously packed a strand of Black Cat firecrackers or some Roman Candles that he'd bought at some stand set up in a strip mall.

"Dude," Owen said. "What part of 'don't be loud' are you not getting?"

He looked at Steph who seemed to be expressing agreement. Her head was shaking slowly from side to side.

Jake looked as if he'd been denied the right to breathe.

"I'm just trying to have some fun," he said. "Things have kinda sucked lately."

Wasn't that the truth.

"That's why I need to talk to you guys," Owen said. "It's about something important."

"Get on with it then," Ryan said. He acted like he had better places to be, which annoyed Owen.

Owen wasn't sure how to say what he was going to say. Maybe he should have rehearsed some grand speech. Formulated how he would handle the various responses. Treated it almost like some formal class project.

But he didn't need to do that, right? These were his friends. They didn't want to hear some logical arguments stating X, therefore Y. They would want to hear what Rocket Man had to say from the heart.

"There's something bad going on."

The words sounded stupid. They were generic. They meant nothing.

The blank stares on his friends' faces seemed to confirm that feeling.

"Something *evil*." His emphasis on the last word made Owen feel like he was telling a cheesy ghost story, only this wasn't something being done for fun and amusement.

He glanced at Jake. "Jake knows what I'm talking about. I'm not the only one."

Jake looked away. He was sitting up now, fully at attention, massaging his knees nervously with his hands.

"Right, Jake?"

Jake cleared his throat. "I don't know. I guess."

"What do you mean 'you guess'?" Owen fought not to raise his voice. "We've both seen it. The Wienermobile."

Jake flinched at the word.

There was no immediate response from the rest of the group. Ryan picked absently at the calluses on his palms while Steph switched between paying attention and drifting off into her own thoughts.

The magic energy that Owen felt earlier disappeared, replaced by a nervous tension.

Finally, Steph said, "I think I saw it too. At the mall this afternoon."

That couldn't have been good. The more of them that saw the Mysterious Mariska and her vehicle from Hell, the more Owen felt like it was building up to something really bad, just as John implied in their chat.

"We seem to be the only ones who can see it. Kids, I mean. Or at least us kids."

"I'm not a kid," Jake said, piping up like he'd been accused of stealing something. "I'm thirteen. Practically a man."

"Whatever," Owen said, dismissing Jake's protest. "I just know my dad can't see it and my friend John can't see it either. John says it has something to do with—"

Owen stopped himself. Was he ready to go there? Ready to suffer what would almost certainly be long-term ridicule from his friends? Maybe even be ostracized for good?

"With what?" Steph asked.

"Magic."

There. It was out there, and he let it hang on the cloud of tension which seemed to have only grown thicker.

"Oh yeah," Ryan said, slicing through it like a blade. "He broke his head good on Saturday. Real good."

He snorted, looking at the others for support. Only it didn't come.

"Okay, so you see this—'magic' car," Steph said. "What does it matter?"

Memories of the car's open door, inviting Owen in at the park, flooded his mind and raised an army of goosebumps across his flesh. He pictured the Rainbow Road and felt its strange pull once again. Crowds cheering his name echoed.

He shut his eyes and fought the distraction.

"It wanted me to get inside."

"It?" Steph asked. "Like the car literally asked you to get

inside?"

Owen realized how childish this all must seem.

But John's warning was urgent. It was real. Owen felt like this was his only chance to convince The Crew that something nefarious was going down and only they could stop it.

"No," he said. "Not like the car itself talked. Well, not really." In his brain, his thoughts and memories were fuzzy. The car didn't talk per se, not in the sense that its fender served as a mouth like some corny cartoon. Or some not-so-corny cartoon like Transformers.

But something had talked to him. Somehow. Words had filtered down through him, and he had listened with an ear that wasn't a normal ear.

"There's this thing, John called it The Worm or The Presence."

Ryan burst out laughing like a wild hyena. Owen wanted to jump up and choke him.

"I got your worm right here," he said, pointing at his crotch.

"This is serious!" Owen said, raising his own voice beyond what he'd told the others not to. "We're all going to die if we don't put our heads together and do something about this."

That shut Ryan up. He looked serious now.

"Die?" Ryan exchanged looks with the others in the tent. "But—but I can't die. I'm too young to die. Especially by a giant wiener on wheels."

The laughing kicked in again, sending Ryan rolling over onto his side.

Owen looked to Jake for back-up. "Jake, tell them. Tell them what you saw."

Jake bit down on his bottom lip. His eyes flicked back and forth between all of his friends before he finally spoke. "I don't know. I mean, I guess I've had some weird experiences, but I think I've just been tired."

"What? What do you mean? Dude, how could we be seeing the same stuff if it wasn't really happening?"

"I don't know," Jake said defensively. Owen didn't know if his interpretation of his friend's body language was correct, but Jake seemed—scared. Like an animal that was caught in a trap, cornered, with nowhere to go.

"You *do* know," Owen admonished him. "You're just being a coward!"

It was a risky word to use. Jake's body seemed to be shaking slightly and his cheeks turned red in the dim aperture of the flashlight.

But he said nothing.

Owen was at a loss. This wasn't how it was supposed to go. He thought he could trust The Crew to be on his side. To believe him.

Everything was falling apart.

"I'm not lying to you guys and I can't believe you don't believe me!" Owen shouted uncontrollably, suddenly not caring if his parents woke up. His heart sank into his stomach. He pictured it floating on top of his stomach acids, slowly being swallowed into the great abyss like a sinking ship.

"Maybe you guys want to pretend like everything's normal. But it's not."

Love Shack had ended at some point and a stream of commercials stopped playing over the radio.

And we're back. We have one more dedication left.

There was a pause.

Aww, guys, this one's really sweet. This one goes out to Owen in Apple Valley. Loretta says she had so much fun chatting with you on the phone. You sent her little heart a'twitter. She can't wait to see you at school tomorrow.

The DJ laughed.

Oh, and you owe her a kiss. Don't leave Loretta hanging, Owen. You heard what happened to Albert's car!

The catchy drum machine pattern and guitar riff from

Young M.C.'s *Bust a Move* came on.

The tension was back again. No one said a word.

Owen was still trying to process what he just heard.

All eyes were on him, but the only ones that seemed to matter were Steph's.

She wanted to say something. Owen could tell. Her face shifted rapidly between stone and fire.

But instead of talking, she stood up with the force of a rocket.

"Steph," Owen said, standing up just as quickly, bumping his head on the tent ceiling. "Where are you—"

"I hate you, Owen Thom," she said as if it were a simple recollection of fact and ran out of the tent.

Bust a Move droned on.

"Whoa," Ryan said. "You and Loretta?" He raised his hand in the air, waiting for Owen's. "High five, man."

Owen barely noticed, leaving Ryan hanging. His heart was fully dissolved by the ocean of stomach acid now. He could only stare at the gaping hole in the tent where one of his best friends had just walked out on him.

He'd never felt so abandoned in his entire life.

"Well," Ryan said, heading toward the exit, "count me out of your crazy little mission. It all sounds like a crock you made up anyway."

"Fine," Owen managed to eke out. "Just fine. I don't need any of you guys for this. I'm going to save you all and you can thank me later."

He threw himself onto his sleeping bag and faced the wall of the tent, listening to the parting footsteps. A few seconds later, Owen heard the last remaining party stand up.

"Owen," Jake said, his voice just at the edge of the tent entrance.

Owen didn't reply. He simply ignored him, staring at the nylon tent material pulsating due to the light breeze.

And then there was the final footfall of Jake walking away, across the backyard and to his bike.

A minute later, Owen turned onto his back. His foot kicked something which crinkled.

For whatever reason, Jake had left the ordinance.

Maybe as an apology.

Owen turned his eyes toward the top of the tent. He violently cranked the radio knob so that it was off. All he could hear now were crickets and the wind picking up, cutting through the air.

He was alone.

Except for John, who apparently couldn't do much for

him anyway, Owen was alone.

No parents to believe him.

No Crew to believe him.

How could he face this monumental task by himself?

It didn't matter, he realized.

If his friends couldn't save themselves, Owen "Rocket Man" Thom would put in the work. He'd figure out a way.

Maybe he could prove to them, once and for all, that the threat was real. He could expose the Mysterious Mariska for who she really was.

But before he could do that, he had to find her. It was time to go on the offense. Time to make her a little less Mysterious.

Time to make her and her stupid Worm scared of *him*.

Thursday, June 22, 1989 - 1:00 AM

The cool night air rushed through the tight gap between Ryan's buck teeth as he pedaled home through the empty desert streets like a mad man. He couldn't stop smiling if someone paid him a hundred bucks to do so.

He knew Owen like the back of his hand. Knew he'd have the radio out. Knew it would be tuned in to KVVQ. All it took was a simple phone call before leaving his house to really set things in motion.

Tomorrow at school, Steph, funny hair and all, would be open to Ryan's comforting arms.

Not to worry, Mr. T.

Not to worry at all.

Ryan wouldn't be playing the fool.

The next morning, Owen sat at the kitchen counter on top of a swiveling bar stool, anxiously kicking himself side to side over a bowl of Honey Nut Cheerios and the Yellow Pages.

His father was getting dressed for work in the bedroom and his mom was in the bathroom, brushing her teeth and getting ready to put on her make-up.

In between the first and second bowl of cereal, Owen flipped between analyzing the stupidly-easy word puzzle on the back of the cereal box and perusing a list of magicians in the phone book.

Owen supposed he could have just asked his parents where they found the Mysterious Mariska, but he didn't want to risk raising any more suspicions. Even if he said something along the lines of, "Oh, Adam Nielsen wanted to have her at his birthday party," Owen was afraid it would create a whole new set of ideas in his parents' heads that he was up to something.

No, better to just find her himself.

Only, there was a problem.

He couldn't find her listed at all.

Owen pored back and forth through various categories: Magicians, Entertainment, Amusement. There was nothing in any of those sections that referred to the Mysterious Mariska.

His parents must have found out about her another way. Owen should have known that she wouldn't have made herself that readily available, if she really was everything John said she was. Probably used some sort of power of influence.

His heart sunk.

What could he do now except ask them?

Was it worth the risk?

He took another bite of cereal, crunching and staring into the kitchen. The counters were spotless. Cleaning them was one of his extra punishments. He'd always had chores, but they'd multiplied since his birthday party.

Between all of that, keeping up with homework, and trying to save the world, Owen was not in a hurry to add to the list.

He noticed a to-go menu from a local Chinese place sitting by the phone. He'd missed it during his sweep of stuffing items into their assigned kitchen drawers—

That was it!

Surely his parents had a receipt. His dad was meticulous about keeping good records, almost to a frightening level. He would have saved the receipt and probably tried to figure out a way to wriggle it into that "tax write off" thing he always talked about but which Owen never quite understood.

He took a final, gulping bite of Cheerios. Milk dribbled off his lower lip and onto his chin. With a single swift motion, he swiped at his face with a paper towel, picked up the bowl, and walked it over to the sink where he turned on the garbage disposal and poured the remains down the drain. The yeasty smell of grinding cereal floated upward.

Noises of his parents getting ready for the day wound their way down the hallway and into the kitchen. There was the turning on of the bathroom faucet and the opening and subsequent closing of sliding closet doors.

He had to be quick.

He shuffled through the first drawer. On top of some papers were a couple of plastic rolls of Scotch tape, a tiny cardboard box holding rows of unused staples, and endless amounts of uncapped pens which had probably dried up their ink supply long ago.

Never before had Owen wished he'd spent more time organizing.

The papers were useless—a pile of pink slips from the dry cleaners, car service records for the Subaru, something on layaway with J.C. Penney, and then finally a handwritten piece of torn-off spiral notepad paper that listed out a recipe for Linda's Low-Fat Cinnamon Bundt Cake.

"Owen, you better be done with breakfast." His mom's words raced down the hall and straight into Owen's ears. "Your dad's taking you to school this morning and picking you up because I have to do set-up and take-down for an office event."

A sense of urgency overcame him. He had to find something, anything, that would tell him where the Mysterious Mariska was. If he didn't find an address, it would be too late.

He jammed the drawer shut and opened the next one.

Owen grunted, feeling despair well up inside—this drawer was even more disorganized than the first.

There was a paper pack of waxy, unused birthday candles. The white and black back of a Polaroid photograph that Owen didn't bother to flip up. And, finally, what must have been hundreds of thin receipts.

Owen released another grunt.

He speed-read the receipts as quickly as he could without losing focus, tossing them onto the carpet and counter without a single thought as to cleaning them up again.

Maybe his dad didn't keep it in here. Maybe this whole idea was stupid and a lost cause.

He didn't stop shuffling and discarding until his eye

caught something interesting on a wrinkled piece of yellow carbon receipt paper.

Owen smiled widely as he took a closer look. Right there on top was a light-purple printed logo of an upside-down magician's hat with a white band across its brim. A pair of rabbit ears stuck out from the hole. Beneath the hat were the words: The Mysterious Mariska — Children's Entertainment.

The rest was a simple listing of services and calculated costs. But at the bottom was a phone number and an address.

The smile fell from Owen's face.

The address was a P.O. Box.

Crap.

Owen heard the bathroom sink turn off. That usually meant he had about thirty seconds before one of his parents would emerge.

He realized that he would have to copy down the Mysterious Mariska's information before the receipt disappeared into a folder in his parents' locked filing cabinets.

Owen looked around the counter top and quickly found what he was looking for right beside the electric can opener. He ran over, grabbed the spiral notepad, and then pulled open the first drawer again, picking up several of the capless pens, praying that one of them would have enough ink to actually write.

His parents' voices were getting louder now. They must have been near the edge of their bedroom door.

Owen's hand shook nervously as he looked at the Mysterious Mariska's phone number and started to copy it down:

6...

The pen wasn't working. Owen tossed it to the side where it clacked on the counter top tile. He grabbed another one.

6...

Still dry.

"Come on, you stupid—"

He almost cursed under his breath, refraining due to his parents' training and reinforcement.

He grabbed pen number three. His parents were walking down the hall now.

619-24...

Hallelujah! Holy Crap! It was working! He scribbled as quickly as he could, copying both the phone number and the P.O. Box number, hoping that whatever he wrote would be legible when he needed it later.

He tore off the piece of paper just as he heard his mom say something to his dad about picking up more slices of deli ham on her way home from work.

The Almost-Apocalypse of Apple Valley

Owen quickly folded the receipt back up and shoved it back in the drawer, accidentally flipping over the Polaroid photo in the process.

He was about to slam the drawer shut, as quickly and quietly as possible, before he froze. He stared at the photograph and felt hairs tingling on the back of his neck.

It was a picture of him standing in the living room during the birthday party. The large window loomed in the background with its window blinds open slightly, providing a bit of a glare.

Owen stood in front of a leaning Mysterious Mariska. She held her hat out in front of him with one hand, the other tucked behind her back.

But that wasn't what caught his eye. That wasn't what sent shivers trailing up and down his flesh like a trail of ants.

It was the glowing red in her eyes. It was the slight plumes of dark smoke that emanated from her body like a barrier—like a shield that morphed and twisted. Owen swore he could see that barrier morphing and twisting in the photograph itself.

Vertigo sent the world spinning and Owen jammed the drawer shut. His breath was short and he gasped for air.

He looked up and saw his mom enter the living room

from the hallway.

As quickly as he could, he tried to act normal, even managing to put a smile back on his face.

His mom paused mid-fumble with her watch, trying to latch it closed.

"Are you kidding me, Owen?" she asked.

"Hmm?" he replied, almost in a dream-like state. His legs felt wobbly, but he propped himself up with his hands on the counter top.

"You have fifteen seconds to clean that up before your father sees and grounds you for another week."

Menus, pens, and other papers surrounded Owen like confetti.

"Oh. Sorry, was just organizing," Owen said, recovering quickly, glad to busy himself and not think about what he'd soon be facing.

Thursday, June 22, 1989 - 8:00 AM

John's truck idled in Tasker's LOTTABURGER drive-thru. Something sounded off with the engine—had since he started it that morning—but one look at the oil change sticker on the inside of his windshield reminded John that he was three months late for maintenance.

A mattress commercial played while his favorite talk-radio program was on break. The sound of the flap-top frying bacon and eggs hissed through the restaurant window.

The perky, blonde teenage girl working the register had handed him his change, two dimes and three pennies, and told him his bacon and egg sandwich (hold the mayo) would be ready in a minute.

John took a quick sip of black coffee from his canteen, then leaned over and stuck his head outside, staring up at the sky. When the previous night's freak rain finally stopped, it almost felt like the town of Apple Valley had been given a permanent reprieve. Now it appeared the opposite was the case. Gray clouds gathered once more around the mountains backing up against the Marianas, seemingly with more force and in greater numbers than before.

Almost like they were preparing for an invasion.

In twenty minutes, John was scheduled to visit an insurance company off Highway 18 and investigate a PC that wouldn't power up. The two older ladies that ran the place, Selma Munro and K.C. McIntosh, were hilarious. They were both heavy-set redheads with the same cropped haircut who wore almost-matching muumuus, and were the owners of two gigantic calico cats that stalked the office like *they* were the owners and the women were the pets.

Normally, John looked forward to visiting them, chatting while he removed furballs from the computer case vents, but his mind was occupied. He knew Owen had his hands full and didn't have the time to dig into the message John had forwarded over, so he'd spent every free moment, night and day, poring over the mass of gibberish, trying to decode it and see if it was useful.

He'd felt like he was on the trail to something at a point early that morning before collapsing into a deep sleep at the desk in his office. Only a screaming modem had woken him up as someone logged into The Desert Oasis.

He couldn't blame Owen one bit for not getting much time in to crack the code. The kid had his computer taken away, for goodness' sake. John felt bad enough as it was—a kid being burdened with what he knew, swept away from a childhood that every kid should experience—but he also knew that such a childhood would be permanently out of reach if The Worm and his Attendant got their way.

The blonde reached across the window and handed him a crumpled brown paper sack.

"Happy Thursday, John."

He smiled, or tried to at least. "Take care of yourself, OK, Leslie? Tell your old man I said 'Hello.'"

She nodded and slid the window closed.

The radio show came back on and John pulled away.

John hit a red light at the intersection of Highway 18 and Rancherias Rd. He slipped a hand into the sack, searching for the source of that delicious eggy, bacony smell. He may have been concerned about everything happening, but apparently his appetite didn't care one whit.

His fingers found the thin paper wrapping of the warm sandwich, started to unravel it, but then felt something pinch down hard.

"Son of a …!"

He yanked his hand away. Blood trickled down his index finger, gleaming in the sunlight filtered through the smudged windshield. His eyes shot toward the bag laying on the passenger side seat and saw something moving inside.

Red light or not, John hit the accelerator and barreled through, avoiding a hatchback that beeped its toy-sounding horn repeatedly as it narrowly missed hitting John's rear bumper.

Quickly, John jerked the steering wheel to the right and pulled over to the shoulder on the side of Highway 18, slamming the truck's shifter into idle. On instinct, he put on his hazard lights and opened his door.

His pulse was racing.

Sweat pooled around the brim of his baseball cap.

Whatever was in the bag continued to move, heading toward the opening.

John's first thought was to haul ass out of the truck and get as far away as possible, but he knew he'd have to get back in eventually, and he'd rather not deal with whatever was in there again.

Besides, what if the thing had wings and took off after him like some kind of mutant wasp?

Instead, his eyes flicked toward the heavy coffee canteen laying on the seat next to the bag. He reached across, picked it up, and slammed it over and over on the bag.

He was unsure if it was having any impact, but after about ten slams, John was breathing hard and whatever was in there should at least be hurting.

Slowly, he lifted the canteen up and held it there.

No movement.

Nothing.

Nada.

John's driver's side door was still open, and now his ears picked up the whooshing of vehicles zooming by. It couldn't have been more than five seconds, but it seemed like an eternity, waiting, thinking, deciding whether he should try to see what was actually in the bag.

His finger started throbbing, and he stuck it in his mouth, sucking on the coppery blood.

Either the courage came or the impatience got there first, but John made a decision. He readied the canteen with one hand, picked up the bottom end of the bag in the other, and poured the contents out onto the seat.

"Raah!!" he screamed, bearing down again, adrenaline-filled fury infusing his cheeks.

Bits of egg and butter-soaked bread splashed around the compartment, sticking to the vents and slightly dusty dashboard like the Tasmanian Devil had stopped in for a bite. A slice of bacon lay innocently on the seat, looking naked and alone.

The canteen flew out of his hand and out of the door. It rolled onto the shoulder, *ting-tanging* until it came to a stop.

John fell back against the driver's seat and took a deep breath. He took off his hat, tossed it onto the dashboard, and rubbed his tired eyes, careful to avoid smearing them with blood.

He looked at his finger again.

No more pain.

No more blood.

The lack of sleep was getting to him.

He closed his eyes and realized just how exhausted he'd become trying to figure out the situation for Owen and his friends.

The Worm.

Of course.

It was so obvious, he felt like an idiot falling for its old tricks. Clearly, things were getting serious now and The Worm was pushing hard to keep John from interfering. He knew it was a risk to confront it at the community center, but the boys being sucked into its trap was the bigger risk.

He'd already been through this game long ago. John finally admitted that a part of the reason he was doing this from the sidelines was because he was scared to fully confront The Worm again. It had taken decades of his life away. An invisible scar ran the length of his body, never to be fixed.

He opened his eyes and slammed his fists into the steering wheel. Crumbs of bun and egg jumped again.

He couldn't be a coward. Not now. He couldn't allow the same thing that stripped him of his youth and confidence to happen to the others.

He wasn't going to let The Worm beat him again.

The insurance ladies and their furry felines would have to wait. John turned off the hazard lights and reached out to shut the driver's side door when the glint of the canteen caught his eyes.

He yawned.

Coffee first, Worm second, he decided.

Just the thought of making The Worm second-tier brought a renewed smile to John's face.

He stepped outside and bent over to grab the canteen handle.

None of what happened after that registered until John

found himself lying between the smooth blacktop and the dirt shoulder.

The sound of a familiar engine revving.

The impact of something knocking into his hips, sending the world into a spin too rapid to keep pace with.

Something warm ran beneath his head, maybe coffee, but his arms were too weak to reach up and confirm.

Before John went to sleep, his eyes caught the rear end of a beat-up Volkswagen Rabbit driving westbound on Highway 18, or maybe...

No, that wasn't right...

The image flickered like a slide show between two slides.

One was the Rabbit.

The other, a giant hot dog on wheels.

Owen barely remembered the day.

Mrs. Kirkwood's class was a blur of health science, history regarding the Iroquois Nation, and something about elementary geometry that he was pretty positive wouldn't matter in this life or the next.

He'd spent most of the day focused on ignoring his so-called friends. It wasn't easy. A part of him was wounded. Deathly wounded.

But, it wasn't hard either—they'd obviously made a similar decision, passing each other silently in class and hanging out at different parts of the playground during recess.

School was out now and Owen sat on a wood-slatted bench just outside of the principal's office. It was the closest place to the parking lot with shade.

Fiddling with the straps on his backpack, Owen stared at the brown stucco walls and rumbling air conditioning units attached to the building opposite him.

That was the kindergarten wing. Owen didn't have any memories of that place. He'd gone to another school for kindergarten, Rancho Verde, before they'd built this one. After being stuffed into portable trailers due to overcrowding, the district finally built Mojave Mesa and Owen got to enjoy the fruits of a fresh environment starting with the first grade. It felt kind of cool to break in the playground, knowing they'd be the first kids to play there.

That's how he'd come to know The Crew. They'd been together since those days. It felt like an eternity. This was where Owen thought the friendships of a lifetime would be made.

Apparently, he was wrong.

A fly buzzed by Owen's ear. Finally, he got so tired of swatting it away that he jumped up, grabbed his backpack and headed toward the curb of the parking lot.

Even though it lacked the shade of the area by the bench, he would sit there for a while and wait for his dad. The sun was shining again. That was one thing Owen *did* remember from the morning—it looked like it would be another day of storm clouds and rain, but in the middle of the first recess, those went away and the summer sun came out again.

It didn't matter. Even sunny days had lost their joy.

On the way to the parking lot, Owen passed a pair of chrome-silver payphones that stood just past the final window of the principal's office. He'd never really used a payphone.

Never had a need to.

But now there was a need.

Owen dropped his backpack onto the ground, crouched, and quickly drew open the zipper. He reached inside and stuck his hand into the tiny pocket which lined the back. His fingers discovered the frilled piece of spiral notebook paper from this morning.

He pulled it out and unfolded it.

He looked up at the pay phone. A little yellow placard just above the handset stated that it cost a quarter to make a phone call.

Luckily, Owen kept a little rubber coin purse inside his backpack, though he never really used it except for the occasional soda machine run.

He thought hard about what he was going to do.

What would be the point in making the phone call?

Say the Mysterious Mariska picked up. What would he say to her? What would he ask her?

He could talk tough. Mention that he and John knew all about her and her stupid Worm. Tell her that they knew what she and her pet were up to and how John and Owen were going to stop them.

But would that even faze her?

Maybe he should call John first. Get his advice.

Maybe John would even talk him out of it. Tell Owen to wait until he could help.

In a snap decision, he dug back into his backpack and pulled out John's business card. Then he unzipped the coin purse and dug out a rough-edged quarter.

He grabbed the handset and held it to his ear. There was nothing but dial tone on the other end. His free ear caught the buzzing fly returning.

He dropped the purse into his backpack and inserted the quarter into the slot. It clicked and clinked its way down the box, slapping the bottom where it met other coins.

The dial tone waited patiently for Owen to push the little chrome buttons.

He looked down at the card and proceeded to dial John's house. Every time he pressed his fingers down, he felt resistance from the stiff buttons as well as from himself. This wasn't going to be easy. Something inside of him, like an old soul, told him this type of thing wasn't *supposed* to be easy.

By the time the seventh digit was plugged in, a massive amount of nervous sweat had gathered on his top lip. He licked it away, instantly regretting the salty taste that stained his tongue. He looked around for a drinking fountain.

The phone rang once.

Twice.

Three times.

After at least ten rings, there was no answer from John or his machine.

He was probably working and forgot to turn on the answering machine. Yeah, that was it.

Owen hung up the phone, picked up the coin purse again, and fished out another quarter. He'd just call John's pager and leave the number printed on the payphone placard.

As he reached for the handset, the phone rang.

Owen yelped and flinched. The coin purse fell from his hand, splashing the cement walkway with nickels and quarters. Butterflies stirred in his stomach.

It couldn't have been John. How would he know the phone number? Or maybe it was a wrong-number caller in general.

A zillion thoughts ran through Owen's mind until he realized that the phone was still ringing and would likely keep ringing unless he took it off the hook.

He lifted the handset and gripped it in his hands. A strong, electrical buzz ran along the silver cord connecting it to the phone box.

Every muscle in Owen's arms were taut, ready to hang the handset back up.

Still, he raised it to his ear and listened. If it was John, he needed to talk to him right away.

The other side was filled with a low hiss.

Owen said: "John?"

"No."

That voice.

Owen pictured himself running away, the phone dangling on the end of its silver cord while he was halfway down the street, hoping to catch his dad before he entered the school's driveway.

Yet his palms and fingers were glued to the handset.

This was the moment he'd been dreading, but knew would come. The confrontation with the Mysterious Mariska. He wanted to talk, but the lump in his throat prevented him from doing so. A word-like thing emerged, but it was unintelligible. Barely even a gasp.

"What's wrong, Owen? Cat got your tongue again?"

The words were interwoven with that low hiss.

Memories of his birthday party made his stomach churn. The butterflies had multiplied into colonies at this point. He was on the verge of bypassing words altogether and just vomiting up the PB&J sandwich that had been sitting in his stomach since lunch.

But he steeled himself. He had to be strong. Had to make sure the Mysterious Mariska knew that he wasn't afraid of her or the thing she hung around with.

"Leave us alone," he said.

There was only the hiss. Owen felt as if he could see her face, stunned into silence. Or maybe that's just what he wanted to see.

"We're just starting to have fun," the Mysterious Mariska said, her voice sounding hoarse now, almost tired. "You don't want to stop playing yet, do you?"

"Leave us alone," Owen repeated like the Terminator. He tried to channel the bad-assitude of the Arnold Schwarzenegger character, only he wasn't coming after Sarah Connor—he was coming after the Mysterious Mariska and her stupid Worm.

"I'm sorry about your friend. I hope he'll be okay."

"What did you do to him?"

Owen knew she was talking about John.

"By the time the ambulance came, I wasn't sure he would survive the ride to St. Mary's Hospital. The EMTs seemed a little concerned."

"If you hurt—"

"Cut the crap, Owen Thom. You're running out of time and you're running out of options. It doesn't have to be this way. You've seen what The Worm can offer. You can ride the Rainbow Road. You can be the hero. You can make this easy and pleasant."

Owen remained silent. Memories of the community center vision crystallized.

"We still have so much to show you and your friends," Mariska continued. "To show this whole town."

"What if I refuse?" he asked.

"If you don't want to give it to us, kid, we can just take it. Only, it will be a lot more painful that way. John was merely a warning. I'm trying to *help* you here."

Owen snorted. The idea of the Mysterious Mariska and her Worm helping him and The Crew was absurd. No, she wanted something only they had, and she was desperate for Owen to give it to her. Despite her efforts to hide it, he could hear it in her voice.

"We're not going to let you take anything, and we're definitely not going to give you anything," Owen said.

He knew that The Crew had checked out. Still, Owen held out hope that in the end, they would all come together against this Mysterious Mariska. Deep down, he knew he wouldn't be able to face off against her alone. That much was written across his heart.

"You're a brave little boy," the Mysterious Mariska said, "But you're also stupid. If you want to die for your stupidity, that's your choice."

Die?

The word shook Owen to his core. He hadn't anticipated such a thing, though it seemed an obvious end to things now.

Something made a noise in the background—beyond the low hiss. A resonant growl or vibrating hum. It was there, but barely audible.

"Suck an egg," Owen said, slamming the phone back on to the hook.

He crumpled down to the ground beside his backpack, barely feeling the cool shaded cement hit his right knee. A little bit of warmth rushed up through his skin, and he knew he'd have to contend with a scrape and yellowed bruise there.

His head swam, feeling fuzzy. He didn't want to move. Didn't want to do anything for the next one hundred years.

But he proceeded to collect the coins that had fallen onto the ground anyway.

What could he do now, knowing that John was hurt? He wanted to visit him in the hospital. Maybe the Mysterious

Mariska was lying and John was just fine. He really was working a job. Owen supposed he could use another quarter to call the hospital and confirm—

A voice shouted in the distance, but he ignored it.

Owen had felt alone before, but now it hit him like a ton of bricks. He really *was* alone. The decision fell on him as to what to do next. He wasn't used to this much responsibility. The thought of rewinding time, going back to riding bikes with The Crew again, getting a do-over on the last two weeks, pulled at him like a pleasant dream.

What he wouldn't give for that ability.

The pleasing image of the Rainbow Road popped into his mind again. Cheering crowds watched as Rocket Man launched across the final jump. What if that was the right thing to do? What if he was *supposed* to sacrifice himself for the good of the others?

He buried his head in his hands and leaned against the office's outside wall, feeling the hard bits of stucco poke into his back like a million tiny needles.

The voice shouted again, only this time he recognized the word.

"Owen!"

Owen tilted his head up and looked out toward the parking lot.

"Owen," his father yelled, leaning across the front passenger seat, looking through the rolled-down window. "Stop wasting time and get in here before your mom kicks both of our butts."

"Who were you talking to?"

Owen's dad had a hand on the knob of the Subaru GL's manual shifter. His wedding band glinted in the tiny bit of afternoon sunlight pushing through both the incoming clouds and the dusty, unwashed windows. The other hand held on loosely to the bottom of the steering wheel.

"Huh?" Owen asked.

"On the phone. I honked like five million times. Who were you talking to?" Suddenly, a grin broke out on his face, and he wriggled his eyebrows. "Was it your girlfriend?"

"What?" That invading suggestion snapped Owen back to reality before he was ready. "No! No...I don't have a girlfriend. I was...I was trying to call you, seeing when you'd get here."

His dad nodded slowly.

"Whatever you say, loverboy."

Owen was too preoccupied to give his dad attention. On their way home, hitting stop sign after stop sign along the intersecting, cracked two-lane roads, Owen dwelled on what would come next.

He thought of John.

He thought of The Crew.

He thought of the word that the Mysterious Mariska spoke:

Die.

The word manifested itself like a wet blanket in Owen's mind—heavy and unshakable.

And it wasn't meant just for him.

It was for everyone he ever knew.

It was for this little desert town that kept their dreams alive.

Friday, June 24, 1989 - 10:00 AM

Apple Valley's post office was a small building. It sat in the central part of town next to the police station and the bank Owen's parents used. Both places lived just across the highway from Bass Hill and the dirt race track that seemed a distant memory now.

The post office's outer walls were faded brown stucco with tall, floor-to-ceiling windows in the front. A towering flag-pole stood out front where a large American flag flapped in the breeze.

Owen looked down at a backpack stuffed with promise. He hoped this all worked out as expected.

Next to it, the Redline lay in the dirt, one handle sticking up in the warm desert air just like the flagpole minus the flag.

The bike was the result of one of several things he'd done that, on a small scale, would probably be considered wrong.

Or disobedient.

Or unethical (thank you for the new word, Mrs. Kirk-wood).

But he felt justified. How he would justify them if he was

caught would be another matter, but that was the least of his worries.

First, he'd forged a note for school from his parents. He was convinced the note would work. Even if there was an ounce of discouragement in his body, he *had* to believe that it would work. He was a good enough student that he wagered Mrs. Kirkwood would accept it at face value and expect him to come back to school on Monday.

His "mom" stated that Owen had more doctor appointments that day to follow up on his accident, but that he would most certainly be back to class the next day.

Then there was the bike.

He'd snuck it out of the unlocked garage after an exhausting run home from school.

If he never had to run another three miles with a backpack bouncing up and down against the back of his skull, it would be too soon.

But he was here now, ensconced behind a grouping of creosote plants just outside of the Apple Valley Post Office, waiting.

God, he hoped he hadn't made a mistake.

What if the Mysterious Mariska didn't come by today?

What if she only picked up her mail once a month and

that was yesterday?

Then there was the trick of not being seen by his dad. What if he popped out of the building at the wrong time and saw the top of Owen's head peeking out from behind the bushes, recognizing it immediately.

Holes began to form in Owen Thom's Magnificent Plan and a shadow of discouragement overcame him.

The sky seemed to mimic his thoughts. Dark clouds gathered around not just the south end of Apple Valley, slightly pushing forward over the Big Bear peaks, but they seemed to be encroaching from all directions now—past the western hills leading to Victorville; in the north near Bell Mountain; and even in the east over the Granite Mountains.

A pinch on his ankle brought him back to the here and now. Quickly, and as quietly as possible, he swept his hand up and down his legs and shoes.

Of course, the only spot useful enough to hide behind managed to also hide an anthill that took up an area the size of a hula hoop.

Owen didn't want to be distracted by them for fear of missing his target, but an irrational fear of the tiny red ants climbing up on him like little soldiers, planting their flags in his skin, overcame him every once in a while.

Owen laughed at the irony of his plan to save the town being shot down because he'd been devoured alive by these little punks.

In between bouts of sweeping the ants away, he thought of his friends. Or maybe ex-friends was the more appropriate term.

They'd all gone their separate ways since their discussion in the tent.

Jake played football at recess and said nothing to no one.

Ryan and Steph continued to hang out by themselves, usually by the swings or near the handball court, though Steph looked miserable while Ryan couldn't stop grinning.

That is, until she caught Owen looking at them. Then she'd start laughing as if Ryan had said the funniest thing in the world and even put a hand on his leg, which made Ryan grin even more.

For reasons Owen wasn't fully ready to admit, that bothered him more than just not hanging out with his friends.

It all seemed to come to a head with that stupid request on KVVQ.

The DJ *had* to have been talking about a different Loretta and Owen. She'd never called him and even if she did, Owen wouldn't have much to say to her. Sure, she was pretty, but she was also boring.

She had every other boy in the class wrapped around her finger. That's fine. Their choice. Owen couldn't imagine having to follow her or anyone else around like a lovesick puppy.

Owen wanted to plead his case to Steph, but she didn't seem interested in listening to him.

He'd worry about it when the Mysterious Mariska was dealt with.

As if on cue, a familiar rumble arose in the street that ran alongside the post office. Owen ducked down and peeked past the left-hand side of the bushes.

There was no Wienermobile.

But there was a Volkswagen Rabbit. It must have been almost cherry red when it was brand new, but had faded over time into more of a burgundy spotted with rust patches.

It was exactly as his dad had said.

So why wasn't Owen seeing the Wienermobile version?

It didn't matter. Not now.

What did matter was the outline of the driver matched that of the Mysterious Mariska, minus her hat.

Noticing that convinced Owen more than ever that it was the key.

No hat, no power.

No power, no Wienermobile.

She'd come to pick up her mail and would inadvertently lead Owen to her home. He'd grab his bike and hope to high heaven that he could keep up with her while simultaneously keeping out of sight.

The whole idea seemed double crazy, now.

What if she lived twenty miles away? Crap, what if she lived all the way down in San Bernardino for goodness' sake? There was no way he'd be able to trail her through the Cajon Pass.

Owen rubbed at his eyes, trying to push the excess of thought away. No, he had to take things one step at a time. Overthinking things would only lead to paralysis. There was one thing he should be doing right now and that was paying attention.

The Rabbit seemed to herk and jerk into a parking space, somewhat catawampus (as his dad would say), and its brakes squealed until the vehicle came to a full stop.

Owen faced the passenger side, so he could only see the top of the Mysterious Mariska's head as she exited. Standing beside the tiny Rabbit, he fully grasped just how short she was. Up close, at the party, he could have sworn she was a giant.

Maybe it was an illusion—one of her or her pet Worm's

tricks.

Now, she was just a frail little human being.

She paused for a moment, turning and lifting her head slightly. She practically sniffed the air like a dog sensing barbecue in the wind. Then she stepped onto the sidewalk and Owen was able to take in the total image.

She wore a pair of neon-green framed sunglasses. Her clothes were plain—a vanilla-white blouse with thick purple stripes running down from front to back, paired with khaki pants that looked like they belonged to someone two sizes bigger.

Owen pictured slobber gathering at the sides of the magician's lips. His heart skipped a beat, fearing that she would turn and look straight at him.

But she didn't.

She slammed her car door shut and walked toward the post office.

Owen started second-guessing himself now. He reached up and felt his beating heart, threatening to launch itself out of his chest.

He had an opportunity to grab his bike and return home now. Hide out in his bedroom all day until it came time to make the hike back to school so his dad could pick him up.

He shook his head, trying to flush the dangerous ideas out before they grew too large and too convincing. There was a mission to be carried out, his own fears and feelings be damned.

Rocket Man wouldn't be scared of doing what had to be done.

He took on the persona like an old costume and felt his confidence renew.

If only he had his helmet, he knew every doubt would be completely wiped away.

Friday, June 24, 1989 - 11:30 AM

Having John there would probably have made him feel a little more comfortable, but Owen didn't come all this way for comfort.

He had a job to do and complaints cost extra—a phrase his father often repeated whenever Owen whined about pulling weeds or raking leaves.

Still, his legs felt like rubber. After seven or eight miles, up Navajo Road and way past Tussing Ranch, he felt like he had pedaled half of his life away trying to simultaneously keep up with the Rabbit yet maintain his distance.

But here he was—here *they* were—having finally arrived at some place up in the Marianas where nearly all the roads turned into sand and dirt.

Owen had been up here before, mainly for soccer games that took place in Mendel Park just outside Marianas' Elementary School. Those were happy memories.

But kids playing soccer on Saturday afternoons would remain memories if Owen didn't do what he came here to do. Still, there were no two ways about it—Owen Thom was scared about what was going to happen next.

He was breathless, leaning down over his bike and nursing one of his calves while hiding behind a large berm of dirt pushed up from the road. Mysterious Mariska finally pulled into the driveway of a weed-covered lot. There was a tarnished, beaten-up-looking single-wide trailer which looked in even worse shape than the Rabbit.

Owen pushed himself and his bike a little closer toward a patch of creosote plants, just past the berm. He used his toes to propel himself forward instead of pedaling. Pedaling would have required him to stand up and make himself all too visible.

He leaned the bike down on the ground. As he did so, a pair of tiny gray-green lizards scattered out of one side of the bush and back into another.

The Mysterious Mariska turned off the engine and exited the vehicle. She walked up the tiny three steps which led to the front door of the trailer and opened it to pitch black.

That's when Owen realized the windows that were visible from this side of the trailer were all blocked out by layers of tin foil, which ordinarily would be kind of weird, but in the grand scheme of things, not so much anymore.

She shut the door.

Owen evaluated the path to the trailer. There didn't appear to be a window on the end nearest him. If he could make his approach from that side, he probably had a good chance of not being seen.

But assuming he made it to the trailer, sight unseen—then what? If the windows were blocked out, he had no way of seeing what was happening inside.

He was hoping the hat would be visible, minimizing the amount of time he'd need to run in and grab it.

Then again, he had The Worm inside to contend with. If he believed John, which he did, he had to believe it couldn't do anything to him by itself. And if Owen was able to get the Mysterious Mariska out of the trailer, all would be well.

Confidence.

That's what he really needed.

He thought back to Cru Jones flying through the jumps at Hell Track.

Time for action.

He dropped the bike into the dirt, tightened the straps of his backpack one last time, then crouch-ran to the rear of the trailer.

It felt like he was running at the beach. The sand was thick and his British Knights sunk into it like a pair of ships caught in a storm.

Still, Owen pressed on until he was at the trailer's end, leaning over and scoping out the other side facing the mountains. He didn't know what he expected, but it certainly wasn't what he saw.

The "back yard" was more unfenced land. A single lawn chair, the kind made of hollow aluminum and green nylon fabric laced over the back and seat, sat and faced the mountain. By itself, it seemed so lonely and for a moment, Owen felt what might be called "sorrow" for the Mysterious Mariska. He pictured her sitting by herself, staring out at the mountains for hours, never moving, never flinching.

Only staring.

Probably cuddling with her stupid Worm.

He pulled himself out of the cyclone of thought and decided to see if the windows on that side were also covered with tin.

His ears perked up as he thought he heard a noise coming from inside. There was a loud click and then a rumble. Owen nearly jumped out of his pants.

Something buzzed from the trailer.

He recognized the sound and felt a palpable sense of relief.

It was the air conditioning unit.

Even though the sound might cover up his steps, he still made an effort to remain as incognito as possible.

Quietly, on his tiptoes, he lifted his already-tired legs up and down with great caution. His hands were at his sides, providing balance to the loose ground. He prayed that he wouldn't step the wrong way or find an extra deep layer of silt and twist his ankle.

How he wished he wasn't alone at this point. How he wished that if not John, at least one, or all, of his friends could be here with him now. They would give him that little extra bit of confidence he was missing. Rocket Man by himself may have still been Rocket Man, but he wasn't *really* Rocket Man without sidekicks. No more than Magic Johnson was Magic Johnson without James Worthy and Kareem Abdul-Jabbar.

He peered upward and saw that there were two matching windows on this side of the trailer along with a back door. He was disappointed to see the windows were also covered in tinfoil, but at least the door was there. That should make the plan a little easier to execute, assuming she came running out that way.

He removed his backpack and placed it on the ground. Slowly, he drew the zipper across, opening the main flap.

Sweat had already claimed every inch of him, but now

it dripped down his forehead in droves. If not for the cooler air near the cloud-covered mountains, he might have passed out.

The brick of Black Cats and Roman Candles tied to it slid out easily. He laid the fireworks down on the sand next to him. Owen was relieved that at least he wouldn't have to deal with carrying them on the ride back home.

At the bottom of the backpack was a green plastic Bic lighter he'd snatched from the fireplace back home.

The question now became placement.

Owen could have just lit the whole thing there next to the trailer, but he'd prefer some sort of cover and distance. The more curious the Mysterious Mariska, the more ground she had to cover to investigate, the more time Owen had to dash inside.

He also hoped his estimates on the fuse were good. If he did place it far away and didn't have time to get out of sight, the whole grand mission would be for naught.

Scanning the back yard again, he noticed a red, dusty, five-gallon bucket turned upside-down. Beside it was a tiny hose connected to a pipe sticking out of the ground. He supposed he could slip the package underneath the bucket, but it would be blown sky-high.

He didn't have time to be picky. There was no chickening out at this point.

Owen grabbed hold of his munitions, scampered over to the bucket as quietly as possible and lifted an edge from the sand. It didn't budge easily. It must have been there for a long time, probably left by whoever owned this place before the loving couple moved in.

He looked back at the trailer. Even though the tinfoil seemed to be serving its purpose of keeping the rest of the world out of the trailer, there was no knowing for sure whether the magician was watching every move, peeking out at him through a solitary crack.

It was a risk he had to accept.

Quickly, he propped the bucket up slightly with the edge of the Black Cats so the extended fuse could run through without dying at the bucket's rim.

The lighter shook in Owen's hand as nerves permeated his entire body. His thumb struck the spark wheel, but he struggled to keep the gas fork depressed as the moisture made it difficult to maintain a grip.

"Come on," he chastised himself.

Sweat continued to rain from his forehead, dripping onto the top of his hand.

There was a loud click followed by the idling of the trailer's air conditioner compressor.

Owen's breath halted.

He swung his head to look, not realizing his success until he felt a sharp heat stinging his thumbnail and smelled the powder of the smoking fuse.

The lighter fell into the dirt, and he instinctively jammed his thumb between his lips.

Realizing he was wasting time, he pushed himself to his feet and hauled ass back to the end of the trailer.

His heart pumped like it was going for a world record.

He had two choices now. He could sit and wait for the Mysterious Mariska to come out when the music started, potentially wasting valuable search time, or he could run to the front door, quietly crack it open and hope she'd gone out anyway.

Owen decided on the second. He'd spent enough time in this miserable place already, and he was afraid his body would revolt and collapse if he stayed any longer.

Halfway to the front door, the snap, crackle, pop, whistle, ting, tang, walla-walla-bing-bang began.

He hesitated a moment, just in case the Mysterious Mariska decided the front door would be the ideal place to check first. Then he moved again.

One couldn't expect to save an entire town if one wasn't ready to accept some risks.

He ran up the three steps and turned the knob.

He suddenly wondered what he'd do if the door were locked.

Luckily, that's as much thinking as he had to give the notion as the knob kept turning and the door jerked open with a little effort.

Directly across from this door was the back door and it was wide open. Owen was grateful for the streaming sunlight, otherwise there was no way he'd be able to find a thing in this place.

Paper plates and plastic cups mingled on the carpet with a menagerie of magazines, paperbacks, socks, shirts, and candy bar wrappers.

What a mess.

Even with the given light, it was needle-in-a-haystack level effort.

At least a magician's hat wasn't the most inconspicuous thing.

The fireworks continued popping off. They even seemed to be shaking the entire trailer, though that may have been his imagination.

Owen realized he was running low on time. He dove right in, happy to use the outside racket as cover. He looked on top and around the tiny couch. Checked around the rack holding up the ancient television set. Swung his hands through every piece of detritus populating the kitchen area.

Nothing.

Owen decided he ought to take a peek out the back door and see what the Mysterious Mariska was up to. Carefully, he edged up to the side.

She was out there, all right. A Louisville Slugger was held tightly in both of her hands, looking just as tall as she was. It was almost comical and Owen wondered if she could actually swing the thing.

The fireworks were still raising hell, but she seemed to be focused on the perimeter of the property.

He felt better knowing he had a little more time. Looking back into the trailer, there was a short hallway to a single bedroom, its door closed.

Last place left.

It had to be there.

But given that Owen hadn't seen any sign of The Worm, chances are it was there as well.

Remember, without her, it's powerless.

No matter what, Owen was out of options. Sitting here, thinking about it, was the worst pick from an array of poor choices.

He almost slipped on some magazines on his scramble over, but stayed upright, propping himself up with his palms against the interior walls.

His shaking hand reached slowly for the door. He was grateful he didn't drink a lot that morning because he probably would have peed his pants right about then.

Go. Just go.

So he did.

He grabbed the knob, twisted, and threw the door open, screaming like a Viking berserker.

It was pitch black.

Darker than dark.

Just like he feared.

His heart threatened to explode just like the fireworks outside.

But then he realized he was an idiot.

First, he opened his left eye.

Then his right.

Though the room was darker than the rest of the house, he could clearly see two things.

An unmade double bed.

And the item he'd come looking for.

The link that he must sever.

Sitting on a pile of blankets was the Mysterious Mariska's outfit, cape and all, with the black hat sitting on top. He realized now that the link between the magician and The Worm could be any one of those things. Or even all of them.

He cursed himself for not having the backpack in which he could stash the items for the ride home, but he'd manage. This was it. This is what he needed.

Without the connection, there was nothing left for The Worm to do but curl up and die.

Owen briefly pictured the awe-filled faces of The Crew when he told them how he valiantly saved them all and the entire town of Apple Valley. If they weren't grateful by that point, there was nothing Owen could do to change that. He'd have to be satisfied knowing what he'd done.

Wasting no more time, he swept his arms around the magician's ensemble and turned to exit.

He screeched and everything fell from his arms.

The Mysterious Mariska stood in the doorway with her arms crossed, her face painted with a look that said she could barely be bothered to react to his presence. Behind her, a shaking, rattling, black plume of smoke darted back and forth. Occasionally, it came to a jerking stop and a pair of red eyes flashed like brake lights.

"Hello, Owen," the Mysterious Mariska said. "Come to get your tongue?"

Ryan was falling again, only this time, he tried to enjoy the ride. The darkness, the twisting and turning and floating which had unnerved him before, started to feel familiar.

Almost fun.

If he was going to have crazy dreams, why not accept them as entertainment? This could just as easily be a ride at Raging Waters.

He closed his eyes and felt the air rush across his bare chest. It was the perfect temperature—not too warm, not too cold.

When he opened his eyes, he was back on the familiar beach, standing with the lapping ocean waves to his back. His toes penetrated inches of sand while foamy saltwater swooshed around his ankles.

Mr. T. was relaxing in his lounge chair, wearing the familiar red shorts, gold chains, and dark sunglasses.

With a cool nonchalance, he barely moved his right arm and patted the empty lounge chair beside him. His chains jingled, sending a quiet song into the humid air.

Ryan looked past Mr. T. and saw the two gangbangers were back again, posed in front of an array of palm trees like bodyguards with their legs spread slightly. Their thick-muscled arms hoisted the AK-47s and each had the black butt of a pistol sticking out of his baggy jean waistband.

This time, one of them was wearing the Blood's red bandanna, the other, that of a blue Crip. They should have been duking it out, but neither appeared to be too concerned with the other.

Two mortal enemies teamed up. It struck Ryan as a funny image.

"Stop admiring the scenery and sit down, kid."

Mr. T.'s gruff command propelled Ryan forward.

Ryan sat down next to him and gazed at the endless azure sea. It felt like a world of possibilities. These dreams. The notion of Owen and Steph going out being a distant memory.

Ryan was practically giddy at the thought of what might come next.

He turned and saw streams of dry blood trailing down the sides of Mr. T.'s sunglasses. He remembered how his idol's eyeballs had just plopped out onto sand during the previous dream, like something out of a cheesy horror movie.

Apparently, some things just stuck in the dream world.

As the thought crossed his mind, two pairs of slick hands reached down and starting massaging his chest.

He smiled, remembering the girls from his class. Looking up, he expected to see Loretta and one of her friends.

He did see Loretta, but his mouth fell open when he saw that the other pair of hands belonged to the person he'd most hoped they would, but least believed they would.

Steph.

She still had that crazy haircut. She and Loretta looked like best friends. If anything gave away that this wasn't reality, it wasn't the crystalline ocean, or undead Mr. T.: it was that relationship.

A part of Ryan liked it.

Mr. T. spoke in his famous clipped tone. "I gotta tell you, kid, you've been top-notch. You're going places."

Ryan wasn't sure if he *couldn't* say anything, or just didn't *want* to say anything, but he simply nodded, basking in the compliments, smiling at Steph with a sloppy grin.

"But there's one other thing Mr. T. needs from you."

"Mmmhmm," Ryan said.

"Hey," Mr. T. said.

Ryan felt something wet plop onto his stomach.

He looked down.

Another eyeball.

He yelped and with the back of his hand, swept the gelatinous orb into the sand. A streak of red blood remained on his torso and Ryan tried desperately to wipe it away.

"Eyes on me," Mr. T. said.

The girls withdrew their hands from Ryan, and he gave Mr. T. his full attention. He didn't know where the extra eyeball came from and Mr. T. still had on his gold-frame shades.

"Your friends are going to try to ask you for help. You gotta give it to 'em, you dig?"

"What? Why?"

"Because your job isn't done. Job's done when I say the job's done, dig?"

Ryan's stomach began to rumble and it wasn't because he was hungry. He felt like he'd done everything that had been asked already, and he was ready to move on to the next stage of his own plan.

"Now you done good with Owen. But I got my eye on the next one—Jake."

Ryan didn't have anything so much against Jake. No reason to come down on him like he had Owen. Even after the fact, there was still a piece of Ryan that clawed at his insides and told him what he'd done was wrong, almost unrepairable.

It was a feeling he was willing to accept though. Rocket Man needed to be put in his place and Steph needed to see that her knight in shining riding gear wasn't all that—that there was someone even better for her. Ryan may not have the looks or the charisma, but he'd been alongside her the whole time.

"I don't know," Ryan said. "I still haven't asked Steph out. I thought I should do it now that Owen—"

"Don't be the fool, kid. You ask her now, you gonna blow it. Have I let you down?"

Ryan didn't think so. He glanced up to see a smiling Steph, waiting patiently for her new hero to wrap up his important conversation.

Mr. T. continued, "I'm gonna give you the opportunity. I'm gonna make you the hero. You just gotta do what I say. Dig?"

Ryan nodded silently again, even though that clawing sense of uneasiness increased its tempo. He didn't like how deep things were getting now. This unwritten deal he'd made with Mr. T. was starting to bother him a little more.

"Now, Jake, he's gonna have some ideas. Some crazy ideas. But you gotta follow his lead, OK?"

"What do you mean?"

"Don't question me, kid," Mr. T. said, tearing off his

sunglasses and exposing the empty sockets. Ryan found himself drawn into them. A sense of vertigo overcame him. "Just trust me. Otherwise, you gonna be the biggest fool there ever was."

Ryan felt like he was going to hurl, but he couldn't look away. A force greater than any he'd ever known was pulling him into the black holes.

Finally, Mr. T. replaced his sunglasses.

"Do we understand each other?"

Acidic bile rose in the back of Ryan's throat.

"I asked you a question, kid, and the polite thing to do is to answer." Mr. T. placed a hand back on his sunglasses frames.

Ryan nodded vigorously, mouth closed to keep the nauseous feelings at bay.

Now Mr. T. laughed a hearty laugh. So much so that his chains jingled and clinked.

"I knew you were the right one," he said. "I knew you had it in you."

Did he?

Ryan wondered if he hadn't bitten off more than he could chew. Like a bowl full of Reese's Pieces, the idea of eating the whole thing was better than actually doing so. Was this notion of going out with Steph worth what happened to The Crew? The magical thing they had going seemed irreparably damaged now.

And would Steph really be willing to go out with her buck-toothed friend? What if she said no? Or worse, what if she laughed in his face and *then* said no.

He chose to trust Mr. T. There was no other option at this point.

He wouldn't be the fool.

Ryan sensed Mr. T. looking at him, almost sniffing Ryan's seditious thoughts out of the air. Ryan lay back on his chair and tried to focus on Steph above him. Though she was smiling as she placed her hands back on his chest, there seemed to be something else there.

A pair of abysses, just as deep as Mr. T's, lurked behind her gleaming eyes. He just knew it.

Suddenly, everything began to melt away from Ryan just as it had done so last time.

He must have been mumbling in his sleep because he awoke to see Gabriela sitting up in her bed, looking at him as if he were a madman. The twins were snoring lightly on each side of her.

Ryan smiled at her, giving her as evil of a grin as he could manage.

Her jaw dropped and as quickly as she could, she threw

off her blankets, rolled out of the bed, and bolted from the bed-room.

Friday, June 24, 1989 - 11:30 PM

Jake was in his bedroom, but it wasn't his *real* bedroom. Instead of lying back on a stained mattress with lumpy springs, he was perched comfortably within red-painted wood paneling designed to look like one of those sweet-looking race cars.

He'd always wanted a bed like this.

And not only that, but it had a television built into the foot of the frame. The screen played the intro sequence for the *Ikari Warriors* video game.

A black cable ran from the bottom of the monitor to a Nintendo controller in Jake's right hand. In the other hand, a not-too-soft, not-too-frozen Neapolitan ice cream sandwich. To his left was a mini-freezer filled with dozens more.

Ice cream truck music jingled and rang just outside his bedroom window.

This was the best dream ever. Jake knew he'd wake up eventually, but he focused all of his mental abilities on keeping himself here as long as possible.

It had been a long time since he'd had good dreams.

He thought about The Crew. Wished they were here, so

they could share in the wondrous moment.

But he'd blown that situation all to crap, hadn't he?

The music outside came to a grinding halt and a sudden shadow fell over Jake. He had had an opportunity to stand up for his friend, to convince the others that Owen wasn't full of it, but Owen went and used the "C"-word. Jake almost socked Owen in the nose then and there, but held himself back because he was afraid he'd cry right after he did it.

Oh well.

Whatever was going on with the Wienermobile and this Mysterious Mariska would go away like a bad dream. Owen was just making something out of nothing and once school ended and summer officially started, things would just go back to the way they were.

Jake leaned down and took a bite of his ice cream sandwich.

Pfft.

Stringy brown strands of fiber fell onto his lap.

"What the—"

He looked down and grew confused. What had been a delicious treat only seconds ago had turned into a little kid's doll. And not a modern-day Cabbage Patch Kid or Strawberry Shortcake doll, but one of those old-looking ones from the 50s or something.

It was hand-painted with giant, bubbly eyes, pursed fire-engine red lips, and curly hair.

The doll was naked. It's peach-colored plastic body felt smooth in Jake's hand.

He stared at it, wondering how this strange turn of events came about when the doll's eyes shifted from staring past him to looking directly at him. A smile formed on its lips.

"Don't you like dollllllsssssss?" it asked in a robotic voice, slurring its words toward the end like an old tape that had been worn over time.

Jake yelped.

On instinct, he tried to toss the doll across his bedroom, but he couldn't get it out of his hand. Its tiny arms were wrapped around his wrist, holding on for dear life. He dropped the Nintendo controller out of his other hand and struggled to pry the doll free.

"Dolls, Jake?"

It was the one thing that could get Jake to stop what he was doing.

He looked up at his bedroom door. His father stood in the frame, watching him, swaying slightly as if he'd just finished pounding the first six-pack of the night.

Before he could get a word out, his father continued, "Seriously? My son is seriously playing with dolls?"

Suddenly, the rest of Jake's bedroom came into focus. There were piles and piles of dolls that looked exactly like the one stuck to his hand—something a little girl might play with twenty years ago. Or whenever they made those black and white movies.

Some of them had on pink and lily-white laced clothing. A few were babies that wore tiny caps and clutched tiny plastic baby bottles with their delicate fingers. Others were older little girls, wearing airline stewardess uniforms or girl scout outfits. Their cheeks blushed red and they had tiny button noses. Just like the one in his hand, they all had those ruby-red pursed lips.

A whiff of warm, rancid alcohol caught Jake's attention. His dad had moved from the door to the side of the bed quietly, almost like he floated there.

He grabbed Jake's chin and spun his head around so that their eyes were locked onto each other's like lasers.

"Answer me," he said.

"Dad, I—" Jake tried to look around again. The dolls were *everywhere*. A group on his dresser. A row on the window sill. Even lined along the inside of the bed like an invading army that had scaled the walls.

"Those aren't my dolls, Dad," Jake continued. There was fear in his voice, quivering, shaking, but there was also defiance. How could his old man think he'd ever played with any of those dolls?

Though he supposed, technically, he *did* play with dolls. He had plenty of little plastic army men that served as fodder for the firecrackers as well as a few G.I. Joe action figures (save me Duke!). Weren't those dolls?

But it wasn't the same, especially in his old man's eyes.

"If they aren't yours, whose are they?" his dad asked. "They're in your bedroom. You wouldn't be lying to me, would you?"

"No!" Jake shouted. "No, sir. I—"

Boom.

Jake's image of the once-perfect bedroom suddenly spun on its axis, swapping up with down and left with right. Jake's right cheek ached like it had been stung by a thousand dull needles. He would have fallen out of the race-car bed and onto the carpet had his dad not grabbed him by the crook of his arm and held him upright.

A symphony of tiny, mechanical giggles coursed through the bedroom.

Jake tasted blood edging out from the corner of his lips.

His dad's face was in Jake's face now. The hot beer breath was amplified with a mix of sour cream and onion potato chips. Jake wanted to turn away, certain he was going to retch, but his dad's eyes seemed to take hold of him even more tightly than the doll which remained clasped to his hand.

"Jake, I don't like being lied to. Just tell me the truth. Tell me that you like to play with these dolls. Tell me that you're a little sissy that likes to dress up in your own little pink dresses and feed these dolls little cookies and sips of tea and treat them like your own babies."

"Dad, I'm telling the truth! I—"

He felt an open palm come down across his right cheek. There was more blood.

"I thought you wanted to be a *man*," his dad said, emphasizing the last word as if it was as sacred as the Medal of Honor. "Aren't you the boy I caught screwing around with my razor? Does playing with dolls make you a man? You think that's gonna put hair on your face?"

Jake was whimpering now. Hot tears streamed down his cheekbones and it sounded like each one hit the carpet with a deafening boom. He didn't have an answer for his dad. He couldn't come up with one that he knew wouldn't wind up with another slap across the face.

"No," his dad continued. "I'm going to make a man of you, Jake. You always wanted to shave. I'm going to teach you how to shave, you little shit."

He yanked Jake by the grip he had on his arm and pulled him out of his bed with little effort—like Jake was a doll himself.

(Save me Duke!)

"Dad, I—"

"Oh, no, son. No, no, no. Crawford men don't play with dolls. Anyone that does ain't a Crawford man after all. Crawford men do shave though. Yep, yep, they most certainly do."

"Dad, I swear. I don't know where—"

They paused in the hallway, halfway to the bathroom, just long enough for another slap on the same cheek with the same open hand. This one felt like it went all the way to the nerves in Jake's teeth. He howled in pain.

"Maybe you really are a girl, Jake. Maybe I'll change your name to Jackie. We could buy you dresses to wear to school."

He said that with an insane-sounding giggle. There was a delirious look on the old man's face. Spittle was flying every which way.

"I bet your friends would like to see that, right? Oh, how I would love to show off my little girl. You bet I would. I would pull up to the school playing the shittiest pop song you can think of—you know, the one I hear you playing all the time through your bedroom door—and blare it as I kicked your ass out of the passenger seat and onto the curb. Right in front of all your friends."

The expression on his father's face grew even more maniacal, if that was possible.

"'This is my little princess, everyone!' I'd say. 'Treat her real nice now. She's a delicate little flower!'"

Jake couldn't recall when they got there, but before he realized it, they were facing the wide bathroom mirror. His father still had the death-grip on Jake's arm.

In the mirror, Jake saw someone he was ashamed of. Not because of the doll situation, but because of the tears running down his face and the beet red pallor his skin had taken on.

The long and short of it was that his dad was winning and that made Jake sick to his stomach.

His dad let go of him and opened the mirrored medicine cabinet hanging on the wall to the right of the larger bathroom mirror.

Inside, surrounding the deodorant and toothpaste and shaving cream, were more dolls. Their eyes were focused on him.

Staring.

Gawking.

The high-pitched, mechanical giggles started again.

"Are you ready, sweetheart?" There was an eerie red glow behind his old man's intense look. "Are you ready to become a man?"

Jake tried to swallow the lump in his throat. It was stuck there, weighing him down like an albatross. He kept his mouth shut, still. There was nothing he could say. He only wanted this dream to end.

To end before it got worse.

A gleam of light sparkled on something in his father's hands now.

It was the chrome silver straight razor.

His old man held it up to the twin light bulbs hanging over the center of the mirror, twisting it in the radiance, admiring it like it was a fine piece of jewelry.

"I think we ought to do this raw, cutie pie. Real men don't need shaving cream, right?"

Jake pleaded with himself.

Please, please, please, wake up.

(Save me, Duke!)

"Hell," his old man said, "we don't even need any stinking water." His eyes returned to his son. "Just raw, puddin' pop.

Just nice and raw."

He dropped the razor down to his son's stinging cheek and held it there. Jake tried to make a run for the door, but his father was too fast. He gripped his arm again, this time twisting it behind Jake's back and pushing upwards. Jake's body bent forward over the sink to try to compensate. Screams of pain rose once more from his vocal cords.

His face was inches from the mirror. His forehead was pulsating pink. Sweat poured down his hairline, mixing with his tears to form a sad concoction.

There was no hiding from his shame or what was about to happen.

"I know you don't want to do what's needed," his old man said. "But, honey, you're my little girl, and Daddy knows best."

"Dad!" Jake screamed. "Please! I'm already a man! Please! I don't need to shave. I swear, I won't ever touch your stuff again!"

Jake's old man clucked his tongue. "It's not about touching my stuff, honey. It's about me doing the right thing as a parent. Lord knows, your mom wouldn't do this for you. I'm only looking out for you. I'm only looking out for my little girl. I wouldn't want you to end up like your little friend, Rocket Man.

Everyone knows that *he* plays with dolls. That kid's a bad influence. You really ought to stay away from him and his dolls."

The words were rotten, twisted. His dad's face was a ragged mess, splattered with rage. Jake wouldn't have been surprised to see yellow venom streaming out from the corners of his father's lips.

Jake couldn't go anywhere or do anything now. He could only endure until some benevolent part of his subconscious would release him from this hell.

(Save me, Duke!)

The razor came down slowly, like it was being dragged through thick water. His old man twisted it back and forth, causing the glint to occasionally blind Jake.

"Now be a good girl and let Daddy do what needs doing."

The razor made contact against Jake's skin.

And then it made its descent.

Deep.

Sharp.

Full of hate.

Jake screamed as he saw his skin peel away from his face like the rind of an orange. Beneath was another layer of skin— fresh and untouched by the world. Crimson blood emerged from the pores beneath. Sweat and tears rolled into the newly exposed gap, stinging like a fire that could never be quenched.

Jake screamed until his lungs ran out of capacity, leaving him gasping for breath.

"For you, sweetie. For you!" his father shouted over Jake's screams, the perfect image of a maniac.

The mechanical laughter. A hoard of dolls magically appeared on the bathroom counter.

Eyes, everywhere. His father's. The dolls'. Something black in the doorway, smoke-like, without form.

All glowing red.

All menacing.

All to make sure Jake did what he was told.

His eyes rolled into the back of his head.

There was sweet blackness.

And there was the sound of birds chirping a familiar song.

Jake shot up from his bed, hearing a familiar groaning spring, and grabbed at the flap of skin hanging on his cheek.

Only there was no flap there.

The pain still radiated, but his hands felt nothing but moist flesh.

And he wasn't in the bathroom.

It was still nighttime. Silver moonlight illuminated his bedroom through the thin brown curtains.

There they were—the old, familiar things:

A pile of dirty clothes on the ground next to the closet.

The line-up of tarnished G.I. Joe action figures standing at attention on the top of his thin bookshelf.

Posters in the room of a sneering Motley Crue and Poison.

But no scary dolls.

THE ALMOST END

Sunday, June 26, 1989 - 6:00 AM

Steph's heart ached as three-fourths of The Crew sat on their bikes at the track below Bass Hill, rolling back and forth listlessly across the dirt.

It was almost a replay of two weeks ago, only their spirits were miles away from the high they'd experienced then. The skies were also clear and beautiful then. Now, dark clouds gathered all around the landscape like a thick, suffocating coat.

The magic was gone and so was Owen Thom.

No one had seen him since Friday morning.

The town of Apple Valley was abuzz with the news of his disappearance.

It was in the Sunday edition of the area's most prominent, and only, newspaper, *The Daily Press*. Kids usually checked *The Daily Press* to see their names in the local sports section for soccer games, but in the Sunday edition, on a front-page sidebar, just above a forecast about an unusual, but not extraordinary, summer storm, was every parent's worst nightmare.

Heading the article was a black-and-white print of Owen's sixth-grade photo, its pink and blue laser background reduced to mere lines.

The final paragraph noted that if anyone had any information on Owen's whereabouts, they should contact the San Bernardino County Sheriff's Department.

After the police left Steph's apartment on Saturday afternoon, finished with their questions and searching her room, she called Jake and Ryan to give them fair warning of what was coming and told them they all ought to meet as soon as possible.

Jake suggested the track and they all agreed.

"Something happened with that magician lady," Steph said. "I know it."

"I don't know," Ryan said. He looked dead tired, but less so than Jake.

"What do you mean you don't know?" Steph asked, bewildered. "That's all Owen talked about in the tent."

She hadn't spoken to Owen since Wednesday night—the night everything seemed to swell together into a nasty, messy explosion of feelings.

She last saw him at school on Friday. Now, she felt absolutely miserable about not only the cold shoulder she'd been giving him, but also her attempts at making him jealous by snuggling up to Ryan whenever she thought Owen might be looking.

The whole thing was a bucket full of wrong and Steph felt sick to her stomach that she'd even led Ryan on a little bit just to make a boy jealous that she wasn't even sure she really wanted to like more than a friend.

Who cared if Owen wanted to go out with the girl who represented everything Steph was against? Steph would eventually get over the idea. If she wound up stuck in the sixth grade again, none of it would matter anyway. She wouldn't have to see him again. She'd make new friends.

Maybe then she would get decent grades.

Steph shuddered to think that maybe her mom was right and The Crew was the main reason she wasn't making progress in school in the first place.

No, she wouldn't believe any of that. Not yet.

"We should have listened to him," she said, shaking her head. "Why didn't we listen to him?"

The question was not quite rhetorical.

Ryan said nothing.

"It doesn't matter," Jake said, adjusting the ragged Jansport backpack on his back. "We need to find him now."

Steph's heart lifted a little bit to hear him side with her.

Ryan shook his head. "Guys, let the Five-O do their job. I barely snuck away from my parents this morning as it was. I should still be sleeping now."

"We can't just abandon him," Steph said.

"Why not?" Ryan said. "Owen did something dumb to get himself into this in the first place. Actually, he's probably just messing with us all. Trying to pull a fast one. The cops said he was probably mad at being grounded."

"No way," Steph said. "No way he'd get the cops and everything involved. That's not Owen. We knew he was going to try to look for her. Maybe we should do the same thing? Or at least tell the cops what he'd been saying about the magician."

"That's crazy," Ryan replied. "They'll just laugh at us."

"Well, give us some ideas, smart guy," Steph replied. "We can't just abandon Rocket Man."

She grew increasingly irritated with Ryan. Why she ever thought to make Owen jealous with him was beyond her.

Before he could reply with what would be another excuse, Jake piped up, "I have one."

Both Ryan and Steph stared at him, waiting for him to continue. Jake's eyes were focused on the buildings across Highway 18.

"Well?" Steph asked. Impatience made her voice shrill.

"I think he's there," he said, pointing.

"Where? The post office? The bank?"

"No," Jake replied, jabbing his index finger forward as if it clarified things. "The building over there."

Ryan piped his head up, looking past the obvious and out toward the old airport. "The old doll factory?" he asked.

Jake nodded.

Behind a tall Joshua tree and set of creosote bushes, the three of them crouched over their bikes, fifty yards from the outside of the creepy, pink building.

The old Terri Lee Doll factory wasn't big. It was a single story, narrow—maybe a hundred feet wide and a couple hundred feet long—with a flat tarred roof and a rusty weather vane spinning on one end. The few dark windows that hadn't been become jagged flesh-slicers—thanks to years of kids throwing rocks—were caked in dust. Broken bits of blacktop and weeds sprouting through the cracks surrounded the building like a sea of history.

The place had been in Apple Valley for decades: around forty years, Steph had heard. It was a ghost of a building now, having long been shuttered and allowed to enter a dilapidated state. It stood as a testament to the town's past that none of the kids really knew anything about.

"Tell me again why we're here instead of letting the cops handle this?" Ryan asked.

He sounded almost bored.

"I don't know," Jake said. "Other than to say, it has to be us. This is where we'll find him and it *has* to be us."

Steph pierced Ryan with her eyes like they were needles full of truth serum. "Don't you want to find him?"

Ryan almost choked on his response with disdain. "Duh! Yeah! Of course, I want to find him. I just don't see why he'd be at some dirty old place where people used to crank out dolls. It doesn't make any sense."

"Since when does any of what's been happening lately make logical sense?" she asked. She glanced at Jake. "I trust Jake. We don't really have any other options."

It looked like Ryan was going to protest once more, but maybe he was tired of additional admonishments, so he left well enough alone. His chest rose and fell in resignation. He placed his hands back on his bent kneecaps like a football player preparing to run, and stared back at the factory.

"Well, if we're going to go," he said, "what are we doing out here? The place looks dead, but who knows—maybe Mama Fratelli and Sloth are hiding inside."

Ryan laughed at his own stupid Goonies joke, but Steph and Jake didn't bite. This was too important.

Ryan tried to recover, "Plus, I don't want to ride home in the pouring rain."

They all glanced up and saw that the menacing clouds had drifted past the borders of the town that failed miserably to hold them back.

Would Owen really be inside?

And would he be alone?

Steph tried not to think too hard about what was coming, because she was afraid she'd make the wrong decision.

The three of them circled around to the narrow north side of the factory, their backs toward the old airport. Gravel crunched beneath their feet as they made a mad dash toward the building.

They almost slammed into the pink walls and then stood deathly still. Steph worked hard to listen to any sounds that might be coming from inside, but it was difficult to hear over the thrumming pulse in her ears. Her heart felt as if it was going to punch its way out of her chest.

They were only a few feet from the back door. It was white, or had been at one time. Now it was roughly peeled paint and splintered wood, barely attached to the building by rusted hinges.

Trying to be quiet seemed a fool's errand at this point. Swinging that thing open would announce their presence to anyone within a five-mile radius.

Either Jake didn't think about that or didn't care as he reached across and flung the door open. As expected, the hinges screamed.

The door came crashing down, clapping and echoing across the parking lot, all while kicking up a sizable cloud of dust.

"So much for subtle, dufus," Ryan said.

Jake ignored him, coughing because he'd inhaled too much dust.

Steph admired Jake for the courage he showed. It reminded her of Rocket Man.

She only hoped Jake's instincts were right and that Owen was there.

They all poked their heads into the dim opening. Steph crinkled her nose as a musty smell penetrated her nostrils.

"Owen!" Ryan yelled.

The sound carried through the opening.

There was no reply.

"Shhh!" Jake chastised him when he managed to stop coughing.

Ryan rolled his eyes. "Yeah, because no one knows we're here now."

Past the little entryway, it was pitch black. On both sides of the door was old wood shelving—planks held up by metal posts that had been secured into the floor of the has-been factory. The shelves were filled with taped-up cardboard boxes. Everything was layered in an inch-thick pile of dust and accompanying dust bunnies.

Steph looked up and saw that the shelving went up to at least three times her height, stretching toward bare rafters that sagged across the ceiling like tired arms.

Her eyes returned to the dark inside.

"How are we going to see anything in here?" she asked. Despite the numerous broken windows, the overcast sky blotted out any useful light that might poke through.

Jake smiled. "Never fear, Jake's here."

He pulled his backpack around to the front of his chest, unzipped a small pocket, and pulled out what looked like a large pen. With finger and thumb, he twisted the end.

A beam of light shot into Steph's eyes, forcing her hand up to shield the glare.

"Oops, sorry," he said. "Present from my mom."

"So, are we going in or what?" Ryan asked. He shuffled

back and forth on his feet.

Waves of uneasy nausea swept through Steph's stomach. It wasn't just the potential hundreds of black widows, rattlesnakes, and God knows what else living in this broken-down building that struck her with fear.

It was a fear that they would actually find Owen. Because finding Owen meant that Jake's feeling was correct. And if Jake was correct, that meant something larger than all of them really was at play here.

Steph wasn't sure she was ready to face that.

"Come on," she said, steeling herself, taking one step onto the cracked cement floor inside the building. "We have a friend to save."

Ryan noticed the flashlight jiggled in Jake's hands, despite his best efforts to keep the thing from shaking.

There was little movement inside. The moldy smell was five times stronger than it had been through the gap in the doorway.

Ryan wondered what he was doing there. What he was *really* doing there.

A part of him said it was because Steph had called on him and Jake to find their friend. Despite the jealousy and difficulties with Steph, Owen *was* his friend, wasn't he?

But Ryan had strands of memories of dreams that urged him to be here for another reason. There was the vague notion that the issue with Steph would be resolved if he came along.

Maybe this was an opportunity to be the hero. If Ryan found Owen, if Ryan *saved* Rocket Man, then surely Steph would find Ryan more attractive. She wouldn't be able to help herself. She'd definitely want to go out with him.

They were probably ten feet inside the building now, still surrounded by those towering racks of shelving. Ryan pictured the days when they were crowded with dolls, both whole and their parts. Images of glass mason jars filled with plastic eyeballs and arms and legs and heads that had yet to be painted brought a deep shiver down to his soul.

This was the type of place that seemed small from the outside, but practically cavernous once you stepped in.

"Where do we look?" Steph asked, looking to Jake.

"I don't know," he said. "I just have this feeling—"

"You're the one who told us to come here," Ryan said. "Maybe I should be leading this search and rescue mission."

Despite the threatening look in Jake's eyes, Ryan felt

braver by the minute. Like he was destined to be here.

He snagged the flashlight out of Jake's hand.

The big guy was too stunned to react.

Ryan extended his arm, pushed Jake and Steph back, and stepped out in front of them like a general leading his troops.

"I'll find him," he said. "Just get behind me."

Steph looked slightly annoyed, but Ryan chalked that up to her frustration with Jake. He crept forward, hearing their footsteps lag slightly behind him.

A gap existed at the end of the shelves which led to another row of shelves. They were at a crossroads in the middle of the building. The flashlight illuminated the opposite side of where they came in. It was a good thing they hadn't tried the front door. Heavy-looking steel file cabinets were pushed up against it that would have prevented even Mr. T. from punching through.

A loud bang from the north side of the factory distracted Ryan from his thoughts, causing the three of them to jump and yelp.

Ryan's fingers lost their grip on the flashlight and it hit the cement, knocking out the light and rolling away somewhere unseen.

The three of them were left in the gray dark.

Ryan felt someone's hands grip his arm. He almost yelped again until he smelled Steph's shampoo lingering beside him.

A smile hit his lips instead.

Only the aftermath of the startling sound remained, wobbling through the thick air like someone had struck a piece of sheet metal with a hammer.

"Owen?" Steph asked.

No reply.

"It's probably just a rat or a possum or something," Ryan said, not so sure himself, but feeling a little more reassured with Steph still hanging on to him like he was her bodyguard. "We probably entered its home and scared the crap out of it."

He felt Jake's elbow bump into his. Heard his rapid breathing. "We need to go," he said. "I think I was wrong."

"No!" Steph said. "We can't. Not without Owen."

"She's right," Ryan added, struggling to hide his giddiness. "You can go home if you're afraid, but we're not going anywhere."

"I'm not afraid," Jake said, "but we can't see anything without the light."

Using the toes of his Keds, Ryan searched for the flashlight with no avail.

He leaned over and whispered to Steph. "You'll need to let go of my arm so I can try to find it."

Ryan thought she nodded in response, though he couldn't really see. She released her death-grip and Ryan dropped to his knees, feeling around the dust-covered floor for the flashlight. His fingers searched and searched, accumulating decades of dirt. It didn't bother him. He'd never been bothered by getting a little dirty.

He stretched one hand into the three-inch gap between the floor and the bottom shelf to their right. Images of black widows sinking their teeth into the back of his hand flashed into his mind, and he pulled back.

"Come on," he said, getting back onto his feet. "I don't know about you guys, but my eyes have adjusted. We don't need the light."

He was half-telling the truth. His eyes had adjusted and it was a little easier to see things in general, but it was mostly vague outlines. The light would have been more useful to see what was actually there, but—

Thoughts of the spiders intruded again. Black, furry things with distended bellies. Thousands of red glowing eyes, watching his every move. He would be unable to escape them. They would find him, cowering, running away. They would shoot their webs out and stick him.

Don't play the fool echoed in Ryan's mind.

Thoughts of Mr. T. and the gangstas steeled Ryan's resolve.

He led them toward the source of the sound. Once they passed two more rows of box-filled shelves, they came upon three rows of workbenches—six of them, two to a row, with more dust on top as well as spare parts and partially composed dolls.

Ryan thought he heard Jake gasp.

The dolls were posed in different positions: some were on their backs like helpless children; some were actually standing on their heads, using their hairless scalps to balance. But all of them had painted eyes that appeared to be following The Crew, much like those paintings which hung in haunted mansions.

On the other side of the desks was a wall of three doors. Each appeared to lead to an office of some sort. They had yellow stained-glass inset from top to middle, all still surprisingly intact.

In fact, they looked brand new.

But they were all closed.

"Now what?" Jake asked.

"Now we pick a door," Ryan said.

The world was a jumble in Owen's head.

He bolted upright, happy to be free from his nightmare in the desert.

There was no chain of spiraling events that kicked off at the track near Lion's Park.

There was no Wienermobile.

There was no Mysterious Mariska.

It was all fake. None of it had happened.

Owen swept his arm across his forehead and wiped away the sweat. He'd go back to sleep in a moment. He'd grab his pillow, flip it, and lay his head back down on the cool side, knowing he'd wake up later to a risen sun and singing sparrows.

But his arm felt gritty. When he wiped his forehead, he seemed to leave more behind than he'd removed.

"What the—" he croaked.

He set himself to coughing and gagging on his own words, wondering what in the world was going on. If he wasn't careful, he was certain one or both of his lungs would come flying out, splatting on the floor like a wet piece of flesh.

God, his throat hurt. It felt like someone had taken long fingernails and dragged them across his esophagus.

He still hadn't opened his eyes, but he decided he didn't need to yet. His ears informed him he was in a room that was not his.

Next, the nagging pain in his lower back announced its renewed presence. He wasn't lying on his soft bed after all. There was some kind of material there, but it was more like a piece of canvas that had gotten all jumbled up when he laid on top of it. He stretched his hands out and rubbed his palms around the cold, stiff floor.

Slowly, he blinked his eyes open. He found that it didn't take long to get adjusted to the light because there wasn't much light to adjust to. The room was dark and with little shadow.

He looked up and around. The ceiling was probably fifteen feet over his head and bare wood frame. The area of the room itself had to be less than fifteen square feet. It was mostly open space, but piled in one corner appeared to be old office furniture—a pair of old desks that were pushed against the wall with several metal filing cabinets sitting on top.

The air was stifling. Thick. There wasn't even a hint of movement.

Owen's thoughts and ideas had arrived at the sorry notion before his eyes: the Mysterious Mariska; The Worm; they were real.

And they'd put him here.

Wherever *here* was.

He wanted to cry, but he wasn't even sure he could. It would be too painful, physically and mentally. He just wanted to rewind. To go home. To see his friends again.

Low shuffling noises bled in from outside of the room.

Owen stiffened up, wondering if he should be silent or shout. He was with it enough to reason that if it was Mariska and The Worm, his saying something wouldn't change his circumstances. But, if by amazing luck, it was someone else who didn't know he was there and could help him, then he'd be a fool to pass by the opportunity.

He tried to say, "Help," but nothing came out except more hacking coughs.

Hopefully, they'd hear at least those.

Water. He desperately wanted a glass of water. There was no bathroom next door to run to, like there was at his house, so that he could stick his head underneath the faucet and let the tap flow between his lips.

The image made Owen realize just how parched and cracked they felt. It was if he'd spent the last month roaming the Mojave.

As much as his head and body pounded, he came to the

realization that he had to get up. He had to do something.

He pushed himself slowly onto his feet. His knees were a little wobbly. The feeling was familiar and now it was all coming back to him—he felt just like he'd been taking the pain pills again that he'd taken for his back. Partial loss of motor control and waves of vertigo sloshed through his head, threatening to break the levee of his mind and spill out into the real world.

Staggering, Owen scrambled toward one side of the room as it tilted. He nearly kissed the wall with his face, crashing into the grime-covered wallpaper that was peeling down like torn blisters. Luckily, his hands shot up in time for protection.

To his right, he saw a door he hadn't noticed before—old wood with a stained yellow glass inset that waved and skewed like running water. It was opportunity waiting for him. He reached toward the rusty, dust-covered knob, but hesitated.

He still felt unsteady, so he paused for a moment. He pressed both hands against the wall like he was going to do a push-up, and tried to steady his breathing.

You're okay. You're okay and you're just in a room and nothing else is here. It's just you and there's nothing else here. Nothing that can hurt you.

And he believed it, too. The sense that the Mysterious Mariska was here—or worse, that black thing with the red eyes—was missing. Neither of them was there. In fact, neither of them was anywhere near. Though there was a trace of something in this place. A trace of something wrong and yearning and wishing to be set free.

Maybe it was him?

Another sound from outside—a muffled bang that sounded like it was echoed underwater. And then what he thought were the muted voices of people.

He couldn't make out the words, but the timbres of the voices were familiar.

In fact, he thought he knew exactly who was outside.

"Steph!" he tried to scream, and it sort of came out, covered only by a gurgle and a sharp intake of breath.

He coughed more and tried again.

"Jake! Ryan!"

The pain in his throat was excruciating, but no more so than the feeling of being trapped inside here.

Despite the muted tones, he was positive he'd heard all of them. Their words floated over each other like the instruments of a band playing music together.

"I'm in here!" he said. His voice felt whole again. Finally, feeling brave and steady enough to free at least one hand from the wall, he shuffled toward the door and started banging his fist against it.

He started gently, afraid the inlaid glass would come crashing down at the slightest disturbance, shattering into a million shards that would slice through his skin and leave him bleeding to do death.

But when the glass did nothing, only vibrated slightly, he increased the strength of his hits until the entire door was shaking.

Owen only realized after he was gasping for breath that he'd been banging with both fists as hard as possible, even slamming them into the glass.

It was the strangest sensation—like punching a giant sponge. There was a little bit of give to the glass, but it didn't feel real.

On the other side of the door, Owen heard more echoing, strangled voices.

"I'm in here!" he shouted, which sent him hacking coughs again.

Despair began to settle on him once again. Something told him that there was no use in banging away anymore. They either didn't hear him or didn't care to hear.

The whole notion sent Owen back to his makeshift bed, where he collapsed and whimpered lightly. His chest heaved as it tried to take in as much of the thick, wet air in the room as possible. His night sweat had since been added to by the sweat of his physical output. Owen suddenly realized just how exhausted he was again. His stomach groaned.

When was the last time he'd had something to eat?

Forget food, he thought. What he wouldn't do for a single drop of water.

That's all he wanted. Just a single drop.

In a bid of desperation, he almost shouted out for the Mysterious Mariska. He was on the edge of begging her for something to parch his throat.

But he didn't. Something stopped him. Thoughts of his friends just outside of the door, maybe even John was there, or on his way, to come and save Owen.

John, I wish you were here. I wish you could come and save me.

Owen had to believe.

Had to believe that his friends were coming.

Rhythmic beeping surrounded John. The notes were somehow dull and shrill at the same time, but distant like a tornado siren heard several miles from its origin.

Maybe the sound was lessened by the fact that he was somewhere else in his mind.

He was dreaming.

Or maybe dead.

Wearing cowboy boots and blue jeans, he crouched beneath the late morning sun. A well-worn baseball cap shaded his face. The sky was nothing but a hole seen through a thin fog wrapped around him, thickening out past a hundred or so yards.

Everything was familiar to John: from the pungent odor of cow manure floating up from the pen just above the alfalfa fields to the feeling of the hardland soil he rubbed between his thumb and fingers.

He was back in the world of his youth—his father's dairy farm in the flats of eastern New Mexico, just north of Clovis, and within spitting distance of the Texas border.

John remembered it all, of course. Not just about the farm, but how he'd ended up here.

The Worm had gotten him. John had been careless, thinking it held no power over him anymore. Yet, he'd been fooled by its old tricks.

Probably, it was for the best, if this was how things

turned out. He had happy memories of this place before The Worm went and turned everything terrible.

He twisted his head and looked back at the tiny two-bedroom adobe house which harbored his parents, two older brothers, Chuck and Ronald, and one younger sister, Sandy.

Smoke rose from the brick chimney. Mom was cooking dinner with Sandy. In about an hour, Dad and the boys would be trudging up to the porch after a long morning of loading the cow feed and, presumably, Dad banging away on the churning machinery that always broke down.

A screech issued from the fence behind him. John wiped his hands against his jeans and stood up.

Even as the boy closed the gate, his back to John, Richie Trujillo was instantly recognizable—it was the combination of a dark-skinned, rail-thin boy in a red-and-black flannel shirt that was too big and a brown, ten-gallon hat that tipped down so often, Richie's constant motion of pushing it back up was forever etched in John's mind.

As soon as Richie turned around and approached him, John knew he never wanted to leave this place. His old friend's familiar smile was big and bright.

Richie pushed the hat up from his eyes. He looked a little tired, but no more so than a ranch hand who'd been up and at'em since 4:30 a.m.

"John," Richie said.

John hadn't heard that voice in a long time, but it curled around him like a warm blanket.

"Richie," he replied.

A stiff silence hung in the air, leaving just enough gaps for the distant beeps to weave their way in. They were still low, maybe even fading.

"It's good to see you," Richie said.

"It's good to see you, too."

John hesitated for a moment. He stuck his hands into his back pockets and kicked at the ground with his boot tips. He turned and looked at the tall wood-framed barn standing fifty yards past the house. "Hey," he said, turning back around, feeling a little bit crazy. "You wanna go running off the loft and leap into the hay bales? It's been a long time."

Richie's smile somehow grew larger. "I'd love to, *amigo*. And we will. I promise we will. But, right now, we gotta help him."

John almost said, "Who?" but he knew exactly who Richie was referring to. There was more hesitation.

"He can't do it on his own," Richie said. "Not now."

"But I can't," John said. He truly meant it. "I think it's

over for me."

"The Worm's still got you, John."

"It *already* got me."

"I mean It's still got your mind. You feel limited. You can't see what's possible."

John wasn't sure about all that. He took a deep breath through his nose, inhaling a smell that he'd once been used to, a smell he'd once thought he couldn't wait to get away from, and then realized he yearned for like his mother's kisses or his dad's campfire stories.

"I miss this place, Richie. I miss what we had."

"I know, John. I know." Richie took off his hat and wiped away the forehead sweat with his arm. "All the more reason we can't let it happen to him and his friends, *amigo*. They're only the beginning. You know that, right? The Worm's not stupid. It knows that if it picks off the strongest elements first, the rest will fall."

"But what can I do?" John asked, anguish clear in his voice now. "I'm tired, Richie. I'm tired."

Richie ambled over, and John, looking down at the boy's thick head of black hair, realized the awkward height difference between them now.

"They'll be plenty of time to rest. I promise, *amigo*. But

only if we make it happen."

It was settled then. Richie was right. John couldn't abandon Owen now. Not if there really was an opportunity to save him and his friends and the world in which they lived.

"What can we do about it here?"

"We just need a little help from our friends," Richie said.

The distant beeping retreated even further from John's ears, replaced by a cacophony of whispers. His vision expanded to see a contingent of children emerging from the fog.

A mixture of boys and girls, some covered in furs and threadbare clothes like they'd stepped out of a museum's prehistoric exhibit, others wearing soccer uniforms, presented themselves. A couple of girls carried skateboards. Another pair swung a jump rope between them for an invisible partner.

But as they approached Richie and John, John saw black rings circling their eyes like those of a raccoon. The kids may have been smiling, but they all had the same tired look as Richie, only more so.

In each one of their hands was a tiny piece of torn white paper. One by one, they walked up to Richie and handed them to him. There must have been fifty pieces in all.

Once it was done, Richie crumpled them together in his fists, only to unfold them as a single piece of paper.

He handed it to John.

John's fingers shook as he took hold of it. His heart nearly stopped pumping.

"You—You sent this?"

"With a little help. We tried to get word to you as quickly as possible. Not quickly enough, unfortunately. And it came out scrambled. A problem with the lines between here and there. But now you can do your part."

John looked at him. He wanted to collapse. "But, it's too late. If this was a warning—"

Richie placed a hand on John's. The shaking stopped.

"The message adjusts to fit the circumstances. We just need to get it to him in a way that he can read it. Right now, you're between worlds, John. You're our conduit now. This is the final push."

John looked down at the paper. He'd recognized the text because he'd pored over it for hours. Suddenly, the symbols, the jumbled characters, they twisted and shifted, rearranging themselves into something that resembled a set of assembly instructions combined with lines of poetry.

"I don't get it."

"You don't have to. It's for him, not you."

"So, how do I give it to him?"

Richie smiled again.

"Like I said, *amigo*. With a little help from your friends."

The surrounding children grinned widely as they approached John—some had all their teeth, some had none. Theirs were the faces of those who'd finally found an ounce of hope in a desert of despair.

They surrounded John. Touched him. Fed him their dreams and memories that had been stolen all too soon.

Sparks exploded within his entire body.

He knew it, now. Knew this would be their only chance at redemption.

John closed his eyes.

The foreign beeping returned with a vengeance, speeding up. It was getting difficult to breathe, harder to focus.

He saw Owen curled up in a dim room that looked like an abandoned office. Tears streaked his dirty cheeks.

"Hold on, *amigo*," he said. "Hold on."

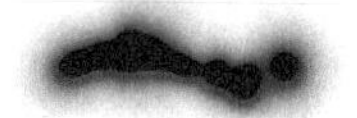

Ryan tried to walk the fine line set for him by his dreams. He trusted Mr. T. The man said to just follow along with Jake's suggestions, but he never said how far. Was being at the old doll factory enough? Ryan felt like he had to take charge at some point, before his newfound advantage with Steph slipped away.

Indeed, the seed of heroics was planted before they arrived, but feeling Steph's hands around his arms made Ryan's ego bloom like a Chia Pet.

Surely, he could take charge at this point. They were in the right spot and now it was up to Ryan to lead.

Only, Jake didn't see things that way.

They'd been arguing over which door to tackle for the past five minutes until Steph finally let go of Ryan's arm and grabbed her hair in frustration.

"Guys! Seriously! Shut. Up."

Her voice carried across the building and introduced silence. Outside, a rumble of low thunder rolled across the land.

"I had the dream," Jake said. "I'm pretty sure I know where he's at."

"You don't know Bo Diddley," Ryan said.

Steph grunted. "You're both acting like idiots. The longer we argue, the more we put Owen at risk. The more we're *all* at risk."

Her scolding left Ryan feeling sheepish. He couldn't have that. He felt opportunity slipping through his fingers like the dust that caked everything in this place.

"He's behind the door on the right. I know it."

"No," Jake said. "The middle. He's behind the middle one."

Ryan and Jake went at it again.

If it came down to it, Ryan would take on the big guy physically. He may have been reluctant to fight his friend in the past, but things were different now. The stakes were high enough that Ryan couldn't back down.

He was so engrossed in his argument that he barely noticed Steph walking toward the left door until Jake turned his head as well.

"Wait!" he and Jake said simultaneously, catching up to her.

"Wait, nothing," she said. "You boys are being stupid."

Her hand was already reaching for the polished knob, inches away from making contact, but tiny strands of electricity shot out at her fingers.

For a second, it reminded Ryan of the crystal plasma ball they sold at Spencer's in the mall—the one that shot out harmless bolts of purple electricity when you rubbed your fingertips along the outside.

Steph yelped and pulled her hand back toward her chest, cradling it.

"Holy crapola!" Jake said. "Are you okay?"

The wince on Steph's face told Ryan that this one wasn't so harmless.

"Yeah," she said, gritting her teeth. She pulled her hand away and shook off the pain. "Felt like getting bit by something. That's all."

"I told you we should have picked the one in the middle," Jake said.

"Right," Ryan said, looking past Steph.

"Back up," Steph said.

"What?" Ryan asked.

"Back. Up."

She was already standing where they had been previously, next to the workbenches covered in doll parts. She held a tiny doll skull in the palm of her hand, bouncing it lightly, feeling its weight.

Ryan didn't like this. He felt like he was losing control of the situation. This was supposed to be his time to impress Steph. To show her his manly leadership skills.

He started to second-guess himself. Started to wonder if he got it all wrong. Maybe Steph was impressed with Rocket Man all because he didn't *try* to impress her. He just acted like Owen.

Don't be the fool rattled around in Ryan's noggin as he caught up to Jake, who was at Steph's side again.

"What are you think—" Ryan started to ask.

Not every question required a verbal response.

Steph angled back like Doc Gooden getting ready to throw a heater and launched the skull at the door on the left.

Ryan wondered if she'd ever played baseball. She'd never mentioned it before, but it was obvious she had skills: the skull connected dead center with the yellow glass.

Ryan put his hands to his ears to dampen the inevitable shattering, but it didn't happen. The skull made contact and bounced off onto the floor.

He smiled, feeling confident again, until the strain of cracks spiderwebbed out from where the doll's head made contact. Thousands of fault lines spread out toward the wooden frame.

Then the glass just disintegrated, falling to the ground like powdered sugar. Ryan shivered. The sensation took him back to the beach in his dreams.

"Holy crapola!" Jake said.

Steph started rushing toward the door.

Thinking back, Ryan didn't quite know what drove him to do what he did next. Was it him? Was it Mr. T? Was it the

Mysterious Mariska and her Big Bad Worm?

His hand shot out and grabbed hold of Steph's wrist.

She twisted her head and gave him a surprised look.

"Hey, what are you doing?" she asked.

Ryan said nothing. He struggled with the words forming in his mind. There was nothing coherent there. He managed to spit out some things.

"Don't...making a mistake...not right for you."

She twisted and turned, trying to escape his grasp, but there was no escaping the death grip Ryan employed.

"Let...go! You're hurting me!"

Somehow, her words both pleased and pained him at the same time. He didn't want to hurt her. Only wanted her to see that Rocket Man wasn't the guy for her. Wanted her to see that she wasn't thinking clearly.

It took a second for Ryan to register that it was Jake's fist that came down on Ryan's forearm with the most powerful Monkey Bite he'd ever felt.

Pain radiated outward. Ryan released his grasp.

"Dude, what's your problem?" Jake asked.

He looked at his big friend as if he were looking at a stranger. Then he turned to Steph.

He wanted to apologize, but the words weren't coming.

Even worse, he wanted to cry, but cutting open his own skin and pouring a gallon of salt on the wound would have been more preferable.

So, instead, he smiled dumbly, shrugged, and ran for the door.

"Ryan!" Jake shouted. "Come back!"

As he flew past the workbenches and ominous shelves, he thought he heard Steph yelling for him as well. Even if that were the case, he'd need at least a month to recover from the hair-trigger crying reflex and overall embarrassment.

As dim as it was, the cool daylight felt wonderful on his skin as his feet met the cracked blacktop once again. The clouds which had gathered around them before were now hovering above like a puffy, gray drop-ceiling. Ryan was pretty sure the sun should have been shining at this point, but the world appeared to be stuck at dawn.

Thunder rumbled in the distance and a flash of lightning zapped across the sky just beyond the old airport, not far from Ryan's house.

In the short duration between escaping the building and grabbing his bike, Ryan's shame was replaced by self-righteous anger.

"Man, don't you guys realize he set this all up?" he said

to no one but himself. "Ever since he hurt himself, he's been the center of your attention. Mr. Show-Off. Mr. *Rocket Man*."

He laughed like a mad scientist and straddled his bike.

"Even when he's injured and not at school, he's the center of attention."

Don't play the fool, Ryan.

"Oh, don't worry, Mr. T." His feet pushed up and down on the pedals, propelling him home. "No sir. I don't buy any of this. This was a total setup. Owen's probably been planning this forever. Jake was in on it. I know it."

He stopped and placed his tiptoes on the ground to maintain his balance. Something struck him.

Oh my God.

He *had* played the fool. All along, he'd been the target of Mr. T's pity.

"Steph. She was in on it the whole time, too."

A gust of wind kicked up and a tiny dust devil spun past Ryan. A little cyclone that represented all of Ryan's stupid life in this stupid desert town.

Why couldn't he live somewhere else? Why couldn't he be down in Los Angeles, a part of a gang where he'd have some real respect. He'd have guns and power. He could get any girl he wanted.

The Almost-Apocalypse of Apple Valley

Don't play the fool, Ryan.

He wiped away the tears that had shown up during his distraction and turned to look at the factory, the pink pit of despair that had actually opened his eyes to the truth.

He turned his bike around and went back to the spot where they'd all parked their rides.

There they were, Steph's and Jake's bikes, lying next to each other like boyfriend and girlfriend.

Reminders of Ryan's humiliation.

A giant grin spread across his face. He dropped his bike, sniffed away his tears, and proceeded to unscrew the valve caps on his friends' tires.

Then he pressed down on the valve tip. Air came hissing out.

He wasn't worried about either of them coming out. Not if they felt Owen was really inside.

And he probably was.

For the briefest second, Ryan felt like he was making a big mistake.

But that feeling disappeared as quickly as it arrived, replaced by the fervent heat of before.

"You should have wanted to rescue *me*," he said to a Steph who couldn't hear him.

No one was coming for him.

Owen felt pathetic.

Next to useless.

For the briefest of moments, he examined the filing cabi-nets and desks, wondering if he could impale himself on one of the sharp edges so that he could put an end to the pitiful mop-ing.

Still sitting against the wall, Owen rolled his head in cir-cles, stretching out his neck muscles. The whispers and shuffles continued from behind the glimmering door window, but now they felt commonplace.

Whoever was out there either couldn't hear him or chose to ignore him. Whatever the situation, help wasn't coming.

He was so tired. Sitting around in a dark room, doing nothing, made a person more tired than Owen ever conceived possible.

The urge was strong to crawl back to the canvas and just fall asleep. Maybe he *was* still dreaming and needed to wait a little longer.

All dreams, all nightmares, had to end sometime.

Or maybe that's just what the Mysterious Mariska wanted. For him to fall asleep forever and never wake up.

Owen dug into his cheeks with his fingernails and screamed until his ears hurt.

It felt good to get that tension out, but otherwise, it did nothing for his situation.

Sleep, then.

That's what he would do.

Maybe his friends would show up. Maybe they wouldn't. Maybe this would all be over soon. He'd sleep until this thing passed, for better or for worse.

He got onto his hands and knees and crawled like a dog toward the blanket. The strength in his youthful muscles just wasn't there anymore. There was no reason for them to carry the body of a dead man.

Owen straightened out the lumps in the canvas, lay down on his back, and stared at the rafters until his eyes decided there was no reason to remain open.

Steph's stinging arm was her only reminder of Ryan at this point. The rest was practically a distant memory.

She and Jake stared at the rectangular black hole that

existed where the office window once was. It didn't make any sense. Even the little bit of light shining through the factory's broken windows should have illuminated the inside of the office.

But it was like gazing into tar, or a night sky where someone had turned off every single star.

Mesmerized, Steph approached the door.

She thought she heard Jake call her name, cautioning her. At least he had the good sense not to try to hold her back physically. She was drawn to the door like an iron filing to a magnet, and she would have hauled up and punched Jake in the nose if he'd tried to stop her.

In a flash of a moment, she was looking into the dark. Like an old light bulb slowly warming up, a picture began to form on the other side.

As it became clearer, hopes that it would be Owen faded.

Steph didn't like what she saw.

One time, last year, her fifth-grade class had participated in a field trip to Paramount Studios in Los Angeles, where they got to sit in the audience for a live television sitcom taping.

She remembered being enamored with the set and how it appeared so strange compared to how it looked on TV. The living room, looking so small and isolated, disconnected from the kitchen by only a thin wall.

On TV, it was a living, breathing, place. But in person, it seemed less...real.

This is what she was seeing now, only the living room wasn't the set of a silly TGIF sitcom, but was, in fact, the living room of her apartment.

And there was nothing at all funny about her mother sitting in the middle of a couch, surrounded by the Aqua Bitches, all of them painting their toenails with tiny little brushes.

"It's too bad Steph couldn't be here, Ms. Morris," Loretta said.

Her voice sounded as if she were speaking underwater.

Steph's mother shrugged her shoulders, smiling away among her true group of friends.

Among her *real* daughters.

Seeing her mom with the girls revealed the harsh truth— her mom was an Aqua Bitch too.

Just as that thought solidified, Steph's mom looked up and stared right at her. Steph felt as if her heart would leap from her chest, and she grabbed onto the wall to keep from collapsing.

She felt someone's hands, hopefully Jake's, come up underneath her arms to hold her up.

"Steph," she thought she heard him say in the vague distance.

Now Loretta's eyes landed on Steph, and as they did, she leaned over and cupped her hands around Steph's mom's ear and whispered something.

Steph's mom started giggling. It escalated and didn't stop until the tears were rolling down her cheeks. The whole time, she never let go of her nail polish brush. Ruby red paint streaked up and down her feet, leaving streaks that looked like blood.

All the Bitches joined in the laughter now, staring hard at Steph, making her feel like the center of so much unwanted attention.

Then the laughing stopped abruptly. "Steph," her mom said. "Honey. Don't you want to get your toes painted?" As she said it, a cruel smile formed on her face.

Steph found herself shaking her head. The familiar feeling of the tips of her bangs tickling her cheeks was gone, reminding her once again of the horrible thing that had been done to her hair.

Steph's mom rolled her eyes, and she looked at the Bitches. "I try, girls. Lord knows, I try. But she insists on being a boy. She insists on running around with those little shits when she should be back home with us, doing what good girls do."

The girls all clucked their tongues in disapproval. The clucks were so loud. They echoed until they grew to such intensity that Steph felt as if her eardrums were going to burst. She clapped her hands to her ears to keep out the sounds.

But it was useless. The noise pushed through. It penetrated down to her bones, grinding her defenses into powder.

"And now she's going to be held back a year." Her mom released a sort of yelping sound. "My daughter, the disappointment. Maybe she'll learn her lesson, but I doubt it."

Steph's mom paused her painting for a moment to look at the end of the brush.

"Girls, looks like we're out. Hit me," she said, handing it to Loretta.

"Sure thing, Ms. Morris." Loretta grabbed the brush from her hand and reached down to pull up Steph's mom's blouse, revealing her stomach.

What Steph saw was not what she expected to see—the stretch-marked flesh of a middle-aged woman who had given birth and gone through life's hardships. Instead, there was what looked like one of those anatomy illustrations in Steph's health textbooks from school—as if someone had sliced away the flesh and displayed the organs as clear as day.

There, as clear as a colored-pencil drawing, was the perfect sketch of a womb. And in that womb was a tiny baby covered in blood and gelatinous slime. Its body was curled up in the fetal position and its face was hidden away in its tiny hands.

"We're running out," Loretta said, dipping the brush into the red slime. The color glinted in the light of the tiny stand-up lamp perched next to the couch.

Steph's mom shook her head and clucked her tongue again while keeping her eyes locked onto her daughter. "Come on, girl! Even in the womb, you were a disappointment!"

The tiny baby's head turned, and this time, Jake, or whoever, wasn't prepared to hold Steph up. She crashed onto the hard factory floor with a shriek.

Dust kicked up around her, entering her lungs. She coughed as she spoke.

"It was me," she said, her lips quivering. "It was me."

"What?" she thought Jake asked, yelling as if she couldn't hear him and she was miles away. "What was you?"

But Steph was out of breath. Out of words.

Out of time.

She felt his hands beneath her again, pulling her up against her will, but she was too weak to fight.

Something had drained her.

Something had been drained *from* her.

She didn't know where to start answering either of those two mysteries.

But she knew something. It had been building that whole time she'd been exposed to that spectacle and only now did it become obvious.

Anger.

She *knew* that she was angry.

Her mom had the gall to call *her* a disappointment?

It couldn't stand, and even though Steph barely could either, she decided that she was going to give her mom a piece of her mind.

"Hold me up," she said to Jake.

"What?"

"Hold. Me. Up."

Jake must have complied, because she didn't fall.

"Hey!" she shouted at the image through the door, wobbling still, catching her breath.

The Bitches had resumed their little party, but now they were frozen in place. Their television-like projection faded in and out like the signal was being interrupted.

"Yeah," Steph continued. "Listen up, you fat cows."

If her mom was wearing her fake pearls, she would have

clutched them. "Don't you dare—"

"Shut up!" Steph said, an utter fury barely contained in her voice. "Shut your stupid fat mouth. You're going to listen to *me*, now." Her eyes scanned the rest of the Aqua Bitches. She thought she even heard one of them, probably Big Kim, squeak out a tiny, nervous fart.

"I'm sick and tired of the way you treat me. No more." She focused back on her mom. "I'm not your little princess doll to mold and dress up and make how you want. I'm my own person, Mom. Do you get that?"

More silence, broken only by Loretta, who started laughing. "What's her problem?"

Steph glared at the Queen Bitch. "And you. You may think you have everyone fooled, hanging on your little pinky finger, but one day, it's all going to come crashing down. The way you treat others is going to bite you in the ass and I hope it hurts like a sonofabitch!"

The girls gasped collectively.

"That's right! Sonofabitch-sonofabitch-sonofabitch!"

Steph was breathless again, but she noticed the oddest sensation.

She was *smiling*.

It wasn't until that happened that she realized just how

long it had been since she'd done so.

"Steph?" she barely heard Jake say.

She was floating. Absolutely floating. It was like she'd spent years holding someone else's groceries, and they'd finally been taken from her.

"What?" she asked him, staring into the facade that was disappearing as slowly as it had manifested.

"Who are you talking to?"

"Huh?" She turned to Jake. His eyebrows were scrunched.

He released a nervous laugh. "You're freakin' me out."

Steph glanced back through the black portal, but it was no longer there. It was just an empty office with a couple of stiff wooden chairs stacked in the corner.

"Dude," she said. "There's nothing to be freaked out about. Absolutely nothing."

Jake shook his head. "I wish that were true. We still haven't found Owen, and we have two doors left."

Was this delirium?

Or was he sleeping again?

Dreaming?

Owen watched as the faded outline of a man material-
ized, standing in front of one of the office desks shoved up
against the wall. He was looking down at a piece of paper held
in his hands.

As the man came in to focus, recognition struck Owen.

First came the hat. Then the flannel shirt and slightly
bent-over posture.

Oh my God.

It was John.

Owen strained to call his name, but nothing came forth.
His throat felt like he'd gargled gravel again. Also, his body was
stiff. He'd heard of something called night terrors before, where
the mind was aware of everything around it but the body was
unable to react or move, but he'd never experienced it.

He could do nothing but watch John, or John's phantom,
go through the motions. John didn't even seem aware of Owen
lying a few feet away. His focus was on the paper in his hand.

John took the paper, folded it a few times until it was the
size of a credit card, and opened one of the file cabinet drawers.
The rusted contraption whined. John popped the paper into the
drawer and closed it.

The whole time, John's lips were moving silently. Almost

like he was mumbling a prayer.

John turned and looked around the room, but it was like he was staring out into an area much larger.

Again, Owen tried to reach out, tried to speak.

Failure.

He couldn't even generate tears.

"Owen," John said, speaking to the room as a whole. His voice was light and airy. "I don't know if you can hear me. I have to go now. Don't worry about me. I'll be just fine. But before I go, I wanted to tell you that you're a special boy. You and your friends. You're all special. There's something you kids have, especially when you're together, that others will try to take away. They may not even know they're doing it or *why* they're doing it. And it's not just Mariska and The Worm, though right now, they're the number one threat."

Please, John.

Owen was begging him in silence to stay.

"But no matter who it is," John said, "you can't let them take away your magic. You absolutely cannot let them."

John paused for a moment, then continued.

"I have faith in you," he said. "I have faith in Rocket Man and The Crew. A lot of people do. We know that you'll be the ones to do what needs doing, *amigo*."

And with that final word lingering in Owen's brain like the sugar-filled bits of soaked hot chocolate powder at the bottom of a mug, John popped out of existence, leaving behind the empty office.

With John now gone, it appeared Owen could move again. His muscles felt relaxed, and he flexed his arms up and down a few times as a test.

His first reaction was to cry.

A horrible feeling welled up inside of him—somehow, he knew that he'd never be able to talk with or see John again. He was partially angry, partially distraught.

How could he do anything in this condition? The Owen Thom of the moment was the furthest thing from Rocket Man that he could imagine.

He turned his head toward the spot where John's ghost had been standing.

I have faith in Rocket Man and The Crew.

How did John know Owen's nickname? And that he and his friends referred to themselves as The Crew? This must be a dream.

But what if it wasn't? Or what if it was, but it was a real message from his friend, nonetheless? Owen already felt as if he'd let John down before, the one grown-up in his life who seemed to get him.

He closed his eyes and thought of his helmet. He'd last seen it in his bedroom, a place of comfort that he realized now he'd taken for granted. Visions of the *RM* glowing in the stormy evening told him that there *was* indeed magic involved in his life and in the life of The Crew.

Memories penetrated his core now: days spent riding beneath the blue desert skies; warm summer evenings at the community center; cool, star-filled nights camping out in his backyard.

His thoughts then moved to each of his friends.

Jake and his love for all things that went *BOOM*.

Ryan and his love for all things movie-related.

And, of course, Steph. Things seemed to be changing between her and Owen, but it didn't feel like it was in a bad way.

Just awkward.

As these thoughts raced through Owen's mind, the more obvious it became that lying down and taking what the Mysterious Mariska and The Worm threw at him was the worst possible thing he could do.

They were holding him here for a reason, and at the very least, he had to free himself from whatever plans they'd concocted.

Cru Jones wouldn't put up with a situation like this.

Cru Jones wouldn't curl up and let himself be beaten.

He'd face the fears that piled up around him without batting an eye.

And so would Rocket Man.

Owen, as weak as he felt, struggled and pushed himself onto his British Knights, dusted his hands off as much as he could, and took a hard look at the file cabinet where John had placed the note.

He ambled over to it and pulled at its handle.

No dice.

It was either stuck with superglue or Owen was weaker than he thought. He placed the bottom of one shoe against the desk and pulled hard on the drawer handle. Sweat poured down his forehead. He clenched his teeth together.

"Come on," he pleaded.

As if the words had induced a little bit of that magic John mentioned, the drawer screamed open, and if it hadn't been for the stopper mechanism, Owen would have landed flat on his back.

Owen recovered, then looked inside. He felt as if he was going to faint, so he steadied himself on the desk.

There it was.

The folded piece of paper, waiting for him, as real as anything in this room.

He grabbed it, unfolded it, and scanned its contents.

His enthusiasm diminished like the fizz from a can of soda that had been sitting out all day.

What was he supposed to do with an owner's manual for a doll?

"Two doors left," Steph said, walking over to the workbench and grabbing another unfinished doll head. "You said it was the middle one?"

Jake nodded. His entire body was shaking. Whatever Steph had just gone through, it got to his very core. She'd obviously seen something inside that office which he hadn't. Something that affected her, even if it left her filled with newfound confidence.

What if Owen wasn't behind the middle door? Maybe they should try the one on the right—the one chosen by that traitor, Ryan.

Or what if that's what the Mysterious Mariska wanted?

Jake began to feel as if their choices didn't matter anymore. If anything, the second-guessing was slowing things down. There was no specific indication that was what the magician and her pet Worm planned, but Jake had a general feeling.

"Here goes nothing," Steph said, bringing her arm back to launch at the middle door.

"Wait!" Jake shouted, running to her and catching her arm just before she started moving forward.

"I feel like it should be me," he said.

Steph's eyes met his in an "are you sure you want to do this?" look.

But the look on Jake's face was obviously convincing.

She shrugged and dropped the skull into his open hand.

It felt nice and weighty.

"Coming here was my idea, after all," he said.

He was the one that had dreamed of this place. He was the one that had put them all in danger, even if it was for one of their best friends.

Briefly, Jake wondered if Ryan was back home again, pitting ants against each other.

It didn't matter. Jake and Steph were going to save Owen now. They'd worry about Ryan later.

Without further hesitation, Jake pitched the skull right through the middle-door window. He felt as if he didn't even have to aim. It sailed perfectly, just as Steph's had, setting in motion the very same events—skull bouncing, cracks forming, glass disintegrating.

The blackness was there. For a moment, Jake wondered if he would be free from whatever Steph went through.

But then a scene began to form.

He didn't want to step forward, but he felt compelled. That if he didn't face whatever was on the other side, he might as well pack up and go home like Ryan, leaving both Steph and Owen to a horrible fate.

The air hung still inside the doll factory, allowing Jake to hear the entire building creak and shudder as the winds picked up outside.

He stood before the door now, looking into his old man's bathroom. Sounds of the running shower along with puffs of steam floated up from inside. The image of a man emerged from the humid fog. He was standing in front of the mirror, his face full of shaving cream, swiping the straight razor slowly down his jawline.

More hot water streamed out of the bathroom sink. The counter was littered with dozens of open beer cans.

Jake stared silently for a while. At first, he thought it was his dad—he had the body, the stained wifebeater, the hair on his forearms barely covering the smattering of tattoos like long, thin grass.

But he also had hair, blonde hair, that looked like perfect plastic molding.

It was like his dad had morphed with Duke from G.I. Joe.

"Yo Jake," Duke-Dad said. His brown-toothed grin looked eerie through mounds of fluffy white cream. "Where ya been?"

Jake said nothing.

Duke-Dad put the razor down on the counter and picked up a can of beer. He took one sip and kept chugging until the thing was empty. He crushed the can and tossed it in Jake's direction. It bounced off his chest and rattled onto the bathroom tile floor.

God, it felt so real.

Maybe it was.

"Come to see what real men do?" Duke-Dad asked. "You really ought to stick around, you know. The fun's just starting and you are one sorry sack of shit, desperately in need of basic training."

Duke-Dad picked up the razor again and started shaving the cheek facing Jake. This time, the razor cut deep. It sliced away not just the shaving cream, but flesh, which curled away like thin sheets of plastic. Red blood poured forth like a waterfall, splashing on the counter.

Jake wanted to scream, thought he did scream, but nothing seemed to come out.

His resolve began to sag. He really wanted to be anywhere but here.

"Yo Jake," Duke-Dad said, "be a man. I didn't raise no sissy. Maybe if you're a good boy, I'll let you go play with those dolls. Even let you put on a dress and we can have a tea party."

He felt the ground disconnect from his boots, and his legs scrambled for purchase like a cartoon character right before he discovered he'd just run off a cliff.

But then he felt a pair of hands holding him up from the side. They were struggling, but they were enough. He thought he heard a girl's voice, quiet and distant, yet encouraging.

His hands held on tightly to the edge of the window frame.

Duke-Dad stopped shaving, ran the razor under the fountain of blood like he was rinsing it off, and extended it toward Jake.

"What do you say? You ready to stop searching for your little girlfriend, Owen, so you can learn to be a man?"

"You don't know anything about being a man," Jake said.

He didn't know where the words came from. All he knew is that his stomach leapt into his throat as soon as the words came out.

Duke-Dad looked like he'd just been slapped in the face. His eyes grew wide.

"Yo Jake, did you just talk back to your old man?"

Duke-Dad cracked his knuckles. The sound echoed across the tiny bathroom like thunder.

"Damn right I did."

He couldn't stop the smile growing across his face if he wanted to.

Duke-Dad moved across the bathroom so fast, it seemed to Jake that he practically teleported. He grabbed ahold of Jake's t-shirt and lifted him off the ground. His face was inches away. The smell of blood made Jake sick to his stomach.

"You don't know what you're messing with, boy," Duke-Dad said. Spittle flew onto Jake's face. Up close, beneath the peeled back skin of Duke-Dad's face, his body appeared to pulsate and writhe. It was composed of hundreds of tiny worms, all squished together.

Jake started shaking again, but kept the feeling clamped down.

"Let go of me," he said. "You don't own me."

Where Duke-Dad's eyes had shown surprise earlier, now they actually showed something close to fear.

Jake felt himself being let down. The soles of his boots hit solid ground, and Duke-Dad's hand flew off Jake's shirt like it had been burnt.

"Yo, you little shit, I'll tell you—"

"You won't tell me anything, anymore. I'll tell *you* something. And you're going to listen up, asshole."

God, what a feeling. Jake's only disappointment was that he'd waited so long to say something like this.

Jake remembered his mother, the day that she walked out the door and never came back. The day that she told Jake it was for his own good and that she would do everything she could to make sure he didn't have to spend another minute with him.

Unfortunately, it didn't work out that way. It wasn't through any fault of his mom. Some stupid judge thought it was good for a boy to be with his father.

To teach him to be a man.

What a joke.

"I'm not scared of you anymore," Jake said. "Because you don't know anything about being a man. You don't know anything about friendship. You don't know anything about anything! You don't even really work. You're always bitching about something and drinking and running away from your problems. How are *you* going to teach *me* anything?"

Only after his little speech did Jake notice that the steam from the shower had all but dissipated.

Duke-Dad looked furious, but in a way that was so comical, Jake couldn't help but start to laugh.

"What—what are you doing?" Duke-Dad said. "Knock it off."

But he couldn't. He literally couldn't stop now. He was doubling over.

"Stop it, you little shit! Stop laughing at me!"

Duke-Dad's hands went to his ears, trying to clamp out the sound. It made the whole situation even more ridiculous.

Tears were spilling from Jake's eyes now, and they wouldn't stop.

"I...I can't..." Jake tried to speak through heaving breaths.

"I can't help it," he said, finally. "You're just...you're just so stupid."

Duke-Dad was screaming now, only Jake couldn't hear him. He couldn't hear or see much of anything as the image in the door started to fade away.

"Jake?" a voice asked, coming up from the distance.

Jake wiped away the final tears and started to recover.

"Jake, are you OK?"

He turned his head and saw that it was Steph. She had a puzzled look on her face, but touched with a slight smile.

He didn't reply right away, but instead shook his arms and hands like he'd just been released from prison chains.

He leaned in through the vacant office window and scanned the tiny, empty room.

"I'm fine," he said. He was pulling himself together again, despite the fact his gut felt like it had gone five rounds with Mike Tyson. "Never better. Now, let's go get Owen and get out of this stupid place," he said.

Steph smiled back, grabbed another doll head from a nearby workbench, and took Jake's hand as they both approached the final door on the right.

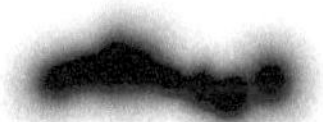

Ryan thought the rain would be the worst of his problems. It *certainly* was a problem, coming down in buckets now, but the fog was worse.

So much worse.

He couldn't see five feet in front of him, and his plans on getting back home with time to spare were blown, just like the sharp-tipped tumbleweeds which he had to dodge every few seconds.

He came to a stop. The doll factory was maybe a hundred yards away. He must have been getting close to Thunderbird Road on the north side of the old airport when he felt a pang in his chest.

He bent forward and clutched at his t-shirt, barely noticing the fog starting to recede a little around him.

What was happening? Was he so filled with guilt that his heart declared a revolt against the rest of his body?

His mind raced, thinking of his friends.

Friends.

The word weighed on his conscience like a heavy stone. After abandoning his *friends*, did they even count as such anymore?

It was bad enough that he left them alone in their search for Owen, but then he was so petty as to let all the air out of their tires.

He'd been mad, all right. Was still mad.

But at what cost?

"I think I made a mistake," he said, shocked as the words flowed out from his mouth.

As soon as they escaped, he felt like he'd released an incantation. Like he'd crossed a threshold that wasn't meant to be crossed—not by him.

And as if he needed confirmation, a volley of thunder boomed from the surrounding fog, followed by an eerie silence.

Then there was another rumble, thinner in form, constant. It came from directly in front.

Breathing heavily now, still grabbing at his chest, Ryan managed to lift his head.

Before him, a group of tumbleweeds parted as if to make way for a procession. A wide pair of low, yellow eyes emerged from the fog. They were encased in a sleek, off-yellow face with a black grill set between them shaped like a wicked smile. Sitting on top of the head was a bulbous, flesh-colored tip with pitch-black windows.

There was someone—some *thing*—inside, watching him, waiting for his next move. He couldn't see it with his eyes, but he felt it on the goosebumps rising across his flesh.

If he had eaten anything earlier, Ryan feared it would have come out of his pants that very instant.

The Wienermobile came to a stop five feet in front of his bike. Sitting against the backdrop of the low mists, it took on a fearsome aura.

It was exactly as Owen described the night Ryan had

made what was probably his biggest mistake.

Ryan snapped his head around and looked back at the Terry Lee doll factory.

He suddenly felt so alone.

It was almost like the town had emptied itself in an instant. He remembered hearing some preacher on one of the TV shows his mother sometimes watched at 5 a.m. on Sunday mornings.

The man had perfectly combed gray hair, wore a charcoal gray sports coat with a button-up shirt and bolo tie. He talked with a Texas accent about the rapture and how there would be two groups of people—Christians everywhere that would just disappear and be swept up to Heaven. And then there were the others—those Left Behind.

Ryan started to wonder if he was Left Behind.

And if he was, maybe his friends were too.

Friends.

There was the word again, stinging him like an army of ants that had slyly marched up his pants leg.

The little engine roared, followed by another bout of rolling thunder.

Ryan couldn't leave them behind.

He had to warn Jake and Steph.

Don't be the fool, Ryan.

He ignored the invasive thoughts. He lifted his bike, turning it around awkwardly, then placed all of his weight onto one of the pedals.

A renewed vigor entered him, refreshing his soul. He'd make up for what he'd done.

He *would* save the day after all.

The fog parted as he started zooming toward—

SNAP.

CLANK.

Ryan's legs suddenly moved at an insane rate as the pedals' resistance disappeared.

Hard-packed dirt and asphalt rose up to meet him.

He tucked his head down, managing to avoid hitting his face, but a burning pain rushed up his forearms and elbows as they took the brunt of the impact.

Groaning, he turned onto his back and looked at the result—bloody scratches ran up and down his arms like he'd dipped them in red paint. He looked over and saw his bicycle on its side. Its chain lay on the ground beside it, broken into one long piece of connected links.

Behind him, the Wienermobile revved its engine again. Then it crept forward, moving with the grace and stealth of a mountain lion stalking its prey.

There was no question in Ryan's mind just who the prey was.

Despite the pain still pulsing through his chest and the newfound pain in his arms, he pushed himself up and broke into a run.

He tried to move fast, but his body refused to cooperate.

Breathing hard, his arms swinging at his sides, he felt the presence of the Wienermobile approaching from behind. He ducked his head and flattened his hands, thinking he'd get as much out of aerodynamics as humanly possible.

He had to get back to the factory. To warn his friends.

There was no idea in his head of what to do once he'd gotten to them, but he knew he had to do at least that.

The fog made it difficult for Ryan to judge how far away they were. His lungs screamed, and he felt as if he were running on a treadmill.

Don't play the fool, Ryan.

He wanted to stop so badly, but he knew if he did, it would be the end. Maybe the end of everything. Tears flew down his cheeks now as the remorse became unbearable. It was as if the whole world was chastising him for what he'd done. The Wienermobile paced behind him, like it was Paulie and

Ryan was Rocky.

But this was no training.

There was no *Eye of the Tiger* to push him onward.

He had to lose the car, unsure if that was entirely possible, but he needed to try.

Ryan did the only thing he could think of and made a quick juke to his right, running off into the weeds.

The idea was ridiculous. Fog parted around him like a spotlight keeping track of his movements.

The Wienermobile maintained its course, it's engine still rumbling behind him.

Ryan's legs were hurting. They felt so weak. A sharp pain stretched out from his hamstrings to his heels, running along what he knew was his sciatic nerve. His head was pounding like a dozen tiny dwarves were taking hammers to his skull.

Everything hurt. He would have cried more, but even that hurt.

It took a moment for his brain to realize that his body had just completely quit. Ryan was on his knees now, only slightly aware of the bits of gravel and goat head stickers digging into his kneecaps.

The Wienermobile came to a stop behind him.

Ryan placed his palms on the ground, trying to catch his

breath, trying to figure out just where he was.

It was futile. The fog covered everything. He may have been even further from the doll factory now, and not even realized it.

As these thoughts sprinted back and forth through his mind like jackrabbits, the Wienermobile's engine cut out.

The eerie silence returned, occasionally punctuated by the low, rumbling thunder that seemed to be getting closer by the second.

He didn't want to turn around. Didn't want to see what his fate would be.

How he wished more than ever that Mr. T. and an army of gangbangers were at his side. Together, they could take on whatever malignant power operated this Wienermobile.

But they weren't here. Ryan was alone—just some poor kid from a poor family in a tiny old house in the desert stretches of Apple Valley, California.

Still, it was the best he could muster.

He straightened up, fighting every ache and pain in his body, got to his feet, and turned around.

There had been no slamming of a car door. Nothing to signify that anyone had gotten out, but there she was, standing slightly bent over beside the driver's side with her full ensemble—black top hat, black coat, black cape.

The Mysterious Mariska looked like she'd been through the wringer. Next to the Wienermobile, she looked minuscule. Large, dark circles ringed her eyes and bags drooped like the jowls of Droopy Dog from one of those old cartoons they played on the UHF stations sometimes.

Ryan wheezed a little. "What do you want?" he asked, quick and sharp, mostly due to the lack of air in his lungs.

He didn't need an answer, though. He knew. He knew exactly what she wanted. She was the one that sent the dreams, wasn't she? She was the one that had sent Mr. T. and the gangsters and the beautiful beach bunnies, one of which turned into the person he truly wanted.

The sweet memories and smell of coconut oil turned sour in his mind, knowing that she was behind it all.

The passenger door to the Wienermobile lifted open gently, rising up to the roof, hissing like it was one of those pneumatic doors the school buses use. A tiny set of steps unraveled itself to the ground.

"Ryan, it's time we go for a ride," the Mysterious Mariska said. Even her voice sounded tired.

Ryan's eyes were pulled into the direction of the dark-tinted windows. It wasn't like he could see through them, at least he shouldn't have been able to, but there was movement within. Or maybe it was the tint itself that was moving like ripples created by wind on a still pond.

"I...I don't want..."

He couldn't get the full sentence out. He knew what he wanted to say, but the strength behind the words wasn't there. His tongue felt like it weighed a thousand pounds.

"I know what you want," the Mysterious Mariska thought to Ryan. "I know *who* you want. And I can't make that happen unless you come along for the ride. Unless you let me help you."

Ryan knew that she couldn't force him into the car. At least he didn't think so. He had to come on his own volition.

How did this stranger know that he had a thing for Steph? There was no doubt that she *did* know. He supposed that if she could send him dreams, she could see all sorts of things happening inside his brain.

He'd never felt so naked and exposed.

A shock of thunder and flash of sheet lightning crashed around them.

"I..."

Still, the words wouldn't come.

"Play this smart," the Mysterious Mariska said. "If you

don't let me help you, you lose it all. You not only lose your friends, who aren't your real friends anyway, but you lose any chance of winning over your little sweetheart."

She paused for a moment to hold onto the car, looking as if she were about to lose her balance and tip over.

"I'm giving you an opportunity, kid. You come with me, you'll have anything you've ever wanted. Power you couldn't even begin to imagine. Don't play the fool, Ryan."

The words struck his very soul. He had been the fool all day. Crap, he'd been the fool for the past two weeks. It seemed no matter what decision he made, he would be the fool.

He looked back to where he thought the doll factory might be. Assuming he made it back to Jake and Steph, found Owen and broke him out, would they even accept him at that point? They'd probably think he was tainted.

He glanced back at the Wienermobile and its inviting steps.

Maybe getting into the Mysterious Mariska's magical car would make him a fool, but at least he would be the fool with power.

Rocket Man used to be the hot-shot here, but he'd be nothing in comparison with Ryan if he stepped foot inside that car.

Ryan felt that deep in his bones.

As if in harmony, a smile grew on the Mysterious Mariska's face with the thoughts forming in Ryan's brain.

Ryan put his left foot forward, paused for a moment, thinking that he saw a pair of glowing red eyes looking back at him through the dark windows. Nerves tingled inside of his body.

And then he carried on as if he'd been planning to get in all along.

I'll show Rocket Man, he thought.

I'll show Steph who the better man is.

Inventory:

300 Heads.

600 Arms.

600 Legs.

Owen was on his second read-through of the paper, trying to make some sense of it all, when a *thwump* on the office-door glass caught his attention.

The sound was dull, muffled, like the whispers and shuffles he'd heard earlier. But a tinkling sound rang out just as a series of webbed cracks spread from the center of the glass to the edges.

Then the glass disintegrated into millions of grains of sand.

The next sequence of events took some time to register, and Owen wasn't quite sure in what order they came.

He blinked, not believing what his eyes were seeing on the other side of the door.

He tried to say their names, but started coughing again instead. Tears flushed into his eyes, which he furiously rubbed away.

"Holy crapola." The familiar gruff voice floated over to Owen.

"It's him!" That voice, with its slight California skater-girl inflection, was musical.

Owen wanted to cry again, and if he did, they would be tears of joy. Still, he maintained his composure. There wasn't any time for that sentimental stuff.

"Guys!" he said. "I knew you'd come!"

The words set him to coughing again.

Absentmindedly, he folded the piece of paper and shoved it in his back pocket.

Simultaneously, the three of them rushed to the door and

reached through, touching each other on their arms and faces as if they needed to confirm the other was real.

Steph even leaned through and gave Owen a giant hug through the door, which made his knees buckle a little bit.

"You stink," she whispered in his ear.

"Thanks," he replied, jokingly pushing her away. "Let me try locking you up in some weird little room for a few hours."

"Days," Jake said, digging into his backpack as he spoke.

"What?"

"You've been gone for days, man."

Jake pulled out a clear plastic squeeze bottle filled with water and handed it to Owen, who greedily sucked it down.

After his thirst was quenched, Owen recounted the chain of events that went down, starting from the night of the campout, when everyone abandoned him, ending with his confrontation with the Mysterious Mariska and the thing she lived with.

The building fell silent, punctuated only by the occasional thunderclap outside and howling winds picking up momentum.

"We shouldn't have left you," Steph said. "I was just so... so *angry*...when I heard that crap on the radio."

"Steph," Owen replied. "I don't even know what that

was about. I never talked to Loretta. I can't stand her."

"Really?"

"Really!"

It looked like a weight had been lifted from her after Owen's confirmation. She hugged him again and then quickly backed off.

"I mean, not that I care," she said. "You could talk to her if you wanted to. I'm not your boss."

"Well, I don't want to," Owen said. If there was only one girl in the entire universe he'd ever be allowed to talk to, it was the one standing on the other side of the door.

"I'm sorry I didn't back you up," Jake cut in. "I was scared, dude." His hands were tucked into his pockets and his head was down.

"He's the one that knew to come here," Steph said.

"It's okay," Owen said, placing a hand on his big friend's shoulder. "You're here now."

And it was okay. For some reason, it all felt okay now. All of them were here. All of them, except...

"Hey, where's Ryan?"

"That little punk bailed on us," Jake said, showing feeling again. "He's been getting all weird."

Owen hadn't noticed how much different Ryan's attitude

had been compared to Jake and Steph's over the past couple of weeks, but in hindsight, Ryan seemed to be the one driving a wedge between them all.

"Who cares," Steph said. "We'll deal with him later. Speaking of bailing, we should probably get out of here. This place sounds like it's going to collapse on us."

As if on cue, a chain of thunder resounded outside, followed by those winds. It sounded like an orchestra of chaos. The entire building shook violently. Rusted hinges from every single nook and cranny screamed in response.

They tried to open the door, but it wouldn't budge. Since there didn't appear to be any glass shards that might slice open his hands, Owen gripped the bottom part of the window frame and leapt through.

Rocket Man was back in business.

"Let's go," Jake said.

Something behind Owen hit the floor with a soft slap. He looked back.

"Wait," he said. He leaned over and picked it up.

"I think there's something else we need to do."

"You want to hang out and read this?"

"It has to be important," Owen said. "My friend John left it for a reason."

Owen was glad Jake and Steph didn't ask how. Things were already complicated enough.

"If we go out there now, we still need to face Mariska and her pet. Maybe this is something that will help?"

"We doubted you once," Steph said, looking at Owen and then to Jake. "Not again."

Jake nodded.

"There's a list of...body parts," Owen said. "I'm not quite sure what to make of it. It's followed by a set of assembly instructions. 'Connect these parts here, put this part there.'"

He handed the paper to Steph, who read through it and then passed it over to Jake.

"Well," Jake said, "if this is talking about what I think it's talking about, we're in the right place."

Owen realized he never even asked where he'd woken up. Looking around, the place was old and hadn't been occupied in quite some time.

"Which is where, exactly?" he asked.

"The old doll factory," Steph replied.

Right away, Owen had visions of straddling his bike on the track by Bass Hill, looking down over the desert valley where the factory stood.

It was all coming back to where things started. He wondered if that was significant.

"I think we all have to be a part of this," he said. He just hoped this missing member of The Crew wasn't necessary.

"Let's stop screwing around, then," Steph said, grabbing the note back from Jake's hands.

As if to emphasize the need to hurry, thunder cracked outside again. The wind continued unabated, shaking and rattling the bones of the old building.

What had they wrought?

They'd dug through every single nook and cranny of the building, pulling and emptying all the cardboard boxes from the shelves. Like a well-oiled machine, they worked as a team, piecing together some kind of monstrosity.

One of the workbenches had served as a practical operating table.

Laying before the three of them was a linked collection of various doll parts, all forming a monstrosity that evaded description. Plastic arms were screwed into legs. Heads screwed into those. Some body parts were already painted with eyes and lips and nostrils.

"What was the point of this?" Steph asked.

Owen reviewed John's note, flipping it over and upside-down and sideways, hoping it would reveal something. But it was fairly straightforward. If there was a clue as to what to do next, it certainly wasn't there.

"Well, that was a waste of time," Jake said.

As if to agree, the building shook violently once more as thunder rumbled outside.

The amount of time they'd spent assembling this thing had been a blur. How much time had they wasted?

"No," Owen said, shaking his head, skimming over the instructions again. "It can't be. We're just doing something wrong. Or missed something."

"Hey," Jake said, "I just did what you told me."

"Are you sure?" Owen asked. He stepped back and looked at the whole of their creation. He had no idea what to make of it.

"Dude, do you think I'm an idiot?" Jake said. "I'm—"

"Guys," Steph said.

Owen exhaled in frustration. "I didn't say that—"

"Guys!"

The two of them shut up.

"Stop arguing like a couple of old ladies," she said. "We need—"

Before she finished her sentence, the sound of a loud snap came from above. Their heads turned upward as if they were all attached to the same puppet string.

An eerie silence passed through the building.

Then the roof came peeling back in the wind like a flap of flesh. Old wood groaned and asphalt shingles flew into the dark sky as they separated themselves from the rusty nails that held them in place.

It was like someone had cranked up a hose to maximum strength. Heavy drips of water slammed against newly exposed shelves and cardboard boxes. The three kids covered their heads as the intruding rain mixed with the splintered debris and tetanus bombs, falling on them like it was an air raid.

Owen noticed the somewhat sweet smell of moisture-clobbered dust rising into the air.

"Go!" Steph yelled over the wailing winds.

Owen felt compelled to stay back and finish figuring out

what John had intended, but Steph pressed her hand into his back and pushed both him and Jake toward the open doorway at the side of the building.

The three of them rushed from the building until their shoes hit the torn-up concrete.

They were surrounded on all sides by a ring of dark fog. If he hadn't been locked in a tiny office, Owen would have felt stifled. The environment was practically claustrophobic out here.

A soon as they were ten yards out, the old factory unleashed an angry groan. The kids came to an immediate halt and looked back.

The pink walls were shaking in the violent winds, waving back and forth like thin sheets of plywood. What little bits of glass were left in the windows shattered. A burst of lightning flashed across the sky, charging the atmosphere before a bolt shot down and hit the old weather vane spinning on the roof.

And then everything just sort of fell in on itself.

With a thunderous crash, the walls turned inward, and what was left of the roof dropped down onto the now-exposed shelving and workbenches.

The noise was deafening. Owen pressed his hands into his ears and squeezed his eyes shut. The pouring rain did little to extinguish the explosion of dust and debris that drifted up from the aftermath and set the three of them to coughing.

The doll factory was no longer.

"Holy crapola," Jake managed to say.

Whatever John had intended, it didn't matter now. Owen hoped it wasn't *that* important.

They backed up further from the building in order to get away from the dust clouds.

"Where do we go now?" Owen asked.

"The bikes," Steph said, looking around as if to gauge where exactly they'd left them. "We need to get to the bikes."

She took off running without a further word. Owen and Jake looked at each other, each taking half a second to catch their breath before they followed.

The breakneck pace reminded Owen that he hadn't moved in a while. He felt weak and stiff, but adrenaline took over. The joy of finally seeing his friends, combined with the fear of getting out of this strange experience, compelled him to keep moving.

Somewhere along the way, they ran headfirst into a large patch of creosote bushes surrounding a lone joshua tree. Jake had managed to get ahead of Steph and, too busy looking behind him, launched right into the weeds. The dried bits crunched underneath his body weight. He went tipping over, falling face-first.

Owen reached out and snagged a corner of Jake's backpack, softening Jake's collapse and almost falling along with him in the process. He somehow managed to stay upright in his British Knights.

"Good job," Steph said, half sarcastically. "You found them."

Sure enough, on the other side of the bush was a familiar, warming sight—his friends' pair of bikes. Owen really wished his Redline was there too.

"Come on," Jake said, picking himself up, mindlessly brushing off the dozens of stickers that left his arms covered in bloody pinholes like freckles. "You can sit on my handlebars."

He grabbed his bike and immediately stopped.

"What the..."

Steph grabbed her bike and apparently had the same reaction.

"How did this happen?" she asked.

"What?" Owen asked, identifying the problem immediately after the words left his mouth.

The tires were flatter than pancakes.

"I swear, I'm gonna beat the crap out of that guy," Jake

said.

Owen knew just who he was referring to.

Obviously, Plan A no longer sufficed. He had to think quickly. The rain continued to pour down. Combined with the iron wall of fog, getting his bearings felt like an impossibility. The usual landmarks just weren't visible.

Still, staying there seemed the worst possible option.

"Leave them," Owen said. "We need to get out of here. The police station is right around the corner. If we can get—"

The few hairs on Owen's forearms rose like someone had dragged a balloon across them. Cutting through the continuous rumble of thunder was a more familiar drone.

He turned, his eyes were drawn to the source. Owen noticed Steph and Jake's heads took a similar trajectory.

Emerging from the dark fog was a pair of glowing, golden eyes sitting low to the ground. Above, the familiar round, orangish tip with windows blacker than the darkest night.

A sudden, familiar pain pulled at Owen's chest. He gripped it tightly.

He looked at Steph and Jake.

Again, they mimicked his motions, pressing their hands to their own chests.

"No," he whispered to himself, barely hearing the words

through the cacophony of external sounds. "No. This isn't how it's supposed to end."

THE END

Sunday, June 26, 1989 - ?:??

The engine stopped.

And so did the rain.

Even the thunder that had been ever-present just quit like a Magic Fingers bed whose five-minute timer expired.

Owen noticed with great relief that the pain in his chest left him, too. It was as if someone flipped a switch to "Off."

All that was left were three kids and the car that had brought them back full circle.

"Oh my God," Steph said. "I see it. I see it now. Just like I saw it at the mall."

There was darkness in the windows still, but behind it, the outline of something squirmed and wriggled. Owen knew it was the thing he'd first experienced just after his birthday party. The thing that lived with the Mysterious Mariska and which he'd seen uncomfortably close up.

The Worm.

"Let's go," Jake said, more of a request than a command.

"There's nowhere left to go," Owen said. "We need to stay. All three of us."

The words came quietly, but confidently. Full of power. They surprised even Owen, and they certainly pulled the attention of his friends back onto him.

"What?" Steph and Jake said simultaneously.

"No way," Jake continued, shaking his head wildly. "Uh-uh. We need to get the hell out of here. Now, dude."

"I agree," Steph said. She grabbed Owen's arm and started pulling him toward Jake. "It wants us, Owen. It wants us all."

Owen placed a hand over hers. "I know," he said, "but we can't go."

Owen didn't want to be the one to tell them they had to stay. He was just as scared as the rest of them.

But it wasn't Owen who was pushing to say it at all. It was Rocket Man. The hero had been buried somewhere deep down in Owen's subconscious and was now emerging again, pulling himself from the rubble that had accumulated during the past two weeks like a phoenix from the ashes.

"Don't you see?" Owen asked. "If we leave now, we'll all die. The whole town will die and lose its identity—what makes it special for us and every other kid growing up out here. Besides, we can't run from this thing. It'll find us wherever we go. It *needs* to find us."

"Smart boy," a familiar voice said in the near distance.

Owen and his friends had been so wrapped up in their own conversation, they hadn't seen the Mysterious Mariska exit the Wienermobile, now leaning against its front with her arms crossed.

Owen's breathing came to a momentary halt—it was her, all right, but a version that hadn't slept in weeks. The black hat was missing, revealing mussed hair that went every which way but down. She wasn't wearing her cape or the rest of her outfit either. Instead, she had on blue jeans and a wrinkled, white t-shirt that had long since yellowed. On her chest was a faded logo that said *Atlantic City—America's Favorite Playground*.

A closer look at her face revealed dark circles and no make-up to hide the wrinkles that crept across her face like cobwebs.

"You can't hurt us anymore," Owen said.

He didn't know why he said it. He didn't even know if it was true.

But it *felt* true.

"You don't know everything, *Rocket Man*," another voice said, the final two words spoken with utter disdain.

Leaning out from the Wienermobile's open passenger-side door was Ryan.

"I'm gonna kick your ass!" Jake yelled.

"Come try it," Ryan said. A wisp of black smoke streamed out from the vehicle and circled Ryan like a cyclone. It rose into the air just above his head. A pair of glowing red eyes formed before the shadow settled across Ryan's shoulders like a shawl.

Jake didn't move.

"How could you do this?" Steph asked. "We're your friends."

Owen thought he saw a flicker of conflict cross Ryan's face, but if it was there, it disappeared as quickly as it arrived.

"You were never my friends. You guys just used me."

"How can you say that?" Steph asked, unable to restrain the incredulity in her voice.

Jake followed up with, "Yeah, you're one to talk."

The Wienermobile engine revved on its own, cutting across this tiny slice of existence like a blade.

"Hush," the Mysterious Mariska said. "You all did what you were supposed to do and now we're here. One big happy family. I thank you for that."

She rapped her knuckles on the giant hot dog. "Why don't we continue this discussion in the car?"

A nasty smile formed on her face. Brown rust, almost a

kind of corrosion, ran along her gum line and dripped down over what had been beautiful white teeth at the birthday party.

"We're not going anywhere with you," Owen said.

"That's your choice," Mariska said. "But it would be a poor one. Either you three come along and live happier lives than you could ever dream of, or we drain every bit of wonder and magic from this town, leaving behind an empty husk of despair."

She locked eyes with Steph. "Nice haircut. You looking forward to being an honorary Aqua Bitch for life? I'm sure it will be a wonderfully miserable existence."

Steph unwrapped her hands from Owen's arm and flinched like she'd been stung.

Then Mariska glanced at Jake. "How about you? Ready for manhood and living under your father's angry shadow for the next ten years?"

Owen could hear Jake's teeth grind against each other.

Owen took a bold step forward. "If you really wanted the town, you would have taken it already."

The Mysterious Mariska's sleepy eyes cracked open.

"You need us for a reason," he said. "You need us because we have something—together—that others don't."

The air was eerily quiet once more.

"Like I said, *Rocket Man*—smart boy."

She pushed herself off the car, looking a little wobbly, but quickly recovering by placing a hand on the metal hot dog frame, using it as a crutch as she walked back toward its open door.

"He doesn't know jack crap!" Ryan said, grinning and reminding Owen of a little monkey bouncing around some bigger animal that would protect it.

Owen caught how Ryan's two buck teeth had also taken on the browning, purplish rust color. His face, too, was almost yellow in pallor, accentuating the dark bags which had formed beneath his eyes at some point.

Steph stepped forward to take her place beside Owen. "There are three of us and neither of you look too good. If Rocket Man says we're not going, we're not going."

"Yeah," Jake said, flanking Owen on the other side. "We're a lot more than meets the eye."

A little flourish of the Transformer's electric-guitar charged theme song played out in Owen's mind.

It was a stand-off. Mariska was inside the Wienermobile now, sticking only her head out through the opening. The Worm also hovered and swam in the safety of the cabin. Only Ryan was at the bottom of the steps still, looking to his new boss to say something or do something.

All she did was glare at the three amigos.

"You've made your choice," she said.

She looked down at Ryan. "Come on."

"Hey," he said. "What about—"

But before he could finish speaking, the black smoke jumped out briefly and wrapped itself around his neck. It yanked him off his feet, slamming him onto the back of the stairs.

Owen gasped.

"Ryan!" Steph said, rushing forward, but Jake grabbed her arm before she got too far.

"Don't," Jake said.

Ryan dug his fingers into the fluid noose, but his attempt was futile. It dragged him into the Wienermobile like a lassoed calf. The door came down and sealed shut behind them.

"We can't let them take him," Steph said.

"Why not?" Jake asked. "Little traitor deserves whatever he—"

A shot of thunder rang out all around, and the dark fog lit up like it was electrified. The three of them hunched over, instinctively protecting themselves.

The Wienermobile's engine kicked on with a roar.

Angry pain shot back into all of their chests again. Beneath their feet, the ground shook in violent waves.

Suddenly, the Wienermobile lurched forward with a squeak, then stopped.

Owen and his friends took a few stumbling steps backward, trying to focus.

"She's gonna run us over," Jake said, his voice hoarse.

Owen wasn't sure if that was true, but he wasn't going to chance it. By some miracle, the dark fog started receding around them, sucked back into the wide desert landscape like a film played in reverse.

Despite the agonizing pain, Owen knew that this was their only possibility of escape.

"Come on," he said, vaguely aware of which way the police station was now.

Between the three of them, they may have covered a cumulative ten feet before the Wienermobile made a groaning sound behind them, reminiscent of the doll factory's collapse.

The shock, combined with more shaking of the earth, threw them from their feet.

Owen felt like a crash test dummy being knocked around for fun.

Lightning and thunder cracked again in the sky. The rain

and winds picked back up from where they left off.

Something was wrong with the Wienermobile.

Something very, very wrong.

It tilted and convulsed, pumping up and down like it had been customized with hydraulic switches. Parts of the body buckled. Things popped. Others hissed.

At one point, the car dipped so far to one side, it looked as if it might roll over onto its edge, only to twist itself back into place.

The scraping groans were deafening.

Owen couldn't figure out if his hands were better off keeping his eardrums from exploding or pressing his heart back into place.

He wondered if it was falling apart because of their refusal to comply. Maybe these were the final cries of a dying spirit.

Maybe they were going to win this war, after all.

Just when things started to make Owen believe life was going to be OK, other things started happening that told him he might be completely, unequivocally wrong.

The Wienermobile extended its body from the wheels like it was doing push-ups, and began tilting upward, revealing its greasy, pipe-threaded underbelly. Spurts of oil and fluids sprayed the ground below as cracks opened up in the metal, narrowly missing the three of them.

The wheels and axles of the yellow 'bun' split and shot out to the sides—the rear pair deploying downward like legs and feet, while the top ones projected themselves outward like arms and fists.

Then the body started rotating until the back of the hot dog faced them all. Its curled bottom looked like a wasp's stinger. The top third of the Wienermobile flipped down like a head, rotating so that its passengers were upright, as if in an airplane cockpit.

Owen was speechless, the pain in his chest long forgotten. He looked around at his friends. Apparently, their own aches had been shoved aside as well.

"Holy crapola," Jake said.

Steph said what they all were thinking: "It's a freakin' Wienerbot."

Owen trembled at the sight. His legs and arms refused to pick the rest of his body up from the wet, muddy ground. Pain seared across his chest, making it difficult to breathe.

Judging by Steph and Jake's lack of movement, they suffered from the same paralysis. The hulking hunk of metal must have stood at least forty feet tall, but sitting directly below, its height was amplified.

Owen felt like an ant.

They could only watch as the Wienerbot lifted its right leg and prepared to take a step. The metal on metal joints screeched, piercing the trio's ears once more.

Only a few feet before them, the foot slammed back into the ground. The earth shook as the sharp-edged metal produced more cracks in the already crumbling blacktop. Owen's body bounced lightly as someone jumped onto a trampoline he'd been lounging on.

Then it lifted the left foot into the air. Oil and grease mixed with dirt, concrete, and weeds, making it look like the Wienerbot had stepped in a giant dog turd.

There wasn't much time to make light of the situation as the foot hung in the air just above Owen. Its downward trajectory indicated that he was about to become a part of that turd-like mixture.

This was it then.

It was all for naught.

Apple Valley was doomed to be destroyed by a giant hot dog.

Beneath the foot's shadow, Owen waited almost stoically, accepting his fate.

But apparently fate decided it wasn't his time to die.

A loud pop emerged from Owen's left, followed by a shrill whistle. Something large flew through the air and slammed into the side of the Wienerbot's torso, knocking the creature off-kilter enough to send it reeling sideways where it hit the desert floor.

It crashed hard, bouncing the kids around again and sending up a mix of debris, dust clouds, and splattering mud.

"Holy crapola!" Jake said. "Look!"

He was pointing back toward the doll factory.

Piles of wood and brick and other materials that had once made up the little pink building pulsated like lungs inhaling and expelling air.

Rubble started sliding onto the ground until all that was visible was the thing they had assembled before the collapse, lying naked and unafraid on the operating table where they'd pieced it together.

The thing sat up, creaking and groaning.

From the distance, it all made sense as to what John was thinking. He had given them the ability to create a Transformer of their own—one made of doll parts that looked like something out of a horror movie.

Everything had been pieced together to form a giant body with all the required parts—arms, legs, torso, head. The creature's eyes glowed like headlights, made up of blonde-painted doll heads strung together. And from what could only be described as lips, it emitted a slurred, frightful tone that sounded like a dying voice box.

Coooommme plaaaay with meeeee!

"Dollybot," Jake said, as if reading Owen's mind.

It pushed itself off the table and onto its feet. Then it took a couple of wobbly steps before gaining its bearings and walked in their direction.

Compared to Wienerbot, Dollybot was half the size. Owen hoped it made up for it in determination and strength.

Owen was reminded of what Dollybot would have to face when he felt the ground shake again. He turned his gaze back toward the Wienerbot. During the distraction, it had picked itself up and stood upright once more.

It wasn't until Steph and Jake climbed to their feet that Owen realized the pain had left his chest, and a semblance of muscle control returned to his body.

"We may want to think of getting out of here," Steph said, pushing wet hair from her eyes.

"Where to?" Jake asked.

It was a good question. Owen was on his British Knights now, wiping his muddy palms against his jeans. He was about to suggest going to the police station again, but before he could get the words out, the Wienerbot turned in that direction.

Its legs moved slowly at first, but then it launched into a rapid run toward the town center and Bass Hill. The footfall boomed and shook the ground.

Dollybot apparently knew its mission and chased after its metallic friend, moving as gracefully as a lumbering ape with a bad leg.

Cooooommme plaaaaay with meeeee!

The three of them watched the gigantic freak machines shrink into the distance.

"Where are they going?" Steph asked.

"I don't know," Owen replied, "but we better find out."

Ryan was too busy doing two things to closely follow the action: Trying not to pee his pants. And wiping chunks of puke from his face. Last night's dinner of Mr. T. cereal was still hanging around his stomach after all.

The Almost-Apocalypse of Apple Valley

He'd been unceremoniously dragged into the Wiener-mobile by his neck and told to strap in. Being choked to death wasn't on the agenda for today, so he did as he was told.

If not for the seat belt wrapped around his body, he would have been tossed around the Wienermobile's interior and slammed against its insides until he was just a fleshbag of broken bones.

One minute, he was sitting in the front passenger seat, tears in his eyes as he gazed at his used-to-be-friends through the tinted front window.

The next, he was being spun and jerked around like a passenger in the Gravitron ride at the San Bernardino County Fair, finally coming to rest high above the ground.

They were in motion now.

Even though they bounced and moved at a rapid pace, the ride in what appeared to now be a cockpit felt smooth.

As stupid as it sounded, Ryan had never been in any building taller than a single story—they were rare in Apple Valley, and his family had never taken an overnight vacation that didn't involve a cheap campground.

His new vantage point was honestly as exciting as it was unnerving.

"Where are we going?" Ryan asked.

It was just the two of them—Ryan and Mariska.

Thankfully, in all the chaos, The Worm disappeared somewhere below deck.

"We start at the center," Mariska said, "then work our way out."

Ryan directed his eyes toward the approaching buildings: Gold Strike Lanes, the bank, the post office, the police station. Behind them, Bass Hill loomed large. Memories of The Crew riding together on the trails below almost overwhelmed him.

It was the heart of Apple Valley.

It was the heart of The Crew's childhood.

Ryan's nausea was still present, and his head throbbed. "I thought there was something back there at the factory—"

"Shut up." Mariska cut him off. She glared at him like his dad sometimes did, whenever he tried to catch some Zs before his evening shift and every kid in the house decided it was the perfect time to make the maximum amount of racket possible. "The Worm knows what it's doing. We do what It wants until It tells us otherwise."

She didn't sound convinced by her own words.

Ryan turned around in his seat and saw there was a gap where the car's plush floorboard used to be. The passenger seats had somehow disappeared from the insides, leaving what resembled a hollow elevator shaft to the bottom of the wiener.

Feeling like he was going to retch again, he turned around and focused on the dim landscape outside. It looked like Apple Valley, but there was something off about it. Something he couldn't put a finger on.

"You promised me that she'd be mine," he said. "You *promised*."

Mariska managed a brief chuckle. She was leaning over the steering wheel, peering outside the windshield as if they were taking a Sunday drive. Her eyes were bloodshot. Dried saliva caked the outside of her lips.

"Welcome to the real world, kid," she said. "We all find out at some point that most promises are just so much bullshit."

She looked like she'd been run over by the Wienermobile itself.

"You look sick," Ryan said.

She leaned back into her seat and flopped her head to face him. "You're one to talk."

When Ryan didn't respond, Mariska continued. "I'm tired. It's time for someone else to take the reins," she said.

It became clear, now, what she'd intended all along.

"I'm supposed to be the new you," he said.

"The formal title is Attendant," Mariska said.

Ryan gazed back outside. They weren't far now. He could see people milling about, walking in and out of buildings, cars zooming along the adjacent Highway 18. But like the rest of the world, they didn't appear...real.

They were phantom-like.

"It's not all that bad," she said.

"You think I'm an idiot?" he said. The thought of being tied to that *thing* made him want to vomit again, but his body had already given up everything it had in the tank.

"I can't take it anymore," she said.

Were those tears in her eyes?

Ryan wanted to ask a hundred more questions, but before he did, a loud, vacuum-like sound blasted through the inside of the cabin. He jammed his palms into his ears.

"What is that?" he yelled over the racket.

"It's starting," was all she said.

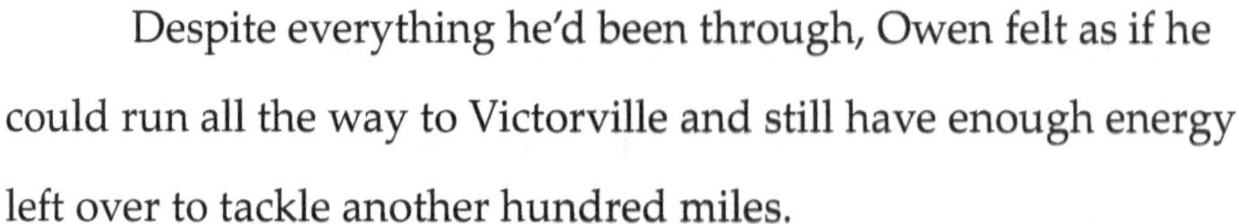

Despite everything he'd been through, Owen felt as if he could run all the way to Victorville and still have enough energy left over to tackle another hundred miles.

He'd heard people talk about "second wind" before,

but this felt unique. Where the extra endurance came from, he wasn't entirely sure, but he wasn't the only one affected.

Steph and Jake kept up the whole way. They smiled, chasing after Dollybot, who was chasing after Wienerbot.

There was no guarantee they'd make it through this, whatever *this* was, but if they did, Owen was positive they'd have an amazing story to tell.

"We're going to beat this thing!" he said. The words came spontaneously.

"The battle's going to be epic," Jake said. "Like Godzilla versus Mechagodzilla."

"Or like Optimus Prime vs. Megatron," Owen said.

It took a second for them to realize Steph was lagging behind a little, no longer by their side.

"Guys," Owen heard her say. "Wait. Everything looks weird."

Both he and Jake stopped and stared at the town through the pounding rain.

Owen agreed. The world had a ghostly quality to it—gray, murky. He was sure it had something to do with the harsh weather, but that didn't seem to explain the almost-transparency of everything around them.

"It's fine!" Jake said. "Come on." He started jogging

again, but stopped after a few feet when he realized no one followed.

"Maybe we should let them do their thing," Owen said.

Hanging back a safe distance from the gargantuan throwdown was probably a good idea. But standing where they were didn't feel right, either.

His vision zoomed in on Bass Hill. The place where everything began.

"The track," he said. "Guys, we need to get to the track."

He was worried he'd have to convince them of his reasoning. The problem was he didn't have any. It was merely a gut feeling.

"Let's go," Steph said, running past them both.

Jake kicked into high gear and followed.

Apparently, the feeling was mutual.

The world below appeared oblivious to everything happening. Pedestrians strolled in and out the buildings like it was any other day.

"Run!" Ryan yelled, his voice hoarse. "Move!"

"They can't hear you," Mariska said. Her voice was quiet,

barely above a whisper. "They don't even know we're here."

The loud vacuum sound increased.

Below, a pair of girls, they couldn't have been more than six or seven, held hands and walked next to their parents on the way into the bank.

They reminded Ryan of his sisters.

His jaw dropped.

A layer of gray flesh tore away from their bodies, like a bedsheet. It wasn't their skin, per se, but a copy of it. The best way Ryan's brain could make sense of it was based on a horror movie he'd rented one time when a vampire bit down and drained not only the blood, but the souls of his victims.

"What's happening?" Ryan asked, afraid he already knew the answer.

"Since your friends are being selfish with their Capability, The Worm is a little pissed off. It's decided to start elsewhere."

Ryan shook his head as the little girls seemed to recognize something was wrong. Their faces scrunched with terror, and they started bawling. The parents stopped and tried to comfort them, but it was useless.

"Oh," Mariska said, "and It's fueling up."

"For what?"

"For this."

The Wienerbot shook violently, rushing forward like it was shoved. The bank building zoomed into view as the Wienerbot sought purchase with its hands. Brick and asphalt crumbled in its hands. Debris fell around an elderly couple walking to their car, blissfully unaware of what was happening.

It pushed itself back onto its feet and turned.

Coooomme plaaaaaay with meeeeee!

Ryan had rented a lot of scary movies in his life, but he'd never seen anything as scary as this.

The three amigos scrambled around the back side of the bank, running through the half-filled Gold Strike Lanes parking lot.

Their eyes were lured by the strangeness as they moved toward the dirt track.

Owen couldn't tell if it was *them* who were the ghosts or everyone and everything else around them. Up close, even the buildings had an odd, wobbly quality to them. It seemed as if a thin film of dark plastic had been laid on top.

People walked by, completely unaware of so many

things: the heavy rains pouring over their heads; Owen, Steph, and Jake traipsing by at full speed; oh, and of course, two hulking giants duking it out above their heads, busting up buildings and concrete.

It seemed to be nothing more to the people than a light summer breeze.

"They're destroying everything," Steph said, sounding wistful even through her labored breathing.

"We can't stop," Owen said. "We need to get to the track."

As difficult as it was not to be distracted by the rock-em-sock-em events, Owen and his friends maintained their stride and started their dash across the busy Highway 18.

It was like playing a real-life game of Frogger. Trucks and sedans zoomed by the double two-lane roads—one northbound, the other south.

They paused briefly, looking for gaps until Jake did both the stupidest and bravest thing Owen had ever seen: he leapt out in front of an oncoming semi-truck.

"What are you doing?" Owen yelled. There was no time to reach out and grab Jake or push him out of the way.

In his mind, Owen expected to hear a blaring horn or maybe a screeching of brakes. The semi-truck blasted through

Jake's body like nothing. Not even a flapping t-shirt.

The grin on his face was enormous. "Haven't you guys been paying attention?" he said.

Owen shook his head, but smiled back. Steph was smiling too.

"Come on," he said, feeling the ground rumble beneath him, hearing another loud crash behind his back.

The outside world was a blur, but Ryan was growing accustomed to the motions. The Wienerbot's cabin shook as the grotesque doll-thing ran toward them and jumped, launching a devastating punch at the front window.

Ryan covered his face and shrank back, expecting the glass to shatter, but it only wobbled.

A rapid motion shook the cabin again.

Something crashed in the near distance.

"It's working," Mariska said, a wheeze in her voice.

Even among the smashing of materials outside, Ryan could hear more and more children crying.

He pulled his hands away. He thought sweat had pooled within them, but when he looked down, he saw a thin layer of black snot covering his skin. It reminded him of the plasticky-smelling slime he'd gotten for Christmas one year. Only, that stuff never tugged at his flesh, peeling the outer layer of his palms apart like pieces of wet paper.

Somehow, it didn't hurt. At least not much.

"What's happening?" he asked, not expecting an answer, but the Mysterious Mariska surprised him anyway.

"Congratulations," she said. Somehow, she sounded even more exhausted than before. "You're being hired."

Ryan didn't need to ask for what. He could see exactly what was happening. He could *smell* death emanating from Mariska's languid body as she slumped back more and more in her seat.

"I don't want this," Ryan pleaded.

"Sorry, kid," she said. She managed to flop her head to the side and look him in the eye. "I really am, you know. But I'm so tired."

She took a deep, labored breath.

"Eventually, you'll find someone else to take your place. But in the meantime, The Worm will take everything it can from you. It's incessant. It's in its nature. It can't help itself, just like its mother couldn't help herself."

"No," Ryan said, mainly to himself. "No. I refuse."

The words felt futile. Any amount of protest seemed use-less. Already, he felt The Worm's power seeping into his body, coloring his outlook.

Conflicting thoughts crowded his mind. Thoughts of The Crew, his sisters, all the kids at Mojave Mesa—all of the young people of Apple Valley.

What about after that?

Who was next?

Victorville?

Neighboring Hesperia?

The Worm could feed forever in this place, leaving be-hind a world in which the magic of youth was but a buried historical artifact, never to be discovered again.

The idea both excited and upset him.

He shook his head, trying to cleanse his mind of The Worm's disturbing notions.

The outside world zoomed into view again as the Wie-nerbot shot forward. The giant doll pushed itself up from the collapsed walls of Gold Strike Lanes, where it had crashed into the arcade and pro shop, leaving behind a trail of rolling bowl-ing balls and a shattered *Street Fighter* cabinet.

There was no obvious indication of pain, but Ryan sensed the doll was meeting its match against The Worm.

The Almost-Apocalypse of Apple Valley

A new, strange idea entered Ryan's mind—that the doll was only serving as a distraction.

He wondered if The Crew was still left behind near the now-destroyed factory. Peering through the windows offered no indication—the view was too narrow.

There had to be something he could do.

As he put his thoughts together, he saw the doll struggling to balance itself.

The Wienerbot vibrated, shook, and rattled every loose piece inside. The tachometers on the dashboard started going haywire, their needles spinning around like sped up clocks. Ryan imagined the feeling was similar to being in a rocket ready to blast off.

Through the side mirror, he watched as the right arm of the Wienerbot reared back.

They stared helplessly from the tiny rise in front of the electrical substation, just above the even-more-ghostly Apple Valley Inn.

"No," Owen said. "No, no, no. Come on!"

Jake and Steph both echoed his words.

"The Wienerbot can't win," Steph said. "It just can't!"

Owen wanted to believe.

He truly wanted to believe.

Apparently, its thousands of eyes were purely cosmetic, because the doll never saw it coming.

The punch was like a flash.

The metal fist careened into the face of the doll, which exploded into a million parts. Arms, legs, and heads flopped out onto the parking lot asphalt like marbles. Others flew into the air, mingling with the rain.

Where they came down, Ryan had no clue.

He looked over at Mariska, expecting her to smile, but she was passed out in her seat. Her mouth was open. For all intents and purposes, she looked dead. Like all the fight had been taken out of her.

The image frightened Ryan. He didn't just see her slouched there like a drained corpse.

He saw his future.

Maybe not now.

Maybe not even within the next year.

But he saw himself, drained of all humanity, wondering if he might be able to convince some other kid to take over for him.

As if she sensed him looking at her, she opened her eyes and glanced in his direction. He swore her lips curled into a tiny smile.

It was over, then.

This was it.

The apocalypse had come to Apple Valley.

THE END END

From the front of the electrical substation, they saw it all go down.

Dollybot, destroyed.

All the hope and light that filled Owen—snuffed out in a single punch.

There we no words to say. No feelings to express.

Owen felt like an empty husk.

John had tried to help them, but it hadn't been enough.

Quietly, Owen blamed his friends. If only they'd listened to him sooner, this could have been avoided.

Then Owen blamed himself. If only he'd *convinced* them sooner, everything would have been fine.

No, that wasn't quite right either.

Owen eyed Steph and Jake, both of whom joined Owen on the ground, having collapsed under the weight of loss. Rain pelted their defenseless bodies.

Maybe this was just how it was meant to be. After all, in the library, John emphasized that there were no guarantees. What made Owen and his friends so special as to avoid the same fate John and his fellow scouts experienced?

Finally, the words that had been there all along, but he'd been too afraid to say, came to Owen. "I love you guys."

They felt sappy coming out of his mouth, and he waited for a stinging rebuke.

"I love you, too," Jake said.

"Me, too," Steph added.

There were no singing violins. No cheesy tears. Everything felt and sounded sincere. The idea of what they were losing seemed to weigh even heavier now.

As questions about what the future might hold floated in and out of Owen's brain, a whistle screamed overhead. Apparently, it wasn't only in his mind as all three of their heads turned up to the sky.

Punching through the dark gray clouds was a blur, increasing in size. Owen thought back to the dream he'd had not long ago—The Crew sitting on the edge of a cliff; Owen tossing a rock which expanded at Bass Hill.

Only now he was on the wrong end.

"Move!" Jake said. Each of them was already scrambling away from the inbound projectile.

Owen rolled and somersaulted across the dirt, narrowly escaping impact. The missile punched into the ground with excessive force. A mix of splattering mud and dust flew into the air and wound its way into their lungs.

They coughed until the dust cloud settled. Finally, it was pounded back into the earth by the pouring rain.

The three of them cautiously approached the result—a pit six feet wide and three feet deep.

Sitting there, steaming under the rain, was a bundle of doll parts, all glowing and shaking like a giant magnet was pulling at them from somewhere.

"Holy crapola," Jake said.

More perfect words were never spoken.

And then the parts started violently snapping together.

An arm to a leg.

A pair of legs to a head.

Each time the pieces came together, the glow increased in power until it became too bright to look at.

Owen and his friends covered their eyes and looked away.

The electrical substation cracked and snapped behind them, just like it had when Owen had gotten ready to break the 'max air' record.

"Owen," Steph said.

His eyes were locked on the hulking steel components behind the fence. Electricity arced between rods.

He felt the hair on his head rising in the air, almost like a cartoon character sticking his finger in a wall socket.

"Owen!"

"Wha—"

He turned and saw Steph and Jake staring into the pit. Their hair, too, stood on end. He looked down and could hardly believe his eyes.

It was his Redline 700SL, resting on its side.

The chrome shined brilliantly, as if there were no clouds in the sky at all, but a beautiful summer sun projecting down.

Something else glinted too.

Something more wonderful.

Something that brought on a strangled, emotion-filled laugh and pasted a smile to his face that he swore would never go away for the rest of his life.

Hanging on one of the handlebar grips was Rocket Man's red helmet. It looked like it had been waxed and buffed a thousand times. The 'RM' stencil glowed and pulsed as if it were imbued with magic.

And it was.

It had to be.

"Oh my God," he said.

In an instant, everything became clear.

Everything.

He scrambled down into the pit, heedless of possibly falling or injuring himself.

He grabbed the helmet.

Its magic seemed to flow into him as he held it in his hands. The heft was exactly what he expected it to be.

He placed it on his head.

It slid on like a glove.

It felt like a crown.

Owen had already started feeling good when Dollybot showed up earlier, but now his body felt completely restored. He turned and glanced upward at his friends standing on the edge of the pit.

They were smiling back at him.

"Rocket Man," Steph said.

"Rocket Man," Jake repeated.

Rocket Man nodded and looked back toward the town center. The Wienerbot continued its rampage, unabated. It smashed into buildings and terrorized the citizens of Apple Valley.

Owen picked up his bike and wheeled it out of the pit. Jake and Steph helped pull him out.

Once he emerged, Owen hopped on the seat—his throne.

He pushed the bike back and forth with his toes, delighting in its smooth movement once more. Then he regarded the arduous blacktop incline heading toward the water tanks.

"I'll be back," he said, flipping the handlebars around. One last flourish before the big event.

He stood on the pedals, prepared to ride away, but something stopped him.

Something that couldn't wait.

Owen wheeled himself over to Steph and pulled off his helmet. Their eyes met, and she gave him a confused look.

He leaned over and kissed her on the cheek, feeling a heat flush over himself as he did so.

Steph obviously felt the heat as well—Owen saw her cheeks turn beet red before she turned away.

"Dude," Jake said. "Gross."

Fear swept through Owen after he'd done it. Had he made a mistake?

She snapped her head back and returned the favor—the feel of her lips on his cheek sent a shiver throughout his whole body.

Electricity crackled throughout the substation once more. The equipment snapped and sizzled as the rain increased its force and tempo.

Owen put the helmet back on his head, stood, and pro-pelled himself up the hill.

Despite the herky-jerky movements of the giant robot, Ryan unbuckled himself, stood, and walked over to Mariska. His legs felt weak. His whole body felt funny—like the time he'd stayed up all night watching the four *Nightmare on Elm Street* movies he'd rented from Prime Time Video.

Mariska was alive—if it could be called that. Her breathing was shallow and wheezy. The Worm was apparently going to drain every last painful bit of her being before letting her go.

He remembered how she looked at Owen's birthday party. She'd been pretty. Probably *really* pretty when she was younger. Now she was hideous.

Ryan stroked the sweat-plastered hair away from her eyes.

"Please," he said. "I don't want this."

Her lips moved as she whispered something, but Ryan couldn't hear. He leaned down and placed his ear closer.

"Capability," she said.

"What?" Ryan asked. "What about Capability?"

"You," Mariska uttered. "Your friends." The words were followed by a coughing fit. Owen shrunk back and watched black bile flowed from between her lips and onto her chin.

The Wienerbot rocked around them, shifting back and forth, forcing Ryan to hold on tightly to the back of the seat. He turned briefly and looked back down at the shaft. If he fell, he'd probably break his neck.

Maybe even die.

As if reading his thoughts, Mariska reached out with her hand and touched Ryan's.

"Sorry," she said. "So sorry. Important."

"What?" he asked. "Tell me!"

He leaned over her face again, feeling the black bile against his cheek, shuddering at the thought that the same vile substance flowed through him now.

Mariska struggled to breathe. "Use it. Capability. Use it."

What did she mean by that?

But she was done speaking.

She was done breathing.

Her body went completely limp. Ryan jerked back and saw her vacant eyes staring through the darkened windshield.

Panic swept down his body like a tidal wave.

"Think, genius, think!"

But all he could think about was how much he had to pee.

There was no turning back.

From the top of the water tank road, Owen looked down at Apple Valley, down at the desert town he'd known and loved and hoped to know and love for many years.

He knew it would change. Everything changes. But there would still be magic here for years to come, if he had anything to say about it.

The Wienerbot was full-on attacking Gold Strike Lanes now. Once it was done with the town center, what next? Owen's eyes drifted to Church of the Valley. The parking lot was full of cars and families walking into the various buildings. He realized that it was Sunday. Of course, families would be heading to service and Sunday School.

It would be a feast for Mariska and The Worm.

And now, Ryan.

An image of his one-time friend popped into Owen's mind. What had driven Ryan to do the things he'd done? Owen had a feeling it had to do with Steph, but still—they were supposed to be friends. They could work it out.

"Doesn't matter," he said to himself, pushing his visor down over his eyes. This time, he double-checked the bolt holding the handlebars into the stem. Seemed tight.

He scanned the distance to the Church from here. He'd have to clear parts of the Apple Valley Inn, and both inner and outer Highway 18, in order to reach his destination. A mere two thousand feet or so.

So, you know, perform the impossible—risk life and limb.

"No guts, no glory," he whispered.

It seemed an appropriate time for a Cru Jones quote.

And with that, he stood and launched himself down the hill, gunning for the tabletop where all the trouble began.

It made no sense whatsoever.

But maybe that's what made it brilliant. It was a stupid kid idea, and despite all his supposed smarts, Ryan enjoyed being a stupid kid.

He stood between the two front seats, pants and underwear bunched around his ankles.

The Almost-Apocalypse of Apple Valley

The bowling alley was behind him now. In front, Church of the Valley loomed. There were children everywhere.

Ryan never felt such relief.

A steady yellow stream flowed from his bladder, splashing across the Wienerbot's dashboard. The tachometers that had been going haywire stopped moving altogether. Sparks popped and snapped. The smells of urine and burnt plastic overwhelmed the cabin.

Ryan hoped his gesture would make up for everything he'd done. Even if he stopped The Worm for mere minutes, it was, as he'd been told many times in his life, the thought that counted.

He had to let go of his wiener long enough to hold onto the seats as the Wienerbot lurched and stumbled in its approach toward the church.

"Gah!" he shouted as his stream went every which way, causing some pee to splash back in his face. "Nasty!"

Something screamed from below.

He felt The Worm's presence shoot up the shaft.

You fool!

The Worm wrapped itself around Ryan's neck again like so much rope. It stung like mad, and the Wienerbot was still staggering back and forth like a drunk. Ryan struggled to breathe.

I need them! I need their Capability!

The voice wasn't emanating from anything in particular. In fact, it seemed to come from within Ryan's head like someone had shoved a pair of headphones inside there and pressed them directly against the sides of his wrinkly brain.

He felt his face turning from red to blue as oxygen was having trouble making its way into his lungs. With his airways cut off, he grew lightheaded.

You can't kill me, Ryan thought back at The Worm. *You need me.*

The Worm began to loosen its grip on his neck.

For a moment, Ryan felt vindication. Maybe he could change things around. Maybe *he* could control The Worm.

As quickly as the thought came, it was dashed when The Worm began choking the life out of him again.

I don't need you. I've got your friends to choose from.

Ryan looked out through the windshield and knew the lack of oxygen was making him delirious—he thought he saw one of those friends, Owen—no, Rocket Man—riding on his bike, flying toward him in the air.

If Rocket Man weren't so focused on controlling his collision-course toward the Wienerbot, he would have pushed up his visor and rubbed his eyes.

Through the thinning black tint on the Wienerbot's windshield, he thought he saw Ryan standing there with his pants down.

"What the—"

The words cut themselves off as Rocket Man used his legs to flip the Redline's frame in a move called a "moto whip."

As he flew past the Wienerbot's head, Rocket Man's back wheel tapped the glass.

The most horrific scream he'd ever heard was followed by a giant flash.

Owen went blind and prayed. Currents of air buoyed him during the descent back to earth.

Landing?

That was easy.

Landing on both wheels and staying that way?

Not so easy.

Somehow, he touched down more smoothly than he could have ever imagined, landing on the blacktop road running behind the church.

He squeezed the rear brake handle and skidded the back of the bike around so that he faced the Wienerbot.

Only, there was no Wienerbot left to face—just a pile of lifeless metal sitting on the ground. A pile of something much smaller than the Wienermobile.

Something like a Volkswagen Rabbit.

Rocket Man flipped open his visor to confirm. Sitting there in the middle of the desert lot behind the church sat a rusted hunk of metal that looked like it had been there for years, stripped for parts, and left for the wildlife to make a home. Most of the paint had peeled away and the one tire that was still attached was rotten. The headlights were shattered and jagged.

The next thing Rocket Man noticed was how the rain had stopped. The sun was shining once again, and the ground was mostly dry as if it hadn't rained since yesterday.

Something honked at him. He looked dead ahead. A man and woman sat in their green Lincoln Town Car, staring impatiently out the windshield. In the back seat were two little black-haired boys with bowl haircuts, playing a game of Monkey Bites.

Rocket Man pedaled off to the side of the road near the wreckage. The Lincoln drove by. The two little boys peered at

Rocket Man through the back window before their car disappeared into the church parking lot.

Rocket Man turned back to the scrap heap.

So, they'd won.

They'd defeated Mariska.

They'd defeated The Worm.

They'd defeated...Ryan.

Rocket Man's heart sank. It wasn't supposed to end this way. Overwhelming thoughts took hold of him—he had no clue how he was going to explain his disappearance, let alone Ryan's.

As if to answer him, the passenger side door of the Rabbit swung open, squealing on rusted hinges. It was followed by a few low coughs and then something plopping out onto the dirt.

Rocket Man dropped his bike and yanked off his helmet. He rushed toward the crumpled heap of flesh splayed on the dirt.

"Ryan!" he said.

Ryan rolled over onto his back, a hand on his heaving chest, and blinked his eyes at the sky.

Owen knelt down and placed his hands on Ryan's shoulders. "Ryan," he shouted. "Can you hear me?"

Ryan groaned. His face was covered in black grease and dirt. "I did until you made me deaf with your yelling."

Owen smiled, despite everything that had happened. He knew that it was mostly a result of The Worm and its malign influence. He also knew that, somehow, Ryan had done something inside that united them—something that gave them the power to defeat The Worm together.

"We won," Owen said. "We beat the friggin' thing!"

Ryan simply smiled.

"Guys!"

Owen looked up and saw Jake and Steph approaching from Highway 18.

By the time they got there, it had taken them a full minute to catch their breath.

"We saw everything," Steph said. "It was amazing!"

Owen fell back onto the dirt, realizing just how tired he was. He gingerly placed his helmet next to him and glanced at Ryan.

"Well, you didn't see everything," he said. "But I think it's done."

Jake walked up to Ryan. Owen tensed a little, thinking Jake still held a grudge about everything that went down.

"Dude," Jake said, "Your pants are down."

They all laughed, even Ryan, as he reached down and made himself presentable again. Then Owen stood up and helped Ryan to his feet.

Ryan looked at his friends and then cast his eyes at the ground. "Guys," he said. "I'm...I'm sorry. I didn't want things to end up like this. I just—"

He interrupted his speech to glance momentarily at Steph. Then he looked at Owen.

"I didn't want her to like you. I was jealous. Jealous of you. Jealous of what you two being together would do to The Crew..."

He threw his hands in the air as if he were searching for the right words, and they just weren't coming.

Owen put a hand on Ryan's shoulder.

"It's okay," he said.

Steph stepped up beside Owen and took his hand into hers. "I'm my own person," she said. "I still want to be your friend, Ryan, but you have to accept me for who I am."

Ryan took a deep breath and shrugged. "I guess you two make a good couple," he said.

Then a smile crept across his face.

"Besides, I think Loretta's more my speed anyway."

Steph's eyes shot wide open.

"Kidding," Ryan said, raising his hands. "Kidding. Though Kim's pretty hot. Long legs. And besides, I come up to the perfect height on her if you know what I mean."

The grin on his face could have told even a blind man what he meant.

Steph rolled her eyes. Owen and Jake laughed.

"And Owen, sorry about your handlebars."

"Huh?" Owen said, not sure what he meant.

"Back at the track. A couple weeks ago, when you ate it. I think that was my fault."

Owen scrunched his eyebrows. "What do you mean?"

"I think...well...when you were coming down toward the jump, I was hoping you'd eat it in front of Steph. I thought that maybe if your handlebars just happened to disconnect, you'd be screwed. I think whatever magic was coming together for us at that point, it had an effect."

It made sense.

Owen probably should have been furious, but Steph squeezed his hand at just the right moment, reminding him that it didn't matter anymore.

"Apology accepted," he said.

It felt like things were returning to what Owen could only describe as "the way they ought to be."

The four of them had single-handedly saved Apple Valley from annihilation.

Would anyone ever know?

He looked down at the rusted-out Rabbit.

Immediately, he remembered Mariska.

He walked over to the open door and looked inside. Laying on the driver's side seat, tangled in springs popping through the cushion, was a dirty old black cape. On top of the shifter knob hung a battered magician's hat.

Owen slammed the door shut, putting a close to this chapter of their lives.

The sun was out, and so was school. In Mrs. Kirkwood's mind, that was the combination of two beautiful things.

She felt relieved that she didn't have to hold anyone back this year. Poor young Stephanie Morris was *this* close until she'd managed to squeeze by on the year's final test. She'd watched Owen Thom helping her study during recess.

It was nice to have friends who cared about you.

She was laying out in her backyard patio, her belly against the plastic strands of the folding tanning chair with her bikini top unstrapped, exposing her back to the warm rays of the High Desert sun.

This was it. This was the life.

There wasn't the slightest breeze in the air. A few flies buzzed around, probably chasing after the sweet coconut scent of her Hawaiian Tropics suntan lotion.

She knew at some point in the distant future, she'd regret laying out here, damaging her normally pale skin, but for now, she was looking forward to a little bronzing. It would look good and maybe even pull some attention from Ms. Berk.

Mrs. Kirkwood could be hot stuff too. She knew that.

As she dozed off to sleep, she was woken up by what she thought was an earthquake.

Around her, the wooden porch supports wiggled, and the wind chimes hanging outside of her kitchen window played their melodic tune.

She pushed herself up and looked around. Her mind went to the earthquake preparedness pack she'd put together based on an Emergency Services guest that had spoken to the kids in her class. It was right by the front door, next to her shoes.

The only problem was she hadn't anticipated having to go *into* the house to get it. Maybe she ought to have put one out here.

Before she had enough time to regret, the shaking had stopped.

"Well, that was fun," she said to only her chair and herself.

She laid back down, right cheek pressed against the beach towel, sunglasses slightly askew.

The breeze picked up a little, sending a small flapping sound from the tree down into her ear.

Something tickled the back of her neck.

It was just the breeze.

Just the breeze.

But someone in the distance must have pulled out the grill and decided to cook hamburgers, because she smelled something like burning fat and flesh, combined with charcoal.

Her nose wrinkled slightly.

She felt bad for whichever neighbor that was—they'd obviously bought spoiled meat and would pay the price later.

Quickly, she fell asleep and dreamed a bad little dream— one involving black smoke and a choking sensation.

FANTASTIC SHORTS

I hope you enjoyed this book. Reviews are always welcome! The following volumes contain more fantastic fiction written by Phillip McCollum:

Fantastic Shorts - Volume 1

Fantastic Shorts - Volume 2

52 Stories in 52 Weeks

My Father's Fire

ABOUT THE AUTHOR

Phillip McCollum hails from Southern California where he shares living quarters with his wife, son, an old cat, and young betta fish.

If you'd like to hear about his latest work, please sign up for the newsletter on his website (phillipmccollum.com). He also pokes his head up on Twitter once in a while (@beatbox32).